Trails of Change
(A New Sunset-Second Edition)
By Lana Lynne

DEDICATION

Dedicated to my daughter and son-in-law, Cheroka and Brent,
May you always share every sunset together
and
To my husband, Rick,
Sharing sunrise to sunset

Author's Note and Acknowledgments

Trails of Change (A New Sunset-Second edition) (2018) remains a work of fiction like my original *Trails of Change (*with the subtitle *A New Sunset) (2010).* All characters are fictional except for known historical figures, i.e., Shanghai Pierce, Robert Todd Lincoln. The interactions or incidents of correspondence with my characters are fictional. Works of literature mentioned or discussed by my fictional characters within the manuscript are listed in the research sources at the end of the novel. Any errors or adjustments made for the purpose of the story are my own.

Please know the ambiguity displayed in regard to both the name of the West Texas town located close to the Kennedy ranch, as well as the name of the specific fort in my story, is purposeful. They are representations. My research found the openings and closings of the forts in our country at that time numerous and finding one within the exact location and timeline needed proved difficult. As this is a work of fiction, it allowed me not to specify in this particular case. I did find the histories of Fort Arbuckle and Fort Sill of particular interest. The other towns mentioned are actual towns, but are used in a fictional sense.

I would like to acknowledge my deep appreciation for the support of my friends, family, and the readers of my first book, *Home Always Beckons (2009)(*with the subtitle*: A New Sunrise; planned release of a Second Edition coming in 2018)*, during the preparation of the original sequel, *Trails of Change (2010) (*with the subtitle*: A New Sunset),* as well as in the preparation of this revised—Second edition. Their many encouragements, along with God's loving and chastening guidance, are the reason *Trails of Change (A New Sunset-Second Edition (2018)* is now in your hands.

One final clarification, I've had the privilege, in my work as a speech-language pathologist, to work with many people, including those with spinal cord injuries. During the course of my research on the Civil War, the magnitude of the injuries suffered and the numerous soldiers who returned home and forged a life post-war reverberated in my heart. In my first novel, readers met Ben Richards, who lost a leg during the war. Now they will meet James

Hawkins in *Trails of Change*. He is one of the most pivotal people for my main character, Boyd Richards, and he will impact the reader. I know he influenced me as the author. The war injury he experienced, as research showed, resulted in a very short post injury survival for the majority. Most died while in the hospitals. The reports I read described the type of injury; surgical interventions, if attempted; and autopsy reports, which specified the damaged neurological systems and organ failures causing the soldiers' deaths. Limited references to or follow-up on those able to survive are available. Please note, available research lists a wide range of different injuries and wounds to the spine.

I am thankful for the help of the librarian at the UT Tyler library and my daughter, during my original research, for helping me locate the microfilm of the US Surgeon General's office, *The Medical and Surgical History of the War of the Rebellion (1861-65)*, Surgeon General Joseph K. Barnes. The exhaustive medical records, opinions, and experiences of the great doctors of that time—including Dr. John A. Lidell, Dr. Chisolm, and Dr. P.F. Eve—facilitated progressive research and changes in patient care. The Civil War forever altered the medical field in America. I once again encourage my readers to reference my research sources listed at the end of my book. I made a definite choice to pursue a character that I knew, outside of this work of fiction, in all likelihood, would not have survived his injuries. However, James has survived within these pages for reasons no one can explain and known only by God as he acknowledges during his conversation with Boyd in Chapter Two. This character would not allow me to file him away, and I hope our country never files away the many sacrifices of its soldiers. I want to take this opportunity to acknowledge the service and sacrifices of all those who have ever served or are serving in our country's armed services. Each deserves our gratitude.

Writing the original sequel, as well as this revised novel, took me on a journey full of serendipity. I delight in sharing it with you.

In Joy,

Lana Lynne

2010 and 2018

Chapter One

The brush flew through the doorway toward Boyd's dusty hat. The well-honed reflexes established during battle did not desert him, and he ducked just in time. Curiosity overcame him, and he proceeded up the stairs as the sound of a distraught female voice, followed by the slam of a door, reached his ears. A bulky man with graying hair lingered just inside the open doorway. He stared at the closed door on the left as one entered the house. The man shook his head and turned to the small woman behind him. She wrung her hands.

"Joe, I do not understand her. What have we done wrong?"

"Agnes, she's a female, so you should know. I'll wait in the wagon. You get her out here, or we'll go alone this morning," Joe said and brushed past Boyd toward the porch. He stopped short, turning his head, fixing a squinted gaze on the newcomer. "Who are you?"

Boyd removed his hat and wiped his dusty hand on his shirt before stretching out his hand. "Boyd Richards. Mr. Pierce sent me. Are you Joe Kennedy?"

"Yes, I am. How is Shanghai? He sent a telegram about you. I'm sure you're qualified for the job." Mr. Kennedy completed the handshake. He motioned for Boyd to follow as he continued his descent to the waiting buckboard. He climbed in and took the reins. "Excuse me." Joe turned his face toward the house and yelled, "Agnes! Lucy! Get out here now. Church services won't wait!" He then fixed his snapping brown eyes on Boyd. "Go out to the bunkhouse and have Ted get you settled. Then go on into town for the day or whatever you like. I'll see you at sunup tomorrow."

"Yes, sir," he said, sidestepping to clear the way for the storm of the two women descending on them. Agnes passed, twisting and

1

pinning the young woman's honey-colored hair, with much difficulty, as they came. Joe Kennedy's daughter jerked away from her mother and glared at Boyd as she clambered into the wagon. Older than her earlier tantrum had indicated and prettier than he cared to admit, he avoided her gaze and assisted her mother up to her seat. The wagon then disappeared in a cloud of dust.

A deep chuckle behind him caused him to turn. A tall, muscled cowboy with twinkling hazel eyes looked over his shoulder. He frowned and then fastened a serious look on his face.

"That female tornado is Lucy Kennedy. Her moods are like Texas weather, ever changing and unpredictable."

"Thanks for the warning. Do you know Ted?"

The man tipped his hat. "That'd be me. And you're?"

"Boyd Richards, new hand."

"Yeah, we've been expecting you. I'll show you where to put your gear and then take you to town. The guys sleep, go to church, or go to town on Sunday. Not much going on, but Hallie will get us lunch and maybe a drink if we ask nice like." Ted slapped him on the shoulder.

Boyd couldn't help but think of his brother in East Texas. The choice would be church for him, as well as his friends there. He left them six months ago. A wave of guilt washed over him. Marc and Florence had married and left Arkansas to help him. His brother and two friends, former slaves on his uncle's plantation, had been so excited at their arrival. The reunion started out well, and he even considered staying for a while. Then a huge confrontation and fight occurred after they forced him to read the letter his wife had written him as she died and the scripture that went with it. A lump formed in his throat at the memory of the printed words; it had pricked his hardened heart and almost broken him. Almost, but he could not, would not, let the God she loved comfort him. The death of his son and wife would never make sense to him. The war took him away from them, and with him, the protection they should have had. Boyd would never forgive himself. He shook it off and tried to concentrate on the information Ted imparted on the way to the bunkhouse.

~

A little over an hour later, they arrived in town. It seemed the saloon doubled as a café on Sundays. They dismounted outside the swinging doors and tied their horses before proceeding inside. A raven-haired woman of an acquired age met them with a practiced smile on her face. "Welcome, boys! Ted, introduce me to your friend. New blood is always welcome." She smiled and slapped Boyd on the backside.

Amusement and offense filled Boyd all at the same time. His genteel upbringing in Georgia had trained him as a gentleman but also taught him to appreciate a beautiful woman. Nancy had captured his appreciation and heart; his affection had been for her alone. Since losing her, he had refused himself all tender feelings. Now might just be the time to amend the situation. Even as he thought it, his heart cried foul.

Ted chuckled, placing a hand on his shoulder. "This here is Boyd Richards. Boyd, let me introduce Miss Hallie Price."

Boyd turned on his most charming smile, bowing over her hand and brushing the back with his lips. "Enchanted, ma'am, you're as fresh as a magnolia." As he straightened, he saw a hint of color grace her cheeks. It pleased him to see her blush.

"Well, well, Mr. Richards. I think we need to have a *long* chat," she said.

Ted cleared his throat. "Let him catch his breath, Hallie. He just got here. Besides, we came for lunch and refreshment."

Hallie sighed and inclined her head toward Boyd. "Just remember, I saw you first. My girls will swarm once they get an eyeful of you, darling. Now, come this way. We've got steak and potatoes."

Boyd and Ted followed her swaying form to a table close to the bar. She left to retrieve their orders. Before long, Boyd noticed the girls huddled at the end of the bar. They whispered and giggled as they cast their eyes toward their table. One rouged blonde soon made her way to them. Ted grabbed her around the waist with one arm. She laughed but kept her eyes on Boyd. Before she could speak, Hallie reappeared with their plates. The tantalizing smells from the steaming dishes reached out to Boyd's growling stomach. He turned his attention toward his food as the two women exchanged competitive glances.

Hallie shook her head at the younger woman. "Not today, dear. He's mine for the afternoon. Why don't you take Ted here upstairs and feed him this fine supper. He might want dessert if you treat him nice."

Ted didn't protest, even though the young woman gave a pretty pout. They soon disappeared. Boyd hadn't seen action this fast since the soiled ladies had descended on the regiments as they entered towns during the war. Hallie had one thing to learn. He hadn't let himself be pushed then, and he wouldn't now.

"If you don't mind, ma'am, I prefer to eat my dinner right here," he said, cutting a bite of steak. He gestured to the seat opposite of him. "However, I would welcome some conversation if you'd care to join me." Hallie smirked but complied.

"What's your story, cowboy?" she asked as she leaned forward on the table.

He presented a masked face at the inquiry. His calculating regard found her waiting with an open expression.

"One best left untold. How about you? Ever married?"

She seemed unruffled. "Yes, I was married once. He died in the war, but it was over in so many ways long before that."

"What happened?" The frankness of these so-called "soiled doves" stirred his admiration. They stroked a man's ego to get his money but didn't build themselves up to be more than they were. Ironic, but it saddened him in a way.

Her chocolate gaze met his golden eyes. "Well, he wanted my body but dismissed my mind and dreams. After a few years, I was shriveling up inside. It may sound harsh, but in a way the war did me a favor. The way I saw it, I could still have men support me and give them what they valued without being disappointed in what they didn't. This way, my thoughts and dreams are mine to have and nourish. No expectation that someone else cares enough to make them come true. Most men are simple enough. They have needs. Once satisfied, they're pretty easy to deal with. However, women are not simple creatures, especially wives. Wives have expectations. As a wife, I expected my husband to value and protect me. My pa chose whiskey as his sole companion once my ma died, and he was glad to be rid of me when our neighbor came asking for my hand. It extinguished the glimmer of girlish hope that had managed to survive my childhood. Now, I take care of myself without expectation of rescue. Why would I ever feel the need to be married? This way I'm happy and the men I serve are happy."

Boyd met her unflinching appraisal as he pondered her words. Quite a synopsis cynical yet not bitter—and, in many ways, accurate. Had he not had a marriage that disproved her theory, as well as observed marriages like Marc and Florey's, he might have agreed. He took another bite of his steak and chewed before responding.

"I have to concede that's true for many of the people I've met but not all. Your husband must have been very short sighted and held more to the image he saw in the mirror than the one in your eyes. I found the most candid view of myself in my wife's eyes. If she lost her smile for me somewhere in the midst of sickness, fatigue, and pain, I wasn't doing my job. Even if I didn't always understand her moods, I had to find a way to know she was content with me."

Hallie exhaled in a gush. "You never failed her?"

A wave of self-hatred cross his face, "Yes, but she never failed me."

"Where is she then?"

"Dead," he bit out. She sure made it easy to talk. It surprised him. He gave her an apologetic smile as he pushed the plate of his half-eaten meal away. "Miss Hallie, you're a good listener. Give me time to settle. You never know."

He saw admiration on her face. She nodded as he rose to leave. "I'll hold you to that, cowboy. I'll tell Ted you had to leave. You come back soon, you hear?"

Boyd gave her a small salute as he replaced his hat and turned toward the doorway. He ignored the female gazes that followed him from the bar.

Once outside, he arched his still trail-weary back and stretched as he appraised the town: store, post office, church, schoolyard … nothing unusual. The more towns he saw, the more he realized the basic places for similar needs stayed the same. Now, people were a different story. People lived in common ways, but their characters differed. He once thought them replicated until the war. The unique compilations of individuals reflected their upbringing, the people who surrounded them, the joys and tragedies through which they traveled. Boyd found two people might go through a comparable situation, but not react, survive, or feel about it in the same way. People remained selfish, short sighted, and judgmental because they found it easier than giving, looking deeper, and forgiving. He shook his head at the last one. It indicted him, forgiveness—the hardest one. After a final look down the street, he pulled down the brim of his hat, done with his philosophies for one day. He stepped down to the hitching post, gathered his reins, and swung up on his horse. A slow canter sufficed until he reached the edge of the town, then he urged his horse into a full run, leaning close against his neck.

~

By the time he reached the ranch, his mood had darkened. He dreaded entering the bunkhouse, and meeting more people. Therefore, he took his time as he watered and groomed his horse. The tension ebbed out of him with each rhythmic stroke of the currycomb. His mustang had been with him for almost two years. They had a loyal partnership. All cowboys knew the value of a good horse.

A hot breeze washed over him as he left the barn. The end of July, with the relentless Texas heat, drained. The water well near the bunkhouse beckoned him. As he drew up the bucket, he glanced toward the main house as a movement on the porch caught his eye. Joe Kennedy's daughter stood on the porch with one hand shading her eyes as she gazed toward the road from town. She remained there a moment before dropping her hand. Her gaze shifted in his direction. She turned and proceeded inside the house. Ted had supplied the name of Lucy. Boyd's first impression pegged her as a spoiled child. Although hard to determine her exact age, her tall stature dismissed his initial summation. He made it a practice to study people and determine their true natures. It didn't take as long with some. This one could take a while—maybe not worth the effort. Boyd took a drink from the dipper, wiped his mouth with the back of his hand, and headed toward his lodgings.

~

Nights had long ceased to be restful and peaceful since the war. Boyd either had dreams of the war or Nancy. He could almost bear the ones of the battles in their graphic detail more than the bittersweet ones of his wife. The Civil War ended, but losing his wife proved an ongoing nightmare. This night's dream returned him to Georgia. Just sixteen, he walked beside Nancy on the plantation road to his uncle's house, the smell of magnolia trees in the air. He pulled a blossom and handed it to her with a gallant bow, his thick blond hair flopping across his forehead. She laughed, and as he straightened with a twinkle in his eye, she reached out and brushed back his hair. He swallowed and held his breath as he took her hand.

"Nancy, I will marry you one day," he declared. Her green eyes locked on his earnest face.

"My Boyd boy, your uncle will never allow it. You and Ben will run his plantation one day. My family rents our farm," she said, her long brown hair blowing across her face. He tucked the dancing strands behind her ears.

The picture waved like looking through water, and scenes continued to flash. Nancy in the small chapel on their wedding day. Nancy when they arrived in East Texas on their new land, jumping out of the wagon, arms spread like wings as she spun around in the yard. Nancy as she worked beside him and Ben to build the house and plow the fields. Nancy's glowing face as she told him he would soon be a father. Nancy smiling through her tears, as she told him good-bye as he left for war. Then he saw her standing at the end of a long road, and he ran toward her but could never reach her. "Nancy, Nancy, Nancy!" Her face loomed in front of him, peaceful, yet sad. "Boyd boy, let me go. Live. Let Him—" Boyd twisted in his bunk and sat upright. The dreams had intensified in the past three months. He hung his head and whispered, "I can't, Nancy." He fell back against his pillow and listened to the snores of the other cowboys.

Boyd didn't sleep after the dream. The eternity between night and dawn seemed endless. Thoughts of the two men he considered as friends occupied his thoughts. John and Marc had made sacrifices for him that no one had the right to offer. They'd stayed with him after he returned home to discover Nancy and his son had died. After their release from Ft. Delaware prison, circumstances and illness prevented his friends' immediate return to Arkansas. He also knew they fled from their own inner horrors at the time. After a few months, they remained by his side and made their way to South Texas, learned to break horses, and herd cattle.

Working cattle sunup to sundown, in addition to the previous years of war served together, had created a bond of steel. He missed them now. Boyd knew he didn't seek to form such friendships again.

He received a letter from John before he left Mr. Pierce's ranch. It announced Dawn, John's wife, expected a baby. Boyd's throat constricted as he read the news. He didn't begrudge his friend, but it renewed the painful memory of the loss of his son.

Going to Arkansas last autumn in 1866 with John and Marc had helped him become more open to family again. It had bred the brief consideration of staying on his farm in East Texas. However, his fight with his brother, Ben, had removed any residual thoughts on the issue.

That's enough, Richards! He sat up, ran his fingers through his shaggy blond hair, and threw off the covers. The rest of the bunkhouse occupants still slumbered for now. He donned his clothes and carried his boots and hat to the door.

The air blew warmth on his bearded face as he closed the door behind him. He placed boots on his feet and headed for the corral. His mustang whinnied in response to the soft click of Boyd's tongue before trotting over to him.

"Hey, boy, you're not sleepy either?" He rubbed his trail companion's nose and patted his neck. The maple brown eyes stared at him in expectancy

"No, boy, we aren't going anywhere today. I have to break a few of your wild friends this morning. Be patient, though. The trail drive days will be here soon."

The sound of the bunkhouse door opening behind him drew his focus. He turned to see Ted emerging.

"Morning, Richards," Ted drawled, pulling his hat down on his head. "I tell you those mattresses get bumpier, but it still beats the ground." He wiped perspiration off his upper lip. "It's too bad it won't start cooling off a bit this month, but it should be brisker, especially at night, on the return trip after the drive."

Boyd grinned. "I tell you, the heat on the trail to Kansas was unbelievable, even starting out in April. I got a bath the day after we got there at the end of June."

"I hear Shanghai's 'sea lions' are pretty wild cattle. It must've been a tough drive north."

"No, they move pretty quick and are strong. The big problem was the scare of Texas fever. They held the cattle in Indian

Territory and will be shipping them from Abilene this month."

Ted nodded. "Still … going north is the way to make money. I mean the average Texas price is about nine dollars for a steer. It jumps to about thirty dollars in Missouri, where we drove ours, and increases to over eighty dollars in the East, I'm told."

"Yeah, we got over thirty dollars a head. At least it's increasing, Ted. We all remember right after the war when we got maybe three to six dollars, or even less a head. I have to help my brother, Ben. The drought this past year didn't help in trying to make the farm work."[i]

Ted whistled. "That's tough. I do remember. I was with Mr. Goodnight then. Being a new drover proved tough, but dealings with Indians made it worse. Still is. I understand you came back on the Kansas Trail, or should I say, Chisholm's Trail." He waited for Boyd to nod. "That's the one we are supposed to take for this drive. I gather your knowledge of the trail is why you're here."

"Yeah, we used to the old Shawnee Trail before, but this one splits off the Shawnee above Waco and goes through Fort Worth, not Dallas. It continues into Indian country after the crossing at Red River, and on into Kansas to Abilene."[ii]

Ted nodded toward the small herd of cattle in the second corral. "Are you recovered enough for this bunch?"

Boyd grinned. "A much more amenable number, pard. It should take a month less to reach market. Are you ready?"

Ted patted him on the shoulder. "Yep. It'll be a more diminished stampede."

Boyd did not grin. You didn't joke about that occurrence.

Ted shook his head. "I'm not funning. We had one on our last drive, and I lost a friend. The herd was massive. Richards, we'll be on this drive together until November. Let's not start out with misunderstandings." Ted stuck out his hand, and Boyd shook it. He didn't stand ready to be Ted's friend, nor did he wish to be his enemy. They both propped their arms on the fence rail, surveying the horses in the adjacent corral.

"You need to break four of those today. Then we have to finish the branding of the remaining cattle to go on the drive. We leave at the end of the week," Ted said, turning all business.

Boyd narrowed his eyes in thought before turning his golden level gaze on Ted. "Let's get to it."

Ted's eyes widened in slight surprise, and he asked, "Before breakfast?"

Boyd fixed his unflinching gaze on him.

Ted put his hands on his hips and turned toward the house for a moment. He turned back to Boyd. "Let's go."

Boyd made a firm but slow approach, talking to the dappled grey mustang in gentle tones before throwing his rope. The whinnied protest and reared resistance dissipated after a few moments. Boyd placed the saddle and the horse reared, pawing the air with his hooves. Boyd continued his gentle address and never let his gaze leave the stormy eyes, which averted to reveal the whites in fear and defiance. He kept one hand on the rope and one outstretched to stroke the neck and nose each time the front hooves made contact with the ground. Once he felt the animal's resolve weaken, he swung into the saddle, prepared for the eruption of new defiance as the beautiful beast fought to maintain his independence and freedom.

The other cowhands filed out to check the noise coming from the yard. Boyd's complete state of concentration made him oblivious to everything around him. He loved and respected each animal he rode. The battle continued with both participants focused on different outcomes until the horse seemed to succumb to the man's immovable presence and ceased his bucking.

Boyd didn't change the pressure of his legs but lessened his pull on the reins as he moved his mount into a slow gallop around the corral. He became aware of his audience, whooping and hollering as he circled the corral. He inclined his head in acknowledgement. A flash of blue drew his gaze to the corner of the fence closest to the main house.

Lucy Kennedy rose from her seat on a barrel at the corner of the house and dusted off her skirt. She held what appeared to be a tablet of some sort in her arms against her sky blue blouse. She smiled at his fleeting regard, flashing a dimple before moving her hands in a silent clapping motion. The oddest occurrence then transpired. Boyd found himself grinning. He remedied the action and averted his head as he slowed to a trot toward Ted. He hoped no one else had noticed. A surge of anger shot through him, and he dismounted.

"Richards, that was—," Ted began.

"Which one is next?" Boyd asked, looking past Ted to the remaining animals in the holding pen.

The look of admiration reflected on Ted's face faltered. A mixture of veiled irritation and confusion followed.

Boyd realized the man struggled to figure out the new hired hand. It didn't bother him. In fact, Boyd preferred it. He didn't do this job for ego, didn't want praise, nor friends.

Ted sent him a warning look and called for their youngest hand, Billy, to get the brown stallion.

All the men, except for Ted Dalton and young Billy Cooper, dissipated and headed for chow, as Boyd addressed his second challenge. Billy appeared about the age of his younger brother. A lanky youth with light sandy-brown hair, a hawkish nose, and earnest, multi-hued eyes, which at first glance were blue then green flecks sparkled as you engaged in longer conversation. The pair remained his audience until the last horse trotted around the corral.

Close to lunch, the hungry trio met up with the rest of the hands. They downed the food before they tasted it. Ted looked up at Boyd and grinned as he wiped his mouth with the back of his hand.

"I got hungry just watching you work. I bet you were plumb caved in after tying up with those broncos."

"Yeah, Boyd, I've never seen anybody do it the way you do," Billy said.

Boyd's gaze narrowed as he judged their sincerity and allowed a slight grin. He gestured to his empty plate with his fork

"You don't see anything left, do you?"

The three laughed and transitioned into good-natured banter as they deposited their plates into the barrel by the chow wagon. They mounted their horses.

The hard, focused work of branding cattle took up the afternoon. The odor of singed cowhide mixed with their sweat lingered at the end of the day. In preparation for the trail drive ahead, all cattle received a trail brand in addition to Mr. Kennedy's brand.

About fifteen men went on the spring trail drive, but the boss signed twelve for the autumn one due to the smaller herd. Ted said Mr. Kennedy debated whether to send the same number of drovers due to the Indian threat but decided to go with the lesser number.

They planned on a hard drive due to the difficulty in trail breaking cattle. It made them unpredictable. However, the challenges to come were what consumed Boyd like a prairie fire. He loved it. While a soldier, he stayed alert at all times. He remained more comfortable, focused, and at home with the flow of adrenaline.

Billy, Ted, and Boyd worked as a team all afternoon. They untied the legs of the last steer branded close to four thirty. Boyd took off his hat and wiped the sweat from his brow with his sleeved arm. An unusual breeze stirred the air and cooled his perspiration-soaked head. He removed his father's pocket watch from his dirty trousers, flipped it opened, and closed it almost in tandem. A good day with no thoughts or dwellings on anything but the tasks to be completed. They planned for an August departure for the trail instead of September, so this pushed preparations. Everything must be ready in four days.

~

None of the men had trouble sleeping that night, including Boyd. Tuesday morning dawned in a wink. Ted enlisted him to go with him into town to pick up the final supplies needed on the trail. They left after breakfast. It felt strange to ride in the seat of a farm wagon after months in a saddle.

Boyd scanned the list: molasses, sugar, jugs of vinegar, coffee, dried fruit, flour—

"We can put the wagon outside of the store. While you get those items, I'll go down and see the blacksmith about those new irons and harnesses," Ted interrupted.

Boyd nodded. "I'll load up and then ride down there to help you."

They traveled in silence the rest of the way to the already bustling town. Ted pulled the reins as they came alongside the general store. He jumped to the ground, gave Boyd a nod as he looped the reins to the post, and headed toward the north end of town.

Boyd removed his hat as he entered the store. The clerk assisted an older lady. She reminded him of his aunt Elizabeth.

"My wife will be right with you, sir," the man greeted him. A woman straightened from behind the counter with a ready smile on her face.

"How may I help you, Mister—"

"Richards. Boyd Richards. I need some things for Mr. K—"

"Kennedy!" she finished and rounded the counter, shaking with excitement.

Boyd stepped back. They must need the business. The woman clapped her hands together.

"I've been just so looking forward to meeting you. I'm Virginia Thornton, and this is my husband, Peter, as well as the sheriff's wife, Bertha Reynolds," she said as she took his arm and pulled him to where the others stood.

How could this woman even know anything about him? Before he had a chance to respond, Mrs. Thornton spoke again.

"The article in the newspaper this morning was so exciting! A real war hero and quite a cowboy from the sketch she drew. I do wish I could see you with those wild horses."

She nodded and smiled so wide it hurt his face just looking at her.

Mrs. Reynolds joined the gleeful tirade. "Yes, yes! We're glad to have someone who's worked with the Pierce brothers."

It kept getting worse. Who had written an article about him?

Mr. Thornton tried to rescue him. "Now, ladies, you'll scare the man out of the store, and then he'll get fired for not doing his job. Give him some room. Mr. Richards, may I please have your list?"

Grateful, Boyd handed it to the man, gathered his wits, and smiled at the now anxious looking ladies. He clasped his hat like a shield.

"My dear ladies, I'm afraid you have me at quite a disadvantage. I have no knowledge of such an article, and I can promise my character is exaggerated. However, I thank you for the kind welcome."

He'd hoped to disarm and diffuse them, but instead, from the close-to-swooning looks on their faces, further infused their rapture. Mrs. Thornton placed a hand to her neck and gazed his way with adoration. If she the woman didn't have fifteen years on him, Mr. Thornton might have asked to see him on the field of honor. The husband in question shook his head as he filled the order behind the counter.

"No, Mr. Richards, if anything, Miss Kennedy did not begin

to do you justice," Mrs. Thornton said.

"Miss Lucy Kennedy?"

"Yes, she works at the newspaper. Didn't you know? Oh dear," she said.

She bustled around the counter and pulled out a newspaper.

Boyd followed her and took it after she turned to the article in question. It included a detailed sketch of him on one of the broncos from yesterday next to the three-paragraph article. It listed his service record in Hood's brigade, his time with the Pierce brothers, and mentioned his childhood on a plantation in Georgia. The well written, and for the most part factual, piece took few liberties. He exhaled when he found no mention of Nancy. The source of Miss Kennedy's information didn't appear in the article of course, but he planned to discover the reason anyone felt they had the right to share anything about him.

"Everything's ready, Mr. Richards," Mr. Thornton said, drawing his attention. "I'll help you get it to the wagon."

He returned the paper to the proprietress. "Ladies, thank you, again." He replaced his hat and went to assist Mr. Thornton.

They loaded the supplies. The storeowner outstretched his hand. "I do apologize for my wife, Mr. Richards. She's always so excited when we get a new person in town."

"Does Miss Kennedy write articles about all the new people in town?"

"Of course she does, unless they're drifters. People like to know the identity of the new faces on the streets. It helps them not be so nervous. You understand, don't you?"

"Somewhat. Thank you, Mr. Thornton. Would you be so kind as to give me the directions to the newspaper, as well as the blacksmith's?"

The information obtained, they shook hands, and Boyd headed for the blacksmith's. He found Ted still waiting.

"It's going to be another half hour before he's finished," Ted said. "We can leave the wagon here and go get any other items we need."

"You go ahead. I don't need anything right now. It'll give me a chance to explore the town."

The two men parted, and Boyd headed to the right side of the street to the newspaper office. Before entering, he stopped by the window and watched the three people inside. As the only female in the office, he spotted Lucy Kennedy with ease. Her profile resembled a fine cameo. Tendrils of honey-gold hair escaped the coiled, restrained silken locks at the nape of her neck, brow, and temples. A squared jaw line, high cheekbones, and a streamline nose with just a slight button-like tip. Then she looked up, turned her head, and saw him. She smiled, and the dimple in her left cheek flashed. Boyd let out the breath he didn't realize he held. He opened the door as she stood to meet him.

"Mr. Richards. What a pleasant surprise! Are you in town for supplies?"

"Thank you, Miss Kennedy, and yes. Ted and I came in this morning."

"Please, have a seat. What brings you to our newspaper?" she asked as she resumed her seat and he settled into the opposite chair. Her blue-green eyes sparkled with good will.

He removed his hat, looking down a moment before returning her direct gaze. Her soft, quick intake of air indicted his advantage and he let his tiger gaze challenge her to look away first. His stare intimidated most men. However, she didn't blink. So he got to the reason for his visit.

"Your article."

"Oh, you read it?"

"I do read, Miss Kennedy."

"I didn't mean to insinuate otherwise. It's just that the paper came out this morning, and I didn't realize you had already seen it. I intended to bring you a copy this evening."

"Pardon my assumption, ma'am. There seems to be some confusion due to some liberties taken. My concerns start with the fact that we've never met, yet you felt the freedom to write about me. How do you know your information is correct?"

The woman sat taller and her eyes flashed with defiance before she looked away. When she glanced back his way, her demeanor had changed, the former sparkle replaced with subtle anger mingled with sadness.

She stretched out her hand. "Lucy Kennedy, at your service. If there are any corrections needed to the information our paper has printed, I'll be happy to oblige. I don't reveal my sources under normal circumstances, and I do like to verify information as much as possible. However, my confidence is high in the information Mr. Pierce sent in his letter of recommendation from which my father employed you. Your skill with horses came from my direct observations and resulting sketches by me yesterday morning. As you are leaving on the trail drive on Friday, I wanted to introduce you to the town before you left. It seems I've made an error in judgment; it's not my first. Please accept my apology."

What gave him the right to steal the joy from a lady who'd meant him no harm? The satisfaction in shutting others out of his life, even his own brother, did not find him. Not today.

He reached out his hand and placed it in hers, receiving a firm shake. "Boyd Richards."

She withdrew her hand and he relinquished it with regret.

"No apology is needed. I made the error in judgment. It seems you violated my desire for privacy without malice," he said.

She didn't respond. Instead, her blue-green eyes held him in steady regard.

Boyd shifted in his chair.

~

Most cowboys wanted to see their name in print. Lucy liked to print any history of trouble so the people of the town knew the risks. Too many took advantage of her being the boss's daughter, and she mistrusted most advances. This one came recommended without reservations. No scandals. Her first hand observation of his patience with and connection to horses furthered her confidence. It never occurred to her that he might object to a complimentary article of introduction. Her mistake. She wanted to dismiss him into the broad box of most men. However, something about him stopped her. Except for the brief instant on the porch on Sunday, they had not met up close until now. His burnished blond head, trim cut mustache and beard, and . . . those eyes. He stood at that moment, she blinked and rose as he tipped his hat.

"Good day to you, Miss Kennedy. Thank you for your kind prose on my behalf."

"You're welcome, Mr. Richards."

She watched him leave. He must be over six feet. Her unusual height of five foot eight inches irritated most prospective suitors. This line of thinking would never do. She looked around to find her editor and typesetter smirking. Mr. Jenkins cleared his throat and stroked his mustache.

"I would say the article didn't capture Mr. Richards to his best advantage. He's even more impressive in person. Would you not agree, Miss Kennedy?"

Her face grew warm. "Yes, sir. I better finish this one on the Andersons."

The two men shared a smile and returned to their own work.

~

Everything seemed out of kilter as Boyd strode down the street toward the blacksmith's shed. He found his self-imposed isolation and control somewhat distasteful at this moment. It irritated him. As he checked for activity before crossing the street, his emotions smoldered like a geyser ready to erupt. He waited for a wagon to pass and stepped into the street. The sound of his name caused him to turn back and squint through the trailing dust. A well-dressed man advanced toward him.

"Mr. Richards, isn't it?" The man gave him a broad smile. He had an unusual light in his eyes. Gray sprinkled hair topped his uncovered head.

"Yes, sir, is there something you needed?" *I'm almost past being polite.* He didn't try to hide the aggravation he felt.

The man continued in a pleasant and patient tone. "No, sir, I just wanted to welcome you and invite you to church services. I'm the town's pastor, Brother Adam Moore. I was planning to ride out to see you today until I saw you leaving the newspaper office."

Boyd frowned. "This town sure is quick on the trigger. Anyway, I won't be here Sunday. We leave on Friday."

Brother Moore nodded. "I know. The church will still be here when you return."

"Why talk to me now?"

The man's gaze penetrated, as if he could see Boyd's soul. "So I'll know how to pray for you." He paused again. "There's something I want you to consider on your journey. We are not unlike the cattle you herd. We're afraid of the unknown trail. We stampede when spooked. We will get lost, kill each other out of ignorance and desperation, or die early on this trail of life. All because we refuse to trust and heed guidance. Sometimes, there's disease that takes us, and we don't understand the futility of it." Boyd flinched, but Brother Moore continued, "However, if we become like the lead steers that have learned to trust the trail boss and his hands, we get to our destination fat and at peace."

Boyd sneered. "Then we die, being led to the slaughter."

The preacher smiled. "We're all destined to die, Mr. Richards. It's who we become on the trail that determines how well and in what condition—in peace or in turmoil. Who we trust determines eternity."

"Trust? A man can only trust others as much as he trusts himself, and it's not even wise to do that. Self-betrayal is always ripe," Boyd stated.

"Is there anyone you trust, Mr. Richards?"

Boyd didn't want to continue this conversation. However, he remained confident in his stance. "Yes, the two men I call friends."

"Why do you trust them?"

"They've fought beside me, worked beside me, and have sacrificed themselves for me."

"So has Jesus. Come see me when you return, Mr. Richards. I'll be praying for you. Good-bye." The man patted Boyd on the shoulder. He turned and retreated up the street.

Boyd's eyes narrowed as he navigated his way across the street to find Ted. Boyd noted everything loaded in the wagon.

"Ready?"

Ted nodded, and they climbed onto the wagon. The foreman reached under the seat and handed him a copy of the newspaper with a caustic grin. Boyd resisted the urge to knock him off his perch.

"Friday can't get here soon enough," he said.

Ted laughed but soon sobered as he caught Boyd's warning glare.

"Richards, you'd better keep that under control. Mr. Kennedy won't be with us this trip. Don't forget who's trail boss," Ted said as he slapped the reins.

Boyd's military service under tougher men might serve him well. All animosities must be channeled into the enemies found on the trail.

Chapter Two

Cowboys had plenty of time for contemplation; that is, as long as the herd and the elements cooperated. The events Boyd had recirculated in his head for the past four hours now bored him. The mild weather calmed, and the cows meandered like a lazy river bumping up against the banks provided by the cowboys who drove them. The drive yielded a peaceful day for once. He should have been grateful, given the events of the past month on the trail.

The first week their targeted fifteen miles a day had been slowed by rain. Wearing slickers got to be tiresome after three days even though they appreciated the moisture. They'd lost twenty-five steers.

The second week stayed routine. Ted maintained excellent control of the outfit. He always scouted ahead for a noon stopping point that had water and a place for a campsite nearby when they'd pushed the herd until they couldn't see well. Boyd and a grizzled hand named Roy rode point each day to guide the herd. Frank, a Swede from the Round Rock area, and young Billy were their swingmen. The rest alternated as flank riders and drag men keeping the herd grouped and moving forward. The men worked hard and had been on two-hour shifts at night. Boyd loved the sound of the hymns and old songs they used to keep the cattle at peace at night. Even though the voices weren't always the best, they brought comfort. The night also echoed with sounds of nature, which nourished his soul. Not much talk on the trail, but plenty of silent communication.

The crossing of the Red River came during the third week. As expected, it turned into an ordeal; some of the cattle drowned when they started milling midstream. Boyd and Roy had saved the majority by untangling the leading cows for the rest to follow.

Such a long day—they'd built a raft for the chuck wagon to cross. Old Amos, the cook, stayed even crankier than usual until the wagon reached the opposite bank. After a new head count, they'd proceeded.

A few days later they came upon a smoking farm. An old woman sat in a rocking chair on a still intact porch. She held a small child on her lap. Part of the roof and front walls remained, but embers smoldered where the rest of the structure should have been.

Ted dismounted and motioned for Boyd to approach with him after instructing the other men to keep the herd contained. Boyd noticed the almost tandem motion of his fellow riders as they drew their side arms as wariness penetrated the air. He'd once carried a pistol but soon opted for a Henry rifle. For some reason, more men challenged him when he carried hand artillery. Bullets, life, and time were too expensive to waste on men trying to make a name with a gun. His gut wrenching memories of watching men die during the war removed the desire to pursue violence. However, if Indians came around, they all needed to stand ready.

The woman lifted her eyes at their approach, clutching the child tighter as she watched them.

She uttered one word. "Indians."

Their eyes darted, scanning the perimeter.

"How long have they been gone, ma'am?" Ted asked.

"First light," she said.

Boyd wondered if the woman had moved from this spot all day. The boy on her lap looked about two years old and seemed too quiet. Boyd used a soothing voice, as if talking to a wild mustang about to bolt, "Ma'am, I'm getting down now." He dismounted, received a nod from Ted, and mounted the porch.

She held the child tighter. Boyd crouched down beside them but didn't touch them. His golden eyes met her brown ones, which began to swim with tears. Still he waited. As the tears began to course down her face, she reached and grasped his arm with one worn hand, not releasing her hold on the boy.

Her anguished-filled eyes locked with his as her broken voice reverberated like a gun shot. "They took my daughter ... his mother."

Then the sobs came, and the boy began to wail. Boyd gathered them both in his arms. He heard Ted grimace and mutter something best left indiscernible. Then young Billy dismounted and hurried forward. The young hand paused by Ted and said something in a hushed tone. Ted waved him forward; Billy pointed at the boy as he approached. Boyd nodded.

"Ma'am, young Billy here wants to cheer up your grandson," he said.

She stiffened for a moment, looking back at Boyd before nodding. The wails rose louder, like a calf caught in a thicket without his mother, as Billy lifted the boy from her lap. However, the young cowhand didn't leave the porch but squatted, taking his harmonica from his pocket. As soon as the first notes trilled, the child's cries dimmed to whimpers, and then a slight smile emerged. Boyd turned his attention back to the grandmother. She struggled for composure, and her words painted the horrible picture of the morning's events.

"We were sleeping. Hank, my son-in-law, heard his horse and the cow raising a fuss. He looked out of the window and saw an Indian sneaking into the barn. Molly came to see, but he motioned her back. He told her to wake me and to take Charlie down into the cellar. We were quiet and hidden, but she heard Hank's gun go off and wanted to check on him. She asked me to stay with Charlie. She covered the opening of the cellar as she left. In a few moments, I heard her scream and many voices above us. It took everything in me to stay put with young Charlie. Believe it or not, he still slept in my arms ... Then I smelled smoke. Hank had made a tunnel from the cellar to behind the well to use for shelter during bad weather. I used it. They were already in the distance; the sounds of their heathen shouts and horses mixed with my daughter's screams and filled the still dim sky as I carried my grandson above ground." She pointed to a coarse barn. "Hank's body is over there."

Ted rode over to the barn and dismounted. Roy and Boyd followed, catching his gaze as he turned. The warning on his face came too late as they looked past him. The man lay just inside the entrance. Insects swarmed the scene. The gruesome work completed after the Indians killed Hank silenced them. Boyd had seen death too many times, but this spectacle pushed him into an abyss in the darkest place inside of himself. He continued to run from the reality of the war, the memory of lives he had taken, the loss of his family, and any chance of happiness. However, a residual hope flickered until that moment. Life held little value to most men. Women cared and gave life, but for what purpose? His mind reeled; numbness and apathy bred of weariness encompassed him.

"Let's bury him and be on our way," he said.

The other two men nodded. They found a shovel and started digging beside the barn.

Billy stayed with Elizabeth and Charlie as they worked. He played the harmonica as the grandmother rocked her grandson. A dust cloud and the sound of multiple horses with riders approaching ended the young hand's attempts of appeasement.

"Ted, riders coming," Billy called.

A cavalry patrol of about twenty men rode into the yard. Ted instructed Roy to help the men keep the cattle from getting spooked as he went to meet the troops. Boyd continued his grim task. He heard Ted and the lead officer talking. As sweat mixed with dirt poured downward, he removed his hat and wiped his eyes and forehead with his sleeve.

"Captain Richards?" a deep, familiar voice like rough granite demanded his attention.

Boyd narrowed his eyes as he replaced his hat and let the shovel fall to the ground. He crossed to stand beside Ted and face the man from his past.

He ignored the questioning looks from Ted. Instead, he met the outstretched hand of Ronald Hawkins. "Lieutenant." The sun-leathered and battle impressed face broke into a rare smile, sending crinkles around piercing blue eyes. "It's Major Hawkins now, Captain, I mean … Mr. Richards. I hope to find the time to inquire about our common acquaintances at the resolution of this imminent situation."

Each previous encounter with this U.S. military officer raised his estimation of him. This time held no exception. The major knew Boyd's preference for privacy, and Boyd didn't fear exposure in front of the cowhands with which he shared company.

"Please continue your report of the events of this unfortunate day," the major said as his attention returned to Ted.

Boyd sensed Ted's irritation. However, the trail boss

complied. Once the summation concluded, the major nodded and turned to his company, giving orders for two men to complete the burial process and then for them to escort Mrs. McDonald and her grandson to the fort. The major motioned for a buckskin-clad man at the rear of his company to come forward. The scout urged his horse toward the major. He escorted a bound Indian. The two horses moved to the porch.

The Indian's gaze went to the cattle and their *remuda*.ⁱⁱⁱ Ted inclined his head toward Boyd and remarked out of the corner of his mouth, "They'd better keep this one captive. It wouldn't be good for us if his group got after our stock."

The scout's slow, meandering voice interrupted their exchange.

"It seems this brave is interested in your friend here, Major." He shook his head and smirked at Boyd. "He says the one with the eyes of the great cat must have a warrior's spirit."

The dark eyes of the Indian fixed on Boyd and didn't relent, even as Boyd fixed his eyes on him. Neither man flinched.

"Tell him I want to know where the mother of this child has been taken. His raid remains incomplete. Is it the way of his tribe to leave the helpless unprotected?" Boyd responded.

The scout translated, and the Indian's expression didn't change. He spoke, and his words confused the men who listened.

"It seems he was part of a scouting party for food and other needs. The group happened on the farm and decided the livestock could be used by their people. When the man came out, he shot one of them, so they killed and scalped him. They looked in the house, but it was empty and then the woman came out. They decided to take her with them instead of leaving her alone. They didn't know about the boy and his grandmother."

Boyd didn't hesitate to push for what he wanted. "Then return her."

The scout hooked his leg around his saddle horn and got comfortable as he continued as interpreter.

"No, we let her have her life. She will become part of the tribe, and this boy will stay in the care of his people."

"What people? You burned the village of this one family. This boy needs his mother." Boyd gestured behind him.

The Indian's eyes flickered toward the porch. "The old one

will care of him."

"Your people don't need her. Return her now, and these soldiers will release you," Boyd said.

The major put a hand on Boyd's arm, "Boyd, you can't promise that. He's my prisoner. We are here to enforce the peace in Indian Territory."

Boyd pulled his arm away. "I don't care about politics. This boy needs his mother. Too many mothers and sons have been separated these past years."

Major Hawkins took in a breath and nodded. "Continue."

Boyd turned back to the scout and moved toward the Indian as he spoke.

"I repeat—have your people return her, and you will go free." Then without asking as the scout related his words, Boyd reached up and pulled the Indian off his horse. The brave stumbled with his bound hands but straightened, eyes flashing as he faced Boyd. Shorter than Boyd but muscled. The two appraised each other, and then the Indian nodded.

"I will tell my people of the one with the eyes like the moon of the harvest and the heart of the great cat of the mountain. We will have many words."

"Your many words must bring the woman back to her son, or you will not remain with your family, as your family will also suffer more loss than you alone. It should end here. You decide," Boyd said.

The scout whistled and darted a quick glance encompassing the military soldiers who listened.

Boyd followed the scout's gaze. However, not one of the soldiers looked nervous or seemed opposed to his words even though it could mean their lives in a fight to come.

The scout turned back and interpreted, and the Indian nodded before responding.

"He says it is understood. He will bring the woman to the ridge behind the fort within five moons; if not, the white men will do what they must."

Boyd nodded and looked toward Major Hawkins. His old friend's face remained grim, but he signaled toward a private. "Release the prisoner and let him keep his horse."

The Indian rubbed his wrists once the soldier cut the bindings.

He swung up onto his horse. He addressed Boyd and then turned his mount out of the yard, whooping as he left. The Scout interpreted once more. "He said, 'You have the word of Runs as White Deer . . . Return in five moons.'" He paused and shook his head. "Richards, I hope this works. This is the most peculiar arrangement I've witnessed."

The major gave the order to mount up, and the soldiers complied. He turned to the woman and boy on the porch. "Ma'am, I need to keep my troops patrolling the area in case there are more Indian parties about. Corporal Case and my friend, Boyd Richards, will accompany you to the fort."

Ted interrupted, "Now, wait a minute. Richards is working for my outfit and has a job to do. We lost enough time today. It'll take a half a day to get to and from the fort if my calculations are right. We'll go ahead and camp here tonight, but Boyd needs to be back before night watch. I don't see that happening. He can't go."

Boyd understood both the major's reasoning and Ted's objections. The Indians would be less apt to attack him due to the agreement, and this would free his troops to protect the few other settler families in the area instead of returning to the fort that night.

"Ted, I'm sure the major will leave a soldier with you to help. I'll stay at the fort tonight and return by first light. It may mean less trouble for us with the Indians this way." He turned to the major. "Is that acceptable to you, sir?"

A sardonic expression danced across the officer's face. "That is the same action I planned to propose if your trail boss had let me finish."

Ted's face flushed, and he surveyed his other trail hands' faces—all remained masked and contained. Boyd hid a smile. He had their support.

"Fine, let's set camp," Ted said as he strode through the horses and soldiers.

The care of the horses and cattle awaited.

~

The grandmother's eyes remained fixed on the fading sight of the now distant horse and rider. Boyd imagined everything inside of her wanted to scream and demand he take these soldiers with him, assuring the safe return of her daughter. He touched her thin,

25

lined hand. "Excuse me, ma'am."

Her eyes turned to him. "Yes, Mr. ... Boyd, wasn't it?" she responded.

"Richards, ma'am, Boyd Richards. I apologize for the rush, but I need you to gather what things you may have. We need to leave for the fort as soon as you can be ready. I'll be happy to help you."

Her eyes assessed him. He reached out as she struggled to her feet and took her hands. She leaned back her head and looked at him.

"Mr. Richards, as you can see, very little is left, but there are a few precious items in the cellar, including our family Bible. I managed to grab it before we went to hide." She hesitated and then asked, "Do you have a Bible?"

Boyd shifted; he averted his gaze as he answered, "Yes, ma'am, it's in my saddlebag."

"Do you read it?"

He turned a hard gaze on her, but she didn't flinch.

"No, ma'am, it was my wife's. She's dead."

She continued to meet his gaze as she nodded. "I'm sure she'd want you to read it. Promise me you will."

Boyd clinched his jaw, and as he did, he thought of his friend Marc, who always showed anger in that way. Marc and John sitting by the fire with a Bible those months before returning home to Arkansas. They'd rediscovered something they'd blocked for a time. He remained unable to recover anything, because he'd never had what burned inside of them, what had filled Nancy before her death. His anger returned. He sensed God's pursuit.

He faced the challenging gaze of Mrs. McDonald.

"Yes, ma'am, I will. Now we need to go."

~

Final arrangements were made between the cavalry and cowhands. Ted set camp, the cook started dinner, and the outfit tended to their duties. Major Hawkins gave the corporal detailed instructions before turning to Boyd

"Mr. Richards, when you get to the fort, you will be taken to my wife."

Boyd lifted an eyebrow in surprise.

Major Hawkins smiled. "Yes, I do have a family. Anyway, she will take care of the boy and his grandmother. Also, tell my son . . ." He paused as Boyd whistled and looked down. "Tell him he's in charge until I get there."

Boyd looked up. "How old is he?"

"You may have faced him in battle, maybe not. Does it matter? I'll tell you this. He's taught me more about courage than any man I've known or now know."

Boyd saw the respect in the older soldier's face and felt intrigued. He met his friend's eyes and nodded.

~

The cries of the child overshadowed their departure. They subsided, and the boy slept as the buckboard jostled along the trail to the fort. Corporal Case rode in the wagon but had his horse tied to the back. Ted had convinced the cook to loan one of his horses to pull the buckboard. Boyd rode alongside and watched for every shadow as the sun began to cover its face with the darkness of night. The bulk of the fort structures welcomed them. Mrs. McDonald, along with little Charlie, had managed to sleep in the bed of the wagon but stirred as the corporal called out to the night watchmen to open the gates.

~

The vibration of the endless conveyance of the wagon ceased. They stopped, and Elizabeth McDonald arose from the wagon bed clutching the now whimpering child. A door opened, and a woman rushed from the fort quarters in front of which they'd arrived.

"Oh my! Please let me help you," the woman exclaimed as she rushed toward them. She glanced at Boyd as he dismounted before ordering their escort "Prepare the extra bunk in my son's quarters for this man, Corporal. I will get this dear woman and child settled. Then I want a full report."

"Yes, ma'am, Mrs. Hawkins."

Mrs. Hawkins helped the travel-weary pair from the wagon, and she glanced at Boyd standing by his horse watching them. She looked away as she placed a sheltering arm around Mrs. McDonald and Charlie, ushering them forward into her home. Boyd followed and stopped in the doorway, watching them.

Mrs. Hawkins guided Mrs. McDonald to a rocking chair. Charlie awakened in her arms and started to cry. A glass of milk and two cold biscuits were set on a small table beside them.

"Share this with him to get something into your stomachs. I'm sorry it's not more. Breakfast will be better in the morning. I'll prepare the bed for you," Mrs. Hawkins said as she turned toward the adjoining room.

Mrs. McDonald frowned as she said, "No, we can't take your bed."

Susannah Hawkins turned back and smiled. "It is warm here, and both of you need to rest. There are empty quarters two doors from here. I will have them prepared for me. You are not to worry. There is a chamber pot beneath the bed for your needs." She smiled again in a reassuring way before leaving the room.

Elizabeth tended Charlie, who ate his biscuit. She also ate a few bites of the second one before giving the rest to him. They shared the milk, and then she began to rock him. His small body relaxed, and his breathing became slow and regular as sleep started to overtake him. Her eyes went to the doorway where Boyd stood. In that rare moment of peace, they shared a smile.

Mrs. Hawkins bustled into the room, breaking the moment. She sent Boyd an irritated look. "May I help you, sir?"

He placed a finger to his lips before pointing toward the sleeping child. She blushed and hurried to help the grandmother who struggled to her feet while holding her grandson. She shook her head and proceeded with her two charges.

Boyd didn't know what to do, so he waited. Mrs. Hawkins returned after a few minutes. She ignored him but glanced at the soldier by the wagon.

"Corporal, Mrs. McDonald tells me this is my husband's old friend. Is Mr. Richards's bunk ready?"

"Yes, ma'am, is there anything else?"

"Corporal, you take care of the wagon and horses; then go to bed and thank you. I need to visit with Mr. Richards a bit."

"Thank you, ma'am. Good night." He turned to Boyd. "Sir."

"Mrs. Hawkins, I couldn't help overhearing your earlier conversation with Mrs. McDonald. Might I go and prepare a fire in your quarters for tonight?"

She smiled up at him, "No, thank you, Mr. Richards. I think I'll just doze in my rocking chair by the fire tonight. It would not be the first time. Please come in and shut the door for a while. It is getting chilled."

Boyd shifted. "I'm sorry. Please let me build your fire a bit."

His spurs jangled as he walked to squat by the fire and reached for the wood box.

"Mr. Richards, I feel I have you at a disadvantage. My husband has spoken to us of you, but I can't help feeling you don't know as much about us. Am I right?"

Boyd stayed squatted by the fire. "Yes, ma'am, the major did ask me to give your son a message. As I am leaving early, might I see him?"

She laughed and he frowned.

"I'm sorry, Mr. Richards. It's just you are bunking in his room and you may not rest that much. Come, I'll introduce you." She rose and started for the door, as did he when she stopped, turning to look up at him. "Please share Mrs. McDonald's story with me as we walk."

"Yes, ma'am." He complied and followed her outside to a door a few feet away. She paused as he finished a brief, mild version of the day's events.

"That poor woman," she said before knocking and opening the door.

A low-turned lantern sat on the bedside table, and Boyd could just make out an empty bunk beside a modified bed with wooden, raised sides. The man in the bed turned his head and smiled.

"Who do you have with you, Mother?"

Something felt wrong. A flash of wounded war comrades caused Boyd to stiffen.

"James," Susannah went to his bedside and clasped his arm as she continued, "This is Boyd Richards. Remember—"

The young man finished for her, "The Arkansas to Texas man. Forgive me for not being able to stand on ceremony." He laughed as he shifted his right arm and hand forward. Boyd moved forward and clasped it in a measured handshake. The man's grip felt weaker than it should have.

"Well, Mother, you'd better turn in and let me get to know our guest. Nate—I mean Corporal Case—told me what happened today and that I had a bunkmate for the night. He just didn't tell me who it was."

Susannah smiled and kissed her son. "Good night, James. Mr.

Richards," she said before departing.

Boyd clasped his hat in the awkward silence after she shut the door.

"Relax. Take your boots off and have a seat. Tonight has been more of a night for thinking than sleeping anyway," James said.

Boyd nodded, relaxing. Major Hawkins's son appeared likeable. James asked questions about Boyd's outfit and the cattle as Boyd removed his boots, pants, and shirt. His long johns weren't clean, but at least the dust that covered his clothes wouldn't be left on the bed. He had not answered so many questions in a long time. This man liked to talk. Boyd decided to ask a few questions of his own. James paused, and Boyd began.

"James, your dad said to tell you that you're in charge 'til he returns. What did he mean?"

James didn't laugh. He sobered.

"That means he may be gone for a while. I'll brief the officers in the morning. I sure hope that Indian keeps his word. It could mean big trouble, otherwise."

Boyd nodded. "It could, but he'll keep his word, if possible. It was in his eyes."

James grew silent for a few moments. He turned his head to meet Boyd's gaze.

"I'm paralyzed, Mr. Richards. My legs don't work, and my arms are weaker than they once were. I stepped on one of those explosives the confederacy went to planting under the dirt. Well, I didn't step on it. My buddy did. I was right behind him. He died, and I was thrown fifty feet. It injured part of my lumbar, and I landed a little wrong, hurting my neck a bit. The doctors would give you more details, but the reality is—I can't walk. I have to have help with part of my private needs. Now, before you start pitying me, don't. Most of the soldiers with spine-related injuries died soon after the incident, after surgery, or within a few months. *I* am still here. No one can explain it, and I don't know how long my life will be, but neither do you. Now, that's out of the way, any questions?"

Boyd sucked in as if hit by cold water. There hadn't been an ounce of bitterness in the young man's story; James had accepted his new life. He hesitated but asked, "Don't you want what you had before?"

James smiled. "Sure. Some days, but I'm learning to treasure what I have now. This world isn't perfect. It never has been, but there are moments of perfection in every day. I've learned to look for them and savor them."

Boyd nodded and somehow felt free to say the next words to this man. "I still want my wife, Nancy, back. How can I—" He stopped.

James's deep voice requested, "Mr. Richards, would you turn up the lamp and get my Bible off the table?"

Boyd complied but wrestled inside. He knew James wanted him to read something.

"Open it."

"Where?"

"Just open the cover. Do you see the small stack of papers there?"

Boyd frowned as he stared at them, not wanting to touch them, but knowing the man wanted him to do just that. He turned and found James's eyes on him. James did not smile.

"I see you found them. Take the top paper and close the cover, please." He waited as Boyd completed his request and retreated to his cot, holding the delicate page in his large hands.

"Thank you. Now I'm not going to preach at you, but I am going to share my experience with you and make a request of you."

James smiled as Boyd raised his eyes to focus on him. "I came to know the Lord about a year before the war started. Everything was wonderful, and for some reason, I now know *people* perpetuate, not the Bible, I thought things always would be. God stayed faithful, and I felt blessed until I became injured. I got angry at God and did not understand how he could let me be incapacitated in this way. I'd given my life to him. Wasn't he supposed to protect me from everything bad? Well, I had to find out so I could plead my cause and know I was right. I did not want my parents to know how I was feeling, so I had the nurses at the hospital start reading the Scriptures to me every day. I found out how wrong I was.

"Time and again, throughout the Old and New testaments, the experiences of God's people aren't easy or perfect, and the trouble or causes of the difficulty start with men not God. He wants the best for us, wants to lighten our burdens, but this world—full of people choosing their own ways and dark principalities—results in the opposite. I cried out and asked for forgiveness. How had I dared to judge and so misjudged my God and Savior? Some of my favorite scriptures I discovered along the way are on that piece of paper. The nurses wrote them down at my request as we read. Then my mother penned copies for me to have and use to share with others as I can no longer turn the pages well myself. Now, Mr. Richards, I would like you to tuck that page inside your pocket and once you are in a place where you can find a Bible, explore those scriptures. I'll pray for you. You are seeking, and you will find the answers," James said, smiling as Boyd reached for his shirt to comply. "Well, let's see if we can get a little sleep before the corporal brings your horse around in about three hours." A small laugh accompanied his last statement.

Boyd groaned and tucked the paper in his pocket. He moved his shirt back to the foot of the cot beside his pants. He blew out the lantern before he stretched out on the bunk.

"Thanks, Hawkins."

A pause followed. "Richards, do you know any nurses?"

"What?"

A deep chuckle vibrated the darkness. "No, seriously, my mother has agreed to let Father hire someone to help with my care. She has overseen me for too long."

Boyd's mind and emotions struggled with the switch in subjects, and then a face flashed in his mind. He smiled. Since leaving East Texas, he'd only opened up to two people about Nancy, this man and—"Hallie Price," he said. "She's not exactly a nurse, but there's something special about her—beyond what most men see. She could use a change." He went on to explain, and they talked and laughed for a while before drifting off to sleep. The corporal knocked on the door in a prompt military fashion, and Boyd donned his gear and bade James good-bye. He left a note for Mrs. Hawkins and a letter for her to mail to Hallie.

~

Ted stomped around as Boyd arrived. "About time," he said before he swung up into his saddle. The older cowboys had the herd and horses ready. Time for the trail to be rejoined.

Boyd passed the day performing all his duties. Ted insisted he pull his night duty as normal, no slack given.

The cows stayed quiet, and he replayed all that had happened since they'd left Texas. The page of scriptures in his pocket from James Hawkins crackled as he shifted in his saddle. Rebellion burned inside of him. No one could make him read anything. His dream about Nancy came to mind, as did his promises to Mrs. McDonald and James. He reached back and untied the flap on his saddlebag, retrieving Nancy's Bible before pulling out the small sheet of paper. The moon shone extra bright, so he didn't have much trouble making out the words as he spent the rest of the night looking up each scripture. Near dawn, everything he read started to circulate from his brain to his heart, and he looked at the twinkling stars in the silent sky. The words from the fragile pages echoed in his head. Two questions made it past his lips: *How? Why?* His insides trembled and churned like they had before battle years ago, conflicting between fear and anticipation of resolution. He whirled and reached for his rifle as he sensed a rider in the shadows. He relaxed at the sound of Billy's voice.

"It's just me. Roy just relieved me and said Frank is headed this way. I thought we'd see if we could sneak a little out of Cook's breakfast pot before the others."

Boyd heaved out a sigh as he slid his rifle back in place. He tensed as Billy reined his horse in beside his. Nancy's Bible lay propped against the saddle horn. The younger man's eyes met his.

"Solid words. My ma taught me to read by the good book."

"I've read many words in my life, Billy. It's just never made sense how these words changed things more than others."

Billy looked up for a good while before turning a serious gaze toward Boyd.

"Words don't mean much until you know the one who said 'em. Boyd, I didn't come on this drive because of my faith in Ted. I came because of Mr. Kennedy. He's proven his word can be trusted. Now, for you, all you know about Mr. Kennedy is what Mr. Pierce told you. You hired on because you relied on Mr. Pierce's knowledge, yet you're still not so sure. "

Boyd frowned as he picked up the Bible and placed it behind him in his saddle bag. The leather creaked as he finished and turned to find Billy grinning at him.

Boyd shook his head. "Billy, you're too young to be a

philosopher. Let's go get some biscuits."

Chapter Three

Hallie Price didn't think her thirty-one-year-old insides would ever stop vibrating. The reverberations from the days of traveling over rough terrain in the stagecoach permeated every muscle and nerve from her unsteady legs to her dizzy head. She decided to forego any future opportunities proposed by gallant men of short acquaintance. Although her first impression of Boyd continued to linger, repeated self-recriminations overcame even his golden image. What had she been thinking? His letter had intrigued her. The son of a friend of his needed a companion and caregiver. The young wheelchair bound, and somewhat isolated man, lived at an army fort in Indian Territory. His mother continued to serve as his primary caregiver and needed assistance. The set pay offered came to less than the potential with her present work, but for some reason she came. The correspondence indicated Boyd wouldn't be there when she arrived due to his part in the cattle drive. His letter gave no explanation about how he'd encountered his friend, the major in charge of this fort, in which she now found herself. His letter indicated Mrs. Hawkins would explain.

The thud of her trunk hitting the dusty ground beside her stirred her out of her dazed state. She shielded her eyes from the swirl of dust as the wind whipped her skirts around her when she bent to set her baggage right. As she straightened, a soldier rushed to help her.

"Miss Price?" he inquired.

"Yes," she responded, straightening her hat, which had been askew all day. It had bounced off every inch of the interior of the coach. Her aching head could testify to its adventures.

"I'm Private Henderson. If you'll follow me, Mrs. Hawkins is expecting you."

"Of course, thank you, Private Henderson." She tried to repress the smile that twitched just inside her lips as she followed the tall, strong soldier who carried her trunk as if it were a box of feathers. This could indeed be enjoyable. No one knew her here. This soldier treated her like a lady. With a little effort, she managed to restrain the practiced sway of her hips and walk with a refined posture.

Her eyes took in the horses and uniformed men moving about the fort. No one stopped and stared, at least not in open regard. Each seemed to have tasks to do or to be on his way somewhere. Periodic gusts assaulted her face. Texas winds did not often equal these.

Private Henderson stopped in front of a small set of barracks. They faced three doors. He pointed to the door on his right.

"These will be your quarters."

He opened the door and entered just long enough to deposit her trunk and shut the door. Hallie waited. He indicated the middle door and then the door to the left.

"These are James's quarters, and these are Major and Mrs. Hawkins's quarters."

He knocked on the door to the left, and a woman with soft, brown hair and welcoming doe eyes opened it. She stood shorter than Hallie, but the firmness of her hands as she reached to take hers radiated a great strength.

"Miss Price, I am relieved you have survived your journey. There have been so many days of trepidation about you traveling to us. God be praised! Do come in and sit with me," she said as she led Hallie to two plain chairs and a small table holding an elegant tea set.

As they settled themselves, Mrs. Hawkins continued, "Oh, where are my manners? I'm Susannah Hawkins. My husband asked that I give his regrets as he was called away from the fort this afternoon. He thinks so much of Mr. Richards and trusts his intuition. That is the reason we agreed to your coming."

Confusion mixed with surprise as Hallie looked at the pleasant, talkative woman. She moved to the edge of her chair.

"I'm sorry. Would you mind explaining your last statement? I thought you had been looking for someone for this position."

The woman's smile faltered, and as her face sobered. Hallie

saw her fatigue and apprehension.

"Well, the major, my husband, has tried to get me to agree to outside help for some time. Any uncertainty came from me. You see, Miss Price, I thought it was my place to care for James, especially here. It's so primitive. We had our house staff to help in Boston, as well as nurses and doctors. However, even then I remained in charge of his care."

"How long have you been here?"

"Eight months."

"How long has your son been unable to walk?"

Susannah looked down at her hands for a moment before she met Hallie's eyes. "Miss Price, my son was injured during the war. He cannot walk, and his arms and hands are weak." She watched Hallie with apprehensive hope in her gaze.

"I am so sorry, Miss Price. Mr. Richards had trusted me to handle this better than I have. Let me start again. James was a soldier in the Union Army. It has been very difficult for him. In all frankness, he has, as a grown man, endured the loss of dignity in having his mother complete his most personal care for long enough. He loves me and would never say those words, but I see it."

Hallie wanted to run back to the bumpy stagecoach. This did not resemble the fresh start she envisioned. She thought Mr. Richards had done her a favor with this opportunity. No, none of this made sense. This felt like a bad dream, and she shook her head to see if she could awaken. The air of expectancy lingered, and the weary brown eyes of the woman next to her didn't waver. She leaned back in her chair for support. Mrs. Hawkins sighed and busied herself pouring two cups of tea. Hallie took the cup passed to her and sought a sip of the warm liquid. It didn't jolt her the way a shot of whiskey would have. Maybe that explained why she continued to sit there, instead of running out the door. She took another sip of the soothing tea.

"Miss Price?" Susannah's voice implored her.

Hallie looked back at the distraught woman. The woman appeared to struggle for composure.

"Miss Price . . . please . . . please stay with us a few days. Meet James. Then decide."

Hallie wouldn't let this woman continue under false

assumption.

"Mrs. Hawkins, I'm not a nurse. This is not my usual line of work."

The brown eyes did not blink. "I know. It seems you are the one at the disadvantage regarding details. Mr. Richards put it in delicate terms."

The warmth in her own cheeks shocked Hallie. This rare state of embarrassment confused her. This woman confused her. Why would a mother consider a "soiled dove" to care for her son?

"Why then?"

A candid smile erupted on Susannah's face. "Because of your experience with men, I knew you would not be uncomfortable with his physical care. Also, he can't …" She looked down and then up. "Now it's my turn to be embarrassed. Let's see, how can I term it? You would be safe with him. Also, you are older than he is. James has endured young nurses who care but show pity even while trying to hide it. Oh, I'm making a mess of this."

The situation became clearer, and she started to see the edges of a possible explanation for them choosing her. She placed her cup on the table, stood, and crossed to the small window by the door. The collar of her society-appropriate dress seemed to cut off all air. A quick pull with a finger swipe failed to loosen the garment's restriction. She licked her lips as her mouth grew dry.

"Mrs. Hawkins," she said, turning, "I would very much like to take a walk and consider all of this."

"Of course." The woman rose and crossed to her with outstretched hands. "Please, go to your quarters and have the dinner I had sent there. I thought you might be tired and not up to our group dinner when you arrived. My husband would prefer you be back from your walk by nineteen hundred hours, I mean seven o'clock. The soldiers here are good men, but they are men, and he does not want to give opportunities for misconduct."

Hallie smiled. "Understood, I'll do as you say, but please know I can take care of myself. Please excuse me and thank you."

Hallie emerged from her quarters after dinner. She inhaled, shutting her eyes and then exhaled as her eyelids lifted. She reached down to smooth the skirt of the simple blue day dress given to her by her one friend outside of the saloon. It had a high neck and conservative cut.

She surveyed the fort yard; little activity at this dusk hour. Guards stood at the gates and on the walls. The sound of the blacksmith's bellows and horses echoed from beside the corral. She reached up to smooth her dark hair and felt to assure it remained secured in the coil at the nape of her neck. She decided to walk toward signs of activity and light near the corral where it would be safer. As she walked, she relaxed a little. She knew how to take care of herself. Her mind replayed the information shared by Mrs. Hawkins. It would be unfair, as well as rude, to leave without meeting James and Major Hawkins. All decisions must wait until tomorrow. So tonight, she wanted to enjoy being in an exciting new place; a place where potential danger lurked just outside the walls, but a place of peace for now.

A buckboard stood outside the corral beside the open-sided shed of the blacksmith's area. Two off-duty soldiers lay propped up on bedrolls in the back. They appeared relaxed and continued to talk, looking up at the dimming sky as she approached. The darkening sky made it hard to make out their features. As she drew close, one of them sat up and jumped to attention.

"Ma'am, may I escort you to Major Hawkins's quarters?"

My goodness, they must have announced her arrival to the entire fort.

"No, thank you, sir, I'm just taking a short walk."

"Begging your pardon, ma'am. It is—"

"Eddie, go see if the blacksmith is finished with the wheel," the other young man suggested with a smile in his voice.

Eddie hesitated for a moment, looking at Hallie, then back at his friend. He ducked his head. "All right, I'll be right back." He headed for the smithy.

Hallie moved forward, waiting for the young soldier relaxing in the wagon to stand. He didn't.

"Thank you," she said.

"Have you ever watched the first star of the evening?"

"Excuse me?"

"Have you ever watched the first star of the evening?" he repeated, lifting a finger toward the sky.

"Young man, I think your friend was right. I'll allow the escort when he returns. You seem a little dangerous."

"What!" He gave a soft laugh. "Miss Price, I assure you, you

39

are safe with me. Eddie is ten feet from us and will be back shortly. As we wait, please do yourself a favor and look up. The best view is here beside me, but that's up to you."

Hallie burst out laughing. This new environment must have given her delusions of grandeur reserved for ladies who protected their virtue. She had none to save. Plus, a small knife tucked in the top of her shoe gave her confidence.

The young man remained relaxed, staring at the sky. He didn't turn to look at her as she climbed in the buckboard, reclined, and adjusted her head on the bedroll. Instead, he lifted one finger toward a bright celestial flicker in the darkening sky.

"There?" She held her breath and turned her head, meeting the young man's gaze. They smiled, sharing a moment of wonder and comfortable companionship, before returning their reference to the sky.

Eddie returned at that moment. "The wheel's ready. We need to go," he said to his friend. "Miss Price, I'm sure the major would like you to return to your quarters."

His disapproval broke the once innocent moment of peace. His disdain reminded her of all the townspeople outside of the saloon. Reality washed over her. She needed to go home to Texas.

"Of course," she said as she moved to stand but paused, turning back to the other soldier. "Thank you." Then she hurried back to her quarters.

~

The quiet soldier turned and looked hard at Eddie. "You had no right to speak to her like that."

"It wasn't proper. It makes me wonder what kind of woman she is," the stocky corporal stated.

"I think she is pretty gutsy. She was uncomfortable but decided to trust me. From what the major shared, she doesn't have much cause to trust men."

"I wouldn't know. You didn't share the details of the major's briefing."

The sound of heavy steps mingled with turning wheels ended their exchange. The smithy, Sergeant Jack, moved behind the wagon. "Here we go, boys; it's ready. Help me, Eddie."

Eddie crawled in the wagon and got behind his friend, raising him to sitting and moving him to the end of the wagon bed. Jack took hold of his legs, and they moved the man into the repaired wheelchair.

"There you go, James."

~

A tentative knock drew Hallie to her door the next morning. She didn't sleep, so she'd dressed hours ago. Mrs. Hawkins stood clasping her hands as Hallie answered. The circles under the older woman's eyes indicated a less than restful repose, much like Hallie's night.

"Miss Price, I know it is just after five a.m., but would you mind helping me with James? You see, his father has still not returned, and I had dismissed the young private who stays with him at night. I mean, I sent him to breakfast. If you decide to stay, we will be sure your nights are restful. The privates take turns with the night shift. It's one of the advantages of living in a military fort." Her lips quivered into a smile

Hallie had decided to leave after last night, but she determined, in view of the woman's apparent need for assistance, to help until the major returned.

"Of course I'll help you," she said as she stepped out, closing the door behind her, and moved to stand with Susannah Hawkins in front of the next door. Male voices had drifted through the walls as she retired last night, but it had been quiet until about four this morning. The thick logs made conversation topics hard to determine.

Mrs. Hawkins put her hand to the latch but turned before lifting it.

"You should know a few things before we start. James has requested a face tent, so to speak, this morning. He does not want to meet you unless you decide to stay. I know it sounds strange, but you must understand the many rejections he has suffered. His care is very involved, as you will see. He's at our mercy, especially when he's in bed. We will be bathing him, and I will show you how to complete everything else necessary for him."

Hallie nodded, never dropping her eyes.

"Ready?" Mrs. Hawkins asked. She lifted the latch and entered.

"Good morning once again, James. I have Miss Price here. We will try to work quickly. I wish you would let us get you into your chair, but Private Simmons promised to let Corporal Rigby know when you needed him after breakfast. He will shave you today." Her voice stayed cheerful and loving as she hurried to his side. "Miss Price, if you will get the kettle off of the fire, it has the water for his cloth bath."

Hallie found the kettle before even registering the sight of the man on the bed in the center of the room. A blanket covered the bottom half of his body, and a thin sheet, fitted over some sort of frame to cover his neck and face, covered the top half. She retrieved the kettle and came to stand beside his mother. Mrs. Hawkins poured the steaming liquid into a bowl on the table, took a bar of soap, and handed the rag to Hallie before beginning her instructions. Hallie felt tension when she first touched the young man's bare chest and began, checking to be sure the temperature of the rag had moderated before applying it. She had touched many men but never under these circumstances. However, the tightness seeped out of her muscles as she progressed. In a strange way, it calmed her to complete the ministrations needed. She took in the weight of his legs, which had no volitional movements, felt slight tension, and startled at the responsive movement in his arms. His hands lay angled and bent, and his fingers seemed weak but still capable of movement. His mother covered him with a blanket after the bath and then showed Hallie how to assist with his other care needs. Susannah watched her as if waiting for her to become embarrassed. Hallie didn't ask questions as they finished dressing him. Susannah had spoken to her son in a quiet voice throughout the procedure, narrating each step for him, as well as Hallie.

"James, we're finished. Corporal Rigby will get you up and about. I'll see you at breakfast."

She nodded to Hallie, and they got ready to leave. However, Hallie turned back toward the bed. "Mr. Hawkins, thank you for the privilege of taking care of you this morning. Oh, in case you're wondering my impressions, as most men would, you are, from a woman's perspective, still a very pleasing sight. In my opinion as a so-called nurse, you could be a pain in the rump if you don't start talking." With that said, she passed the very shocked mother of her charge and heard a soft, low, deep chuckle from behind the tented partition as she left the room. She waited outside with a smile playing at her lips.

A flushed Mrs. Hawkins soon joined her. Hallie gathered this woman had never heard of such boldness. She seemed speechless and not just a little protective as a mother if the look on her face gave any indication. Of course—Hallie thought—the fact that the woman's son had laughed about it, flustered Mrs. Hawkins the most.

"Breakfast will be in twenty minutes," Susannah choked out and went inside of her quarters.

Hallie allowed a spring in her step as she went to tidy up a bit.

She emerged from her room within fifteen minutes. She'd noticed a lower window cut into James's room the night before, the shutters had remained closed until now. A young man sat inside James's room looking out of the window.

"Good morning!" he said with a twinkle in his blue eyes.

His malted brown hair hung over his forehead from under a hat with the corporal insignia above a pleasant and open face. This must be Corporal Rigby.

"It *is* a good morning, sir," she said.

"May I propose breakfast, ma'am?"

"Well, thank you, Corporal, but I'm expected next door."

A loud guffaw sounded, and Eddie from the night before came to stand behind the man seated in the window. The top of his curly blond hair, brushed back and curling at his collar, remained uncovered until he swiped the cap from his friend and placed it on his own head. His green eyes held a secret he didn't seem to want to contain.

"Miss Price, may I introduce myself? *I* am Corporal Eddie Rigby, and this ain't. This is former Private Hawkins of the Union Army, now known to one and all as Mr. James Hawkins."

James moved his head backwards, giving a slight bump to his friend's chest.

"Stop it, Eddie," he said before turning his eyes back to Hallie.

Her mind raced—the man in the wagon last night. It all made sense now. He hadn't moved or stood because he couldn't. Gratitude for the obstruction of his face earlier that morning filled her. He retained his dignity, and she received a first impression not impacted by his physical injuries and limitations. She wanted to know *this* person. A trial period became a real consideration. She decided to ignore his friend.

"I'd be happy to have breakfast with you, Mr. Hawkins. It's time for our official introductions. I'm Hallie Price."

His gaze sobered. "Does this mean you're staying?"

He waited as if daring her to look away and make an excuse, but she didn't.

"Yes, let's give it a go and see if it works," she said.

His eyes never wavered, but hers did at the slow shift of his right arm and forward movement of one hand on his lap. She recovered from her surprise, reaching out to cover his hand with her own.

Her chestnut eyes returned to his azure regard.

"Thank you, Miss. Price. Let me introduce myself. I'm James Hawkins."

His soft and genuine response endeared him to her. Hallie had never received such kind regard and platonic appreciation from a man in her life. She found herself at a complete loss for words, and that never happened.

James's gaze conveyed appreciation for her candor, her humor, and lack of pity. She wanted him to feel like a person with her. This unfamiliar spark held the promise of a pure friendship in addition to the provision of needed care and livelihood. She averted her eyes to find Eddie grimacing and shaking his head. James grinned at him and shifted his hand as Hallie removed her hand.

"Eddie, I'm starving. Please stop being a pain and get me to breakfast."

Hallie laughed her trademark, very unladylike laugh, and soon both men joined her. She waited as Eddie emerged, pushing James in a chair with wheels.

~

Mrs. Hawkins met them at the door.

"Good morning!" She smiled and bent to kiss her son on the cheek. Her eyes shifted between them as they resumed their conversation. "So, you two have decided to make introductions. Does this mean you will stay with us, Miss Price?"

The other woman's eyes met James's before his direct gaze returned to her.

"Let's just say your son has made enough of an impression for me to give it a try," Hallie said with a smile.

"Wonderful!" Susannah beamed at them.

It appeared enough for now. Breakfast awaited and everyone must be made comfortable. Susannah closed the door behind Eddie as he pushed James to his regular place at the table.

"Miss Price, if you don't mind, I've put you beside James so we could share helping him."

Hallie watched to see if this embarrassed James, but he responded with a resigned smile. She noticed three other people at the table as she sat in the simple wooden chair. A small boy sat between two women; who logic indicated as his mother and grandmother. However, her ever-observant mind noted something amiss. The grandmother tended to the boy without any response from the other woman. His mother sat with her eyes lowered toward her lap, not raising them to acknowledge the other occupants of the room. Hallie frowned and turned as James whispered something she didn't hear.

"I'm sorry. What did you say?" she asked and leaned her head toward him.

"Let me introduce you to them, and I'll share their story later," he said in a soft voice.

She nodded, and James cleared his throat to gain everyone's attention.

"Good morning to everyone. We have a new guest at our table this morning. I'm hoping she will choose to remain with us as my companion and nurse. This is Miss Hallie Price."

The older woman beside the small boy smiled. "Welcome, Miss Price. I'm Elizabeth McDonald, and this is my daughter, Molly Scott, and my grandson, Charlie. This fort has become our new home for now, and everyone here has been so wonderful. I know you'll come to love it."

"Thank you. It's nice to meet you," she said.

She noticed Eddie had taken the seat opposite of the too-silent and unresponsive Molly. Her analysis of this ended as the door opened and a very dusty and tired-looking seasoned officer entered the room, an older version of the young man seated next to her.

Susannah Price rose to meet her husband.

"Susannah, I apologize for arriving at your table in this state," he said.

James didn't let his mother respond as he interrupted, "I think we will allow it as this table has been without its head for too many nights. Welcome home, Father."

Susannah smiled as she hugged her husband.

"You just missed all the introductions. I think everyone knows my father except for Miss Price," James said.

Hallie rose and stretched out her hand. The major removed his hat and met her halfway. "Miss Price, I'm glad you made it. We will talk later," he said, sitting at the end of the table beside his wife. "We have so much for which to be grateful. Let us pray."

Hallie bowed her head, but her thoughts were not on his words. She sighed with gratitude when he finished.

The meal began, and she helped James as it proceeded. At first, he held the spoon as he scooped the eggs but soon tired, needing assistance completing the long distance to his mouth. How different from her normal circumstances, but as she looked around the table at the new people in her life, it felt right. Eddie fed Molly Scott, talking in hushed tones and encouraging her. The young woman's mouth opened and closed, but otherwise she didn't acknowledge him. Elizabeth McDonald tended to her grandson, Mrs. Hawkins talked to her husband with happiness glittering in her eyes, and James conversed with her between bites. These interwoven lives served, received, and gave to each other. Hallie thought of Boyd Richards. She wished he could be here. A sense of something *divine* emanated from this situation. A sardonic smile hid just behind her lips. She'd never understood or experienced what people meant when they used words like that, yet being here seemed to actualize it. Maybe if the cattle drive went well, she might have the opportunity to thank Boyd for triggering these events. She hoped so.

Chapter Four

The last steer made its way into the large fenced yard, dust swirling in the air as Billy latched the gate. October arrived with them, and they'd made excellent time even with the short delay. The spring roundup had taken three to four months due to the greater size of the herd. Ted dismounted and pushed down the neckerchief which kept the grit out of his mouth and nose.

"You boys wait here while I go finalize this business, and then we'll see about having some fun," he said with the first trace of a smile in weeks.

Boyd watched him walk toward the shipping office and shook his head. Billy laughed, causing a contagious, reciprocal response from the other men.

"The fun will start as soon as we move downwind of this cattle yard," Frank said, wrinkling his nose in the wind.

"I'll be better when I'm no longer riding downwind of you, Windy," Roy returned, fanning his hat toward Frank.

The others laughed and then grew silent. They'd worked hard and were trail weary. It would be good to have one night in town before they headed back to Texas the next day. The return trip shouldn't take quite as long without cattle to tend, but they'd still have to be watchful and alert as they traveled. The remuda[iv] and their individual mounts could be of interest to Indians and thieves.

~

As they waited, Boyd's mind went back to the night Runs as White Deer appeared during his watch. He'd left the fort seven days ago. His mustang stomped to the side and pulled with his head.

"Easy, boy," he crooned as he checked the undisturbed cattle under his watch and then scanned to see if any snakes or other creatures were the reason for the animal's unease.

Out of the darkness came the haunting sound of a night bird followed by a quiet voice, "Man with the eyes of the big cat. It is done." The Indian appeared after this very broken English announcement.

The brave approached on foot, and Boyd dismounted to meet him. Someone had helped him with the words. Boyd hoped the brave could understand him.

"You released Molly Scott to the fort?"

Runs as White Deer nodded. "Fort."

Boyd nodded in return. "Good."

Their exchange held respect and honor. The soldier who had led Boyd from the fort on the morning after the incident with the Scotts said that Indians appreciated a gift as a sign of respect. He didn't want the Indian to misunderstand him, so he held out his hands before reaching into his saddlebag for his cleanest neckerchief. The man grunted and reached out and touched the one around Boyd's neck before taking the item from his hand. He rolled it and tied it around his head as he maintained the glittering gaze of the giver. Then he turned and disappeared into the shadows.

~

Boyd wished he knew if Mrs. Scott returned to the fort unharmed, but at least he knew she lived and the Indian had kept his word. He spent the rest of his watch that night thinking about the varied characters of men, as well as the plight of Molly, Elizabeth, and Charlie. The Indian had kept his word, and now a family could recover. Elizabeth McDonald had her daughter and little Charlie had his mother. The promise he'd made to Mrs. McDonald echoed in his head: to read the Bible. He did after visiting with James that night at the fort and several times since. He'd tried to pray a couple of times but too much of an inward struggle prevented it.

The wind snatched his hat from his head and his thoughts returned to the present. Before he could dismount, young Billy retrieved it, handed it up to him, and scrambled back to sit on the corral fence. He grinned at Boyd.

"I'm tired of being in the saddle," he said.

Boyd reached out and slapped him with the hat. Billy reminded him of his brother, Ben. Boyd had talked to him about his turmoil. As it turned out, Billy professed as a Christian. Still, he'd suffered his own unimaginable tragedies. They hadn't made Billy weaker but stronger in a different way. He remained humble but decisive; his actions just weren't tinged with anger like Boyd's.

Billy had tried to explain the difference—after knowing the Lord. He'd said, "It's like traveling down the same road but seeing different things." Before, he'd focused more on the snags—the difficulties caused by looking inward—and not God's outward blessings and purposes. The things and people didn't change, only he did. This made his motivations different.

Boyd wanted to get more answers. The other issues during the drive perplexed him. He worked hard and did his job well, but Ted's aggravation didn't lessen. The plans for the evening and return trip interested him. Boyd turned as he heard the trail boss approaching.

"Well, boys, it's pay day."

A myriad of whoops and shouts started, though kept brief—as the men didn't want to incite a stampede from the nearby cattle at this juncture.

"We'll go to the livery stable and get the horses settled for the night. We can leave our gear there. I suggest baths and haircuts first, and then I don't want to know or hear anything until about seven a.m. I would say sunup, but I know that may be tough." Ted paused, becoming serious. "One rule: avoid trouble with the law. I don't want to spend any of Mr. Kennedy's money getting you out of jail, or your pay will not be yours for months." His eyes met each one, and every man nodded.

It took less than an hour to get everything settled at the livery. The ground surface felt funny to Boyd's legs. They hadn't been out of the saddle much the last couple of days, as they pushed to make up for the time they'd lost. He knew where to head. Billy called out to him, and he turned.

"Mind if I come with ya?"

Boyd gave a nod, and they headed toward the opposite end of town with long, quick strides. They didn't slow until the church came into view. Being Saturday, the town continued to bustle, and Boyd didn't know if the town minister would be there. He stopped, taking a deep breath full of relief as he saw a man coming down the wooden steps. He shared a sideward glance with Billy before proceeding.

The man looked up as they approached in their dirty cowhand state.

"May I help you gentlemen?" he asked.

"I hope so. Are you the minister?" Boyd said.

"Yes, I'm Reverend Taylor."

"Might I visit with you for a while, sir? I'm Boyd Richards, and this is my friend, Billy."

"Please come in, young men."

The last time Boyd entered a church, he'd watched his two friends marry their brides in Arkansas. He thought about Brother Moore, the minister in Texas who had spoken to him in town the day before they'd left on the drive. The man had been praying for him. He felt that for sure. He looked around at the simple wooden benches as they entered. Billy took a seat at the back of the building as Boyd and the minister went to sit at the front. The minister picked up his Bible, and Boyd reached to take it from him. "May I?" he asked and received a nod. He went over all the scriptures given to him by James, plus the others read by the campfires during the months on the cattle drive and shared his life story. Reverend Taylor listened and shared more scriptures.

Boyd thanked him and then asked Billy to meet him at the hotel later. Reverend Taylor invited them to stay at his house, so Boyd promised to meet them at the small white house beside the church later.

Boyd kept his head down as he made his way back through town. The preacher's words reverberated to his very soul. He kept moving forward until he sighted the edge of the stockyards. The stench from the animals didn't penetrate as the darkness within his own soul washed over him. It went beyond the embittered man he had become since losing Nancy. He now realized there could have been problems, even between them, had she lived because of the transformation that occurred in her life during the war. Before the war, they'd made a simple life for themselves after leaving Georgia. Although they were good people, their lives had something missing. He'd never believed the show his uncle made of church, so he didn't go and after marrying him, neither did Nancy.

A dry, cool wind battered his hat with dust as he continued on to the livery. The owner lifted a hand from where he worked in the corral, and Boyd nodded before passing into the barn. His horse munched oats in the fourth stall.

"Well, old boy, we made another trip."

A soft whinny of expectancy followed as he stroked the soft nose now lifted toward him.

"No, no, we aren't leaving yet. No, you rest, and I'm going to go see if I can."

Boyd took off his hat and ran a hand through his flattened, sweaty hair. He needed a bath and a meal. A quick look at his pocket watch showed the time as close to four. His stomach growled; his breakfast a distant memory. The sign for baths—hanging outside of the hotel—as he walked through town came to mind. Frank and Roy might be there. Now those two, better known as "Swede" and "Windy," wanted nothing but drinking and cards tonight. They'd tell Boyd to quit thinking so much. Maybe he *should* let the matter be for a little while longer. Eating might help. He headed up the street.

The smells from the log store, also marked as a café, reached him before his feet hit the step by the door. A woman in a calico dress reached the door right before him, and he held it open for her. She gave him a gentle smile.

"Thank you."

"Ma'am," he said, tipping his hat as she passed through the door.

A gust of strong wind blew a wave of dust and he sneezed as it assaulted his nostrils. He turned his head and squeezed his eyes shut as a second wave seized him.

"God bless you!"

His watery eyes opened as he straightened to discover a small girl of about eight years sitting on the seat of a wagon secured to the hitching post just in front of him. A smile found its way to his lips as he looked at her sitting so serene and still with her hands folded in her lap.

"Thank you," he said.

"You're welcome! I'm Emma. What's your name?"

He let the door close and stepped forward.

"Boyd Richards."

A bright smile erupted across her freckled face.

"Nice to meet ya, Mr. Richards. Are you going to the café or just passing by?"

Boyd frowned, his eyes trying to catch her small gaze. The bright blue eyes stared straight ahead, never adjusting to the path of his movement. Realization hit him, and an unexpected lump formed in his throat. His steps slowed, and she tilted her head with a quizzical scrunch to her face.

"What's the matter, Mr. Richards?"

It took a couple of hard swallows before he could find his voice.

"I'm sorry, Emma. I just have never met someone so young without their eyesight."

An impish grin appeared.

"Don't worry. It's not catching!"

A delightful bubble of laughter followed. Boyd couldn't help smiling.

"I know that. I had a friend who lost his sight after an explosion during the war."

Her mouth opened, and her eyes widened.

"You were in that war they talk about?"

"Yes."

"You must have been very brave."

He found her candor contagious.

"Some people say that I was, but I don't think so. It was scary sometimes. Are you ever afraid?"

She pursed her lips in thought before shaking her head.

"Sometimes I start to be, and then I remember."

"Remember what?"

"I remember Jesus is always with me. You see, I met him last year and was baptized. Before that, I got afraid a lot."

Everything in Boyd froze. Absolute silence ensued.

"Mr. Richards, you're still there, aren't you?"

His feet moved of their own volition until he stood beside the wagon.

"Yes, little one, I'm still here."

Her hand reached out searching, and he lifted his to take it.

"Why are you so sad?"

He withdrew his hand. The admission fell from his lips.

"I guess because I don't know Jesus."

"Really? That's all right. He's not hard to find. You just have to talk to him in a special way. My ma says most people have trouble meeting him because they can't see him. That wasn't a problem for me. I can't see anyone that I'm talking to with my eyes. Oh, I can touch them with my hands and hear them with my ears, but I like it best when I see them with my heart. That's the way I see Him."

The door to the café opened, and the woman came toward the wagon. Emma's face beamed at the sound of the steps on the boardwalk.

"Ma, this is Mr. Richards. Did you sell the eggs?"

The woman gave Boyd an apologetic smile before answering her daughter.

"Yes, Emma."

Emma clapped in delight. "Oh, good!"

The woman turned back to Boyd.

"I'm sorry Emma has detained you, Mr. Richards. She loves meeting new people. I'm Etta Madsen."

"Not at all, Mrs. Madsen. In fact, I think, Emma has helped me make a very important decision."

Emma beamed even as her mother frowned in puzzlement.

"How? I don't—"

Boyd smiled at Mrs. Madsen as he reached to squeeze Emma's hand.

"I'll let Emma explain. Thank you, Emma. Allow me to assist you into your wagon, Mrs. Madsen."

The woman blushed and looked not just a little bewildered.

"Why, thank you, Mr. Richards."

Once she reached the seat, Boyd tipped his hat.

"Good afternoon, ladies."

He turned to continue up the street but stopped as Mrs. Madsen's voice called to him.

"Aren't you going into the café or store, Mr. Richards?"

He shook his head.

"No, ma'am, not now. I don't think they have what I need most."

~

Boyd lengthened his stride as he headed to the opposite end of town. He saw Frank and Roy headed into the hotel. They caught

53

sight of him as he passed across the street and motioned to him. He shook his head. They shrugged before continuing inside. As soon as he cleared the corner of the last building, he began to run. He could see Reverend Taylor's small house in the distance and hoped no one stepped out as he approached. The pastor had mentioned he left the church unlocked for anyone who might need a place to pray, and gratitude filled Boyd. His boots pounded on the boards of the steps as he ran up them. A shiver of apprehension raced through him as he reached for the doorknob. The door opened without a hitch and he slid inside, shutting the door behind him.

"Reverend Taylor?"

Silence responded. Boyd wiped his now sweaty palms on his dirty pants before removing his hat. The sight of the wooden cross on the table at the front of the church brought unexpected moisture to his eyes.

He stopped at the bench closest to the front and sat down, but stood up again, and then sat back down again. He folded, rolled, and twisted the brim of his hat a few times before he laid it beside him. Scooting forward on the seat, he looked at the cross as everything inside him went still. An old memory surfaced of his friend Marcus kneeling in prayer, beside a very ill John, inside the damp darkness of Ft. Delaware. It had been right after they arrived at that terrible place as prisoners of war.

Boyd had never knelt in front of any man, but he knelt now.

So much swirled within his head and soul; his very being felt exposed, humbled, and broken. The maelstrom of emotions overcame his battle-weary soul as the toil from the years of running from God culminated in that moment.

"I'm a broken, rotten man, Lord . . . Forgive me. Everyone I love or admire seems to think you want me. I'm not worthy . . . But I'm yours. Please take this darkness from my soul, forgive me and take my life down the trail You have planned." Tears coursed down his face as overwhelming joy flooded his heart. "Amen."

As he stood to his feet, peace overflowed. He turned to find Billy and Reverend Taylor standing in quiet respect and joy with him. They met him with handshakes and pats on the back.

"Mr. Richards, there's a pond behind this church we use for baptisms if you're ready," Reverend Taylor said.

"Whatever I need to do."

"Let's go then."

~

An hour later, Boyd, Billy, and Reverend Taylor sat in the minister's home with his wife serving them dinner. Completeness and joy filled Boyd. He smiled as he pushed his wet hair out of his eyes.

"I've had two baths within an hour, and meaning no offense to your tub, ma'am, but I think the first was the best," he said.

The small woman with plaited golden-gray hair shared a smile with her husband before she responded, "I'm certainly not offended and am so overjoyed for you. I would also like to offer you a trim or shave and a haircut if you young men are so inclined."

Boyd thought for a moment. It had been a long time. He thought of how he once teased John Wilkins, who had insisted on a clean shave as often as possible.

"Yes, ma'am, if it wouldn't be too much trouble, that would be a help," he said before elbowing Billy. "However, I think Billy here just needs the haircut. His fuzz doesn't warrant the attentions of the blade."

They all laughed as Billy swiped at him.

"Please say grace, Edward, before these two upset the table."

"Certainly, Edna."

Boyd and Billy relished the delicious meal in the warm and relaxed family atmosphere; taking their time without being on alert and working the cattle. After dinner, Edna kept her promise and worked magic worthy of a real barber. Boyd's own reflection startled him when she handed him a mirror. He ran a tentative hand across his now smooth face before he caught Billy's open-mouth stare. Boyd met it with an intense frown but laughed.

"It makes you look not much older than me," Billy said. "How old are you anyway?"

"Still older than you, whelp," he said and stood up, rubbing the back of his now bare neck. "It's your turn, and none too soon. That hair is making you look like a girl—all long and curly."

Reverend Taylor chuckled before asking, "Mr. Richards, would you like to sit on the porch for a spell before retiring for the evening?"

Boyd ducked a blow from Billy before nodding and followed

the reverend out the door. The couple had asked them to stay the night. Their grown children no longer lived with them, so they had an extra room.

The brisk night air greeted them, and the stars and moon twinkled as they sat in well-worn chairs.

"May I ask how or if your recent decision will change your plans once returning to Texas?" the minister asked.

"Well, sir, I've been pondering and will start praying about that. This is so new. I plan to write a letter to my brother in East Texas tonight and would like to have you mail it for me if you don't mind."

The white-haired man moved his spectacles down on his nose, looking over them at Boyd before he answered.

"I'll be happy to take it on Monday morning. Mr. Richards, I feel I must caution—no, prepare you—for something."

Boyd sat forward, giving him his full attention.

"Yes, sir?"

"Your joy is all consuming right now. Embrace it, share it, but realize others will challenge it, and many will want to extinguish it. In various ways, your new life journey may be even more challenging but with a big difference. Remember, you aren't promised a life without problems now, but that you will never be forsaken," Edward said.

Boyd started to protest but stopped as he remembered Nancy's letter and how James Hawkins now faced life. He nodded as he looked outward to the yard bathed in the moonlight before turning to meet the man's kind gaze.

"Yes, sir, I do believe there's truth to your words . . . " He hesitated; it seemed asking for help came easier: "Pray for me?"

Reverend Taylor stood and shook his hand. He then patted him on the back.

"Definitely, son, now let's get you to bed. I don't like you traveling on the Lord's day, but you must meet your obligations."

~

The next morning came too soon. If it hadn't been for Mrs. Taylor, they'd have overslept. Cowhands weren't used to the comforts of a bed in a quiet house, and sleep took a firm hold on them. They woke with a blur of sheets, cleaned clothes being donned, and boots pulled on feet. They emerged still tucking their shirts and smoothing their hair. They inhaled breakfast and said quick good-byes. Boyd and Billy dashed for the other end of town. Their hosts shook their heads and smiled as they watched them from the porch.

Ted stood by the livery with his pocket watch in hand. His mouth compressed in a grim line as he measured their approach.

"Get in there, tend your horses, and mount up. I don't want excuses or explanations," he said as he turned on his heels and headed for the corral where a bleary-eyed Roy tried to string the extra mounts together. Frank knelt beside the water trough with his head buried deep in its cold depths. The rest of the men emerged from the barn with their mounts, all reflecting the lateness of the night before.

Boyd and Billy made quick work of things and returned to help Ted and Roy within ten minutes.

They had everything in order when they noticed two men approaching on foot.

"Who's the trail boss?" one of the approaching men asked without a greeting. The stocky man wore a gun on his hip. His companion displayed several missing teeth as he smiled at the cowhands.

Ted stepped forward, flanked by Boyd.

"I'm the trail boss," Ted said without extending his hand. "State your business."

The man hesitated for an instant as he caught Boyd's intense gaze from under his lowered Stetson. He brought his eyes back to Ted, who had not moved one inch.

"We come to get your string of horses. A couple of your men lost them in a game of cards last night."

Ted turned and met each of his men's sobering gazes, receiving a slight negative head shake from each before returning his regard to the man in front of him. His eyes traveled downward to the man's boots and then back to his face, paused, turning to glance at the dirty, toothless man who faced him on the right. Ted sucked in his lower lip, making a calculating clicking noise. He shook his head and met the accuser's steady gaze.

"No, sir, I don't believe that's the case. Most of these men were at the saloon last night and some did play cards, but none lost these horses to you."

The stocky man frowned and narrowed his gaze. "How do you know? I didn't see you there."

Ted smiled. "Oh, I was there, upstairs, and I know if my men were to have done something as foolish as that, one of them would've come to get me. They know the consequences. These horses aren't theirs to lose at any rate, and Mr. Kennedy won't take to us returning without them."

"So you're calling me a liar?"

"Definitely, sir. Now, I understand that's hard to hear, and I'll be willing to admit I'm wrong if—after talking to the sheriff and some others who were present—you're proved to be correct. If that proves I have a liar and cheat in my outfit, that man will be left here to pay his debt."

The pair shifted.

"The sheriff rode out this morning. So you'll have to take our word for it."

Ted crossed his arms, smiled, and rocked back on his heels in a gesture well known to his men, who had moved to stand behind him.

"I don't think I can do that," he said; then slicker than a train on a greased track, Ted rocked forward, removing the man's gun from its holster, and Boyd knocked the other man, who had lunged for him, to the ground. Ted sidestepped as his men grabbed the disarmed man, wrestling him to the ground. They tied them like a cow ready for a brand and took them to the deputy. It seemed these two had tried this swindle on others before.

An hour later, the cowhands hit the trail.

"Well, today is a bust," Ted said as he rode beside Boyd.

"Seen worse," Boyd said.

Ted grinned. "Yeah." His smile lingered a moment as they rode along before he turned a thoughtful stare in Boyd's direction. "Richards, thanks for coming through; I wasn't sure you would."

Boyd frowned. "Why?"

Ted shrugged. "I have eyes. You're different this morning. Something has been working hard on you since you got back from that fort in Indian Territory. It looks like you got it resolved, but—as I suspect you're now more of the mind of young Billy here—don't start preaching at me, and I hope whatever you caught at that fort isn't going to addle the men's wits when we stop by there on our way home." He saw the look of surprise on Boyd's face. "Your friend the major asked we check in on the way back, so he could let us know the status of the Indian activity. I know we're liable to see some of that activity before we get there to hear about it, but—"

Boyd cut him off. "Ted, I better tell you something before we get there. Hallie Price is there."

Ted looked puzzled. "Why? What place does she have there?"

Boyd ducked his head. "She's working. No, no, not like her old job. She's taking care of the major's invalid son."

Ted laughed. "Hallie? Richards, you baffle me. Are you trying to rescue her or something? Well, don't try that with me. I like my life just fine. Let's go." Ted urged his horse into a canter, looked back once to repeat, "Hallie?" before breaking into a deep rumbling chuckle that drew all the men's gazes. They looked at Boyd, and he shrugged before spurring his horse forward.

The autumn night air held a brisk chill as the men from Joe Kennedy's drive sat around the campfire. All quiet except for the sounds of insects, the occasional call of a bird, or nicker from the horses. The men sat in companionable silence as young Billy started to play his harmonica. Even Old Amos, the cook, looked relaxed. Ted had pushed them hard for two days but had relented a bit the third day. He laid with his head propped on his bedroll.

"Hey, Richards!" he said, propping himself up on one arm.

Boyd looked up from his contemplation of the flickering firelight in front of him to the trail boss. "Yes, boss?"

Ted cleared his throat and addressed the group. "Boys, do you know what Richards did?" All eyes turned on him. "He sent for our Hallie Price to go be a nurse to his friend's son at the fort. Ain't that the oddest notion?" Ted smirked as he finished.

All eyes turned to Boyd, whose eyes had not left Ted.

"Why—" started Frank before swallowing as Boyd's eyes halted his words.

"I sent for Miss Price because it made sense to me. She impressed me as someone who could use a new opportunity," Boyd said, and then he frowned as a potential issue occurred to him. "As we're going to the fort, I think it would be best to pretend the rest of you don't know her in front of the soldiers. It might cause her problems. The fact of me recommending her is known."

Ted sat up at this and glared at Boyd. "Richards, don't start telling us what to do. The rest of us have known Hallie in one way or another for a lot longer than you. We think she's a good, straightforward woman. She's never pretended to be something she's not until now. Shoot, she may be so glad to see us that she wants to travel back with us. You boys talk some sense into him. I've got to go check the horses," he said as he stood and turned into the darkness.

Roy, the oldest of the hands, shook his head. "If this don't beat all. Richards, you can't rescue women like Hallie. They don't change."

"Then why did she leave and go to the fort when given a choice?" Boyd asked.

The men stewed on that for a bit.

"We'll play it however you say, but we can't speak for Ted or for Hallie."

"Fair enough," Boyd said.

Old Amos brought him some coffee. "Most people might expect you to think of someone like Miss Lucy instead of Miss Hallie for such a job, but I think you're right. Besides, the boss'd kill ya if you suggested it to his daughter."

A tingle went through Boyd. "I never thought about Miss Kennedy . . . for James. She strikes me as comfortable where she is."

The cook emptied the dregs from the now empty pot. "You'd be right, except if given another chance. Did you know she went to college in the East for a bit?"

The well written, if not ill conceived, newspaper article came to mind. He replayed the memory of her intelligent blue-green eyes meeting his in the newspaper office. Boyd stared into the campfire. "No, I didn't, but I'm not surprised. Is that why she's not married?"

The cook laughed and so did the other men. Frank and Roy stood up and continued to chuckle as they headed out into the skirting darkness to check the horses. Billy stopped playing his harmonica and met Boyd's gaze as it shifted from the fire.

"Mind you, I don't agree, but some people think she's too spirited to ever get married," Billy said.

"I like a little spirit in a woman," Boyd said.

Cook spit on the ground and chuckled again. "You'd better not let the boss or Ted hear you say that."

"What does Ted have to say about it?"

"You're aiming to get on his ornery side, Richards. That's all I'm saying. You sent his first pick to the fort. I'd leave his other plans alone."

"Miss Lucy ain't studying on him, Amos," Billy said.

"Don't make no difference, Billy. Unless the boss says so. Give me them cups, boys. I got to bed down. Get some shut eye."

Boyd resumed staring at the fire. Lucy Kennedy and Ted? Nope . . . but what did he know? Not her, no . . . but something long dormant stirred in him. He *wanted* to.

He glanced at Billy. "You've been with the Kennedy's for a bit. How do you see it?"

Billy tapped the spit out of his harmonica and slid it back in his pocket. He grabbed his bed roll from under the wagon and spread it on the ground. "They've been good to me. Real decent—all except for Jason. He and Ted make a bad combination. I hope Miss Lucy might go back to school or get away from the ranch before her brother returns." He glanced back at the old cook and lowered his voice. "She's not for Ted."

"How about Hallie, Billy? Was I wrong?"

The young man ducked his head with a shy grin. "I've never known her like the other men, but she's been kind to me. She's a good listener. I think you done good by her." He slid down and flipped on his side. "G'night."

"Night, Billy."

Boyd slid his Bible from his saddlebag and looked at his baptism date under Nancy's. It felt good. He flipped it open to his last reading and finished a chapter before returning it to his bags. He felt more certain now than when he had sent for Hallie. She needed this opportunity.

As for Miss Kennedy, he closed his eyes in prayer.

Chapter Five

The lookout soldier over the gate called, "Riders coming in! It's Mr. Kennedy's men!"

Boyd spotted Major Hawkins as the gates opened, admitting them. He relished the thought of a long talk with the man he now considered a friend. The major put his hat on as some other officers emerged from the door in the office behind him. Hallie Price emerged from what appeared to be the blacksmith's shop, pushing James in his chair, and Boyd nodded toward them. Everyone watched their group as they approached and pulled their horses to a halt in front of the group of officers. Ted pushed his hat back and leaned forward on his saddle horn.

"Good afternoon, Major. Where do you want us?" he said.

A flash of irritation crossed the officer's face, however, the major smiled and encompassed all the cowhands with his greeting.

"I'm glad to see you have returned without mishap. The fort welcomes you and invites you to stay the night. Please, excuse me a moment." He dismissed the other officers before turning back to them. "I would like to visit with your boss and Mr. Richards." The major raised his hand toward the corporal accompanying Miss Price as she pushed James toward them. "Corporal Rigby, please take the rest of these men to the North quarters and tend to their horses."

"Yes, sir." The corporal retrieved his horse and motioned the men to follow him. All did with a noted backward glance at Miss Price.

"Mr. Richards!" James Hawkins called out, smiling as Hallie pushed his chair beside where Boyd and Ted had dismounted.

Boyd removed his hat, revealing his shorter hair and a face with only a few days growth on it. A heartfelt smile triggered a reciprocal response as he reached down to cover James's hand with his.

"It's good to see you, James. I see you're in the capable hands of Miss Price," Boyd said and nodded to the woman, who stood behind his new friend's chair.

James smiled. "More than capable, I can assure you. She has been the best nurse I've ever had. The doctor here is so pleased with her, he wants her to be his assistant in Washington. He plans to put her in contact with more experienced nurses who worked during the war, but I won't let him take her away from me. Isn't that right, Hallie?"

Hallie blushed. "That's right, James. I will only consider the doctor's plan if you dismiss me, which I hope never happens," she said as she moved around and looked James in the face before turning toward Boyd. "Mr. Richards, I am so glad to get the opportunity to thank you for sending me here. I have to admit I wanted to run the first day, but that passed once I met James." She smiled a genuine smile, not the practiced one present when he first met her. Her smile faltered a bit when she saw Ted and her old one replaced it. "Well, Ted Dalton, how are you?"

Ted glanced at Boyd before he responded, "Just fine, Miss Price. It's nice to see you again. Mr. Richards told us about your new post here—Congratulations."

Well, well . . . more of a history *did* exist between the trail boss and Miss Price than demonstrated. Boyd appreciated Ted's restraint in front of the major and James.

"Thank you. Well, I have to get James inside for a rest. I'll see you gentlemen at dinner," Hallie said and turned to go, but the major halted them.

"Miss Price, I know you stick to a strict schedule for my son, and I appreciate it, but I would like to take him inside for my conversation with these gentlemen. I'll send him over with Corporal Rigby after our meeting. Please let Mrs. Hawkins know about the dinner plans and then take a rest yourself. We will see you this evening."

"Very well, Major, thank you, but if James gets tired before then, please send for me." She nodded. "Gentlemen."

Major Hawkins turned to consult with the other officers who still stood behind him. He dismissed them and then turned back to the men who awaited the meeting. "Boyd, Mr. Dalton, James, please accompany me inside," he beckoned as he pushed his son's wheelchair, following them inside his office.

The major pushed James inside, placing his chair to the right of his desk before motioning to two other chairs. "Please have a seat," he said as he took his place behind the desk. He removed his hat and leaned forward, regarding each of them. "First, I want to thank you for making this detour at my request. I must confess the original reason for me asking this of you was three-fold: to update you on the Indian situation, to consider sending the family you helped to rescue back to Texas with you, and to ask Boyd Richards to consider returning here as one of my scouts during the spring."

Although Boyd knew he couldn't take the position, a deep appreciation and sense of honor filled him. The chair next to him creaked, and he turned in time to see the perturbed look on Ted's face. He glanced back as the major continued.

"However, this week has changed all but one of those intents." Major Hawkins turned toward James, who watched him with a knowing look. He nodded at him. "Yes, James, there is a new change of which you are unaware. Your mother and I found out two days ago in the letter I received from Washington. Our family will be leaving the fort at the first of December as they are sending me to work with the War Department. This was a temporary assignment, James. We knew that."

The intelligent gaze, so like his father's, reflected understanding and held a question, but before the question could be spoken, the major held up his hand and turned to Boyd. "You see, Boyd, I came here to assist the regular fort commander, and the captain will be capable of completing all we've established. Now, let me finish. Our officers met today as we have been notified the Peace Commission, which formed in July, will meet with the southern tribes in Kansas this month. We hope it will progress things for the better, but it also means changes. They are considering closing more forts, including this one within a year. These events mean a drastic turn of things. Boyd, I will be unable to offer you the position I had hoped. I looked forward to the opportunity to work with you. So, I express my regrets. Furthermore, Mrs. Scott has not recovered from her ordeal, and she is in need of specialized attention. Susannah and I would like Mrs. McDonald to bring young Charlie and become part of our household in Washington with the plan of having Mrs. Scott join us once she is better. So the one original intent I *can* finalize is to let you know the Indian situation is improving, but please be careful as you leave in the morning. I'll have a detail travel with you the first ten miles on their regular daily scouting of the area. Enjoy the afternoon, and I look forward to dinner this evening."

James spoke first, "What about, Hallie?"

Boyd shared his question and also sensed Ted's interest in his answer.

"She will come with us of course." The major smiled at his son.

"Excuse me, Major. I appreciate the information, but I have some things to attend to before dinner," Ted said as he exited.

The tension level dropped as he left, leaving the three friends to visit more.

~

Boyd appreciated his old friend, as well as his new one. Outside of John and Marcus, he had allowed only three other friendships; Billy, James, and the major. He shared his conversion, as well as his tentative plans for the future upon his return to Texas. James expressed how much he valued the care Hallie provided. He didn't try to probe Boyd for information about her past. James told him Hallie had shared small bits about being married and widowed but wouldn't talk about her other work prior to coming here. Boyd respected his new friend even more for his discretion. The trio talked until just enough time to change for dinner remained. They made their way back toward the Hawkins' connected quarters and noted Corporal Rigby propped outside of James's room. He put a silencing finger to his lips and inclined his head toward the cracked door of Miss Price's room. Raised voices could be heard. The group shared the looks of silent communication familiar to soldiers. The major nodded at Eddie, who traded places with Boyd behind James's chair. Boyd moved to the right side of the door as the major flanked the left side. James waited for everyone to be in position before nodding to Eddie, who pushed him toward the door. The corporal knocked for his friend.

"Excuse me, Hallie . . . " he said as the front of his chair knocked the door open to reveal Ted yelling at Hallie with his hands just about to grasp her arms. Their interruption staunched the flow of words and two heads turned toward the door. "Mr. Dalton, this impropriety will not be tolerated. I assure you there was a time when I could have shown you how intolerant I can be, but—"

Boyd and the major entered at that time, flanking his sides.

Ted glared at all of them. "This is personal, gentlemen, and of no concern to any of you. It's between Hallie and me."

"That is where you are wrong, Mr. Dalton. This fort is under my command, and Miss Price is in my employ; therefore, it does concern me," the major said. He turned to Hallie. "Miss Price, we will allow you a few moments in which to conclude this matter, and then I will need you to help James dress for dinner. We will be right outside."

The group left as they'd entered.

~

Hallie should've known Ted would be unable to leave the past alone. She'd tried to make it clear three years ago when he'd asked her to marry him. The idea of ever marrying again didn't sit well with her. She much preferred her independence. Still, his outburst showed he cared, and she used the term in the loosest way possible. Having soldiers, Mr. Richards, and James rescue her flattered her. No one had ever rescued her.

Thank goodness Ted didn't persist after the men left. At least the man wished her well. No illusions or disillusionments existed between the likes of them. She smiled and exited through the still ajar door. The voices from James's room became clear as she closed her door behind her. The shutters stood open to his window. She froze, not wanting to listen, but knowing she must.

"You knew!" accused Eddie.

James nodded. "Eddie, she's not Julia. You have got to quit judging all women by your sister's mistakes, which, I might add, were decisions made out of desperation."

"That was true at first, maybe, but what about when I asked her to let me take care of her after the war? She refused to leave the madam's house in Boston. It's not a saloon; it's worse. It pretends to be a refined business, but in the end it's all the same."

"Eddie, she knew you barely made enough to keep yourself on a soldier's pay."

"I would have left the army in time and found something else.

I've learned new skills and am better than the poor boy you first met," Eddie said

"Yes, you are, my friend. Eddie, Julia has made her choices. I pray each day for her to decide to find you or an opportunity will come along to free her from the life she's living. Julia is one of the reasons I agreed to give Miss Price a chance. I'm just glad she decided she wanted it. I'm convinced this is God's hand at work. Don't mistreat her because you are mad at Julia. Help *her* like you would your own sister."

"I'm already helping Molly Scott because she reminds me of Julia when we were younger. She needs a brother to care for her like Julia used to."

"Eddie, you were the younger brother and did the best you could when your mother abandoned the two of you on the streets."

"It wasn't enough, James. The scrapping, pickpocketing, and whatever else I did fell short of feeding us enough. Julia hated it and got a job with a tailor. It didn't last. That's when she left. I know I've had to be forgiven of many of the things I did to take care of us, but losing my sister to whoring because I couldn't do better by her haunts me. I can never make it up to her. Just like I can't do enough to fix what happened to you. It can never be taken away."

"Eddie, it wasn't your fault. You say you accept God's forgiveness, but you won't forgive yourself. Let it go," James said.

Guilt stabbed at Hallie and she knocked at the door, ending their conversation.

"I came to dress James for dinner. We're expected in ten minutes. Corporal Rigby, would you mind helping me, so we can make it in time? I do apologize for causing a delay."

Eddie looked shocked when Hallie asked for his help. A silent antagonism existed between them, and James knew it. He smiled when his friend nodded. "Of course." As he bent to lift James out of his chair, his green eyes strayed to the window and widened. He looked back at James. She knew they now realized the shutters had remained open the whole time they'd talked.

Hallie bowed her head and started removing James's boots. Perhaps they'd leave it alone.

She held her breath. Eddie crossed the room.

"I think you should wear your uniform tonight, James," he

said.

Hallie exhaled and set the boots to the side.

"No, it doesn't fit. Just get my suit," James said.

~

Dinner went well under the gracious and ever hospitable hand of Susannah Hawkins. Mrs. McDonald expressed her joy in seeing Boyd again and introduced him to her daughter, Molly, even though the young woman gave a mere flicker of an eye in response. Her grandson, Charlie, laughed with delight as Billy played his harmonica for them. They had all bathed and turned out as well as could be expected in their trail gear. All appeared to enjoy this rare glimpse of home life. They exchanged trail stories for soldier stories in an atmosphere warmer than many had known for years. Then the major stepped up to the fireplace with his arm around his wife and raised his hand to get everyone's attention.

"I am so pleased we have been able to share this evening. As many of you now know, my family's time here is very close to being over as we will be going to Washington by, or possibly before, December. Tonight also is the night before my son's birthday. His mother and I are so grateful to have him with us. James, your mother has made a few special pies with the provisions available. We feel the gifts are the kind people present with us tonight. Happy birthday, Son!"

Everyone clapped, and James smiled. "Thank you, everyone. What a wonderful birthday gift—life, family, and friends."

Suzanne Hawkins gasped and placed a hand to her mouth. "Wait, I almost forgot your other gift. Eddie, please bring James up here; this is for you also." She scurried from the room and returned with a paper-wrapped parcel. "Now, Son, this was sent by a young man who made your acquaintance the year you left Harvard to enter the war. He was part of the class of 1864 and received admission to their law school but had to leave before graduating. As a captain on General Grant's staff during the last year of the war, he witnessed Appomattox with Lee's surrender. He graduated from law school at the University of Chicago. I'm not sure how he found you; maybe it's because of your father's impending promotion. Anyway, this is for Private James Hawkins and Corporal Eddie Rigby from Mr. Robert Todd Lincoln. It arrived a few days ago, and I saved it for your birthday. He sent the brief note—from which I have shared his information—to your father and this letter addressed to you." The room had gone silent.

Boyd fought down fires of former war aggressions, thankful for their present bridge of peace.

James looked at his father.

"Did you have *my* letter delivered to him after the president's death?" James asked.

"Yes, Son, just as you asked. I took it to his mother after you dictated it to me," the major said.

"Please, read *his* letter, sir."

The major took the letter from his wife's hand and broke the seal:

My dear friend,

I am sorry it has taken me so long to reply to your most heartfelt letter of sympathy. It echoed the sorrow of a nation and the grief of our family's hearts. The kindness you showed me during our brief days together at Harvard was immense. I have not forgotten how you treated me as a person of the same standing as your other friends, not more, nor less because of who my father was. You may not remember this photograph, which was taken at Cambridge the day you left us. The photographer captured the images of the new soldiers. Your new friend, now Corporal Rigby, had returned with you to gather the rest of your things. The uniforms were so very new. It is my hope this image will bring a smile and not a sigh to you in light of your present state. I was grieved to learn of your injuries but am obliged to thank you on the part of the United States and my father for your service and sacrifice. May the future find you ever in God's care.

Your grateful friend,
Robert Todd Lincoln

Boyd and his fellow cowhands from Texas murmured appreciation of the letter, while Corporal Nate Case cleared his throat and Corporal Eddie Rigby coughed to cover the extent of their emotions. Every military officer and soldier present exchanged meaningful glances. Major Hawkins folded the letter before laying it on his son's lap. He stepped back to put a loving arm around his wife who stood holding the special gift. James nodded to his mother without speaking. She brushed away a tear and removed the wrappings from the parcel. A picture of James and Eddie, both young and strong, with James standing a head taller than his friend emerged. Boyd examined the somber and serious faces still full of youth and vitality. His mind went back to other faces he held in memory. He missed Marc and John the most.

Mrs. Hawkins and the major shared the photograph for a minute before passing it to Eddie, who shared it with James. Memories flashed, and old feelings surfaced and subsided like waves crashing onto the shore before rushing back out to sea.

Boyd watched, frozen in time with these two men who had fought on the opposite side of the war from him. More flashes of faces from the back of his mind emerged and another wave of homesickness for his brother and friends in Texas crashed. He knew the time had come to take out every piece of himself and deal with all of it, this time with God's help. It appeared James also had some remaining inner conflicts, but he somehow knew the man wouldn't sleep until he prayed about them.

Hallie moved behind James, and Boyd held his breath. He wanted to scream for her to wait, but she didn't.

She leaned over James's shoulder and gazed at the picture before asking, "May I?" and took it from his hands to pass it to Major Hawkins. Then she nodded and smiled at the group, "I think these two might have some stories to tell us. Right, James? Corporal Rigby? Or maybe the rest of you fellows want to take a look at this and tell us how much better looking you were in your photographs? The ladies will go get the pies and leave you men to your bragging. Mrs. Hawkins, let us assist you."

Elizabeth McDonald deposited young Charlie in Billy's arms, where he sat beside Molly Scott.

Susannah blinked and then smiled, "Yes, and the biggest piece will go to James. Everyone, we'll be back to serve you."

Boyd released a sigh of relief. He strode forward and asked to see the picture. He stared at it for a while before he handed it back to Eddie, who still stood beside James.

"No, mine was much better. I feel I must remind these gentlemen and all you Union men, and I say this knowing my person may be in danger, that the gray coats of Dixie were much better looking uniforms, especially on the men in Hood's Texas Brigade," he said tongue-in-cheek and with much bravado in order to be taken in good humor.

He knew making that statement in the presence of the officers in attendance held a risk as feelings still ran deep on both sides, but he wanted to switch the focus off of James and what could have become a more awkward situation. As he finished, silence filled the room, even his trail partners who had been unaware of any of his past remained quiet.

Uneasy laughter emerged as more of the men gathered around James to do some bragging of their own. By the time the ladies returned with the pies, they'd shared laughter over several of the exaggerated stories shared. The time passed with the hour soon turning late, and the guests trickled out until only the major, Susannah, James, Boyd, and Hallie remained. Corporal Rigby left, along with Billy, to see Mrs. Scott, Mrs. McDonald, and Charlie home as Hallie and Susannah finished cleaning up the dishes.

Mrs Hawkins turned to Hallie. "The major and I will take care of James tonight, dear. We need to visit as a family for a few moments after everyone leaves. This move will bring many changes, which need to be discussed. I want to offer an official invitation for you to come with us in your present position. Also, please know we want you to pursue the opportunity Dr. Jones has made for you. He's waiting to see if you will accept the position as his head nurse in Washington. Of course, it is with the understanding that James will remain your priority. All of the arrangements are made." She smiled at Hallie.

Boyd hid his smile when Hallie appeared speechless. Moisture reflected in her eyes. "Yes, thank you so much. I'd be honored."

Susannah took both of Hallie's hands in hers. "Good. Now I'm going to shoo Mr. Richards into the night. I'll see if he will see you to your quarters."

The major's wife scurried over to Boyd like a fussy mother hen.

"Mr. Richards, it has been a pleasure to have you with us, but I'm afraid I need to have a few moments with my husband and son. If I do not see you before you leave in the morning, please give the information on how to correspond with you to my husband. I know our family wants to stay in touch," she said. She gestured to where

Hallie stood. "Would you see Miss Price to her door?"

"Of course, ma'am, Thank you for your hospitality. Happy birthday, James! Major, you've been too kind. I thank you, sir, good night." He deepened his voice in heartfelt friendship. "Thank you for being part of changing my life, James."

"Boyd, if our paths never converge again, it's been my pleasure to know you. You have shown me pain beyond my own and have reminded me how priceless the daily grace we live in is. Anyway, as Hallie would say, stop preaching, just talk. Thank you for giving me that opportunity tonight. The stories all the men had would fill volumes of novels but were more fun in the telling. You'll have to forgive me for not writing," James said, flashing a lopsided grin. "Mother will keep you abreast of family events in her letters."

The major extended his hand. "Boyd, I'll just say thank you. You have become a cherished friend. I will see you off in the morning with one of my morning patrols."

Boyd shook his outstretched hand, slapped James on the shoulder, and received the hug Mrs. Hawkins offered.

James managed a slight turn of his head toward where Hallie waited by the door. "Don't keep her up talking too late. I'll need her early in the morning. She's so efficient. My day starts out much better with her care." He grinned, and Hallie smiled in return. "Good night."

Boyd opened the door for her, and she held her shawl around her as they stepped into the brisk night air. They walked the short distance to her door in silence. Then she glanced up at him, her dark eyes met his before speaking. "Mr. Richards, why did you do all this for me?"

Surprise lifted his eyebrows. "I didn't do any more than give you an opportunity. You have done the wonderful job that's gained you praise and respect."

She dropped her head and laughed. "Fine, if you don't want to take the credit, but thank you just the same."

He smiled. "Then I will say, you're welcome, ma'am." Her scrutinizing stare found him through the darkness. "What's wrong, Miss Price?"

"Nothing. It's just you seem so much more relaxed than the first time I met you. What did James do that helped change your life?"

"He shared the scriptures that spoke to my heart to let God have my life. I believe the prayers my wife prayed before she died have followed me, and God used James along with a preacher and little girl in Kansas to lead me to heed his voice."

Hallie walked forward and placed her hands on the hitching rail. "Do you feel forgiven?" she asked before turning to continue. "I mean . . . It's just . . . James has shared the story of this woman named Rahab and one about some woman at a well from the Bible. They seem to have had a past like mine, and they were forgiven."

Boyd stepped forward, hat in hand, as he gazed down at her with a fire burning in his soul. "Miss Price, yes, I do, but it goes beyond feeling to certainty. The events that have brought all of us to cross paths the way we have, go beyond happenstance. The best advice I can give to you is the last words my wife left for me in a final letter: 'Let Him.'" He reached for her hand and gave it a gentle squeeze before he strode toward the barracks for the night.

~

Hallie started to go inside her room but turned and found herself in James's room instead. She made her way to the small table beside the bed, which had a Bible on it, paused for a moment before reaching for it, clasping the precious book to her and leaving. Once she returned to her room, she lit a lantern beside her bed and sat down to read. Her heart raced as she read and re-read the words. Then she prayed from the depths of her soul, tears streaming down her face like a child. As she finished, she heard the door to James's room shut, the muffled voices of his parents getting him ready for bed, and then the sound of the door again as they left to return to their home. Unknown joy and excitement bubbled inside her. She imagined happy little girls felt like this, never having experienced such herself. It bubbled into a feeling too big to keep to herself. She picked up the Bible from her bed and shut her door with a soft click as she left her room. She kept her knock light as she opened James's door and leaned against it, closing it behind her back.

A light stir came from the bed as James moved his head to peer into the darkness. She didn't want to alarm him, so she whispered, "It's Hallie."

"Hallie, are you all right?"

She moved away from the door to stand beside his bed overflowing with excitement. "I needed to tell you something. I borrowed your Bible."

The air seemed to radiate the joy that swirled through her, and his voice reflected her excitement. "You did?"

She squeezed his hand before returning the precious book to his small table. Her hand covered his as she moved back to his side.

"Yes, and I now know Jesus."

He whooped.

"Shhh! Your parents will think something is wrong," she said.

She made out his grin even in the darkness as he whispered, "Does this mean when I ask you to attend chapel with us this week, you will?"

"Yes, I will. Well, I just wanted you to know. Good night."

She turned to go, but he stopped her. "Good night, Hallie! The angels are rejoicing, and so am I!" She hesitated a second before bending to give him a brief hug, which she knew he couldn't return and left.

~

The next morning, Hallie rose right at dawn, the same time she woke every day to start work, but she got up and dressed with more ease. Her schedules in Texas contrasted as she worked until late at night and slept late in the mornings there. So, she'd experienced a profound period of adjustment the first few weeks of her new job, but she came to enjoy her days once she started work. The hardest part of her job remained the physical hands-on care. She completed the tasks James could no longer do alone. Assuring he didn't stay in one position too long to avoid red patches in his skin that could become sores at risk for infection. She checked his output levels to determine if everything remained adequate for the health of his internal organs and worked with the doctor. They reviewed the records she kept each day. Dr. Jones had shared volumes about hygiene, ventilation, and diet from the United States Sanitary Commission, as well as information about the nursing principles of Florence Nightingale in England. These things engaged her mind, and she loved learning and felt proud of herself for the first time in her life. His parents watched to make sure she didn't get tired, and Corporal Rigby helped during his off duty time, as well as the other soldiers who alternated to help her lift James into or out of his bed or chair. James complained little to not at all. He displayed a ready sense of humor when not preaching at her. Until now, she preferred the laughter to the sermons, but this morning, gratitude filled her for that very thing. She wanted to talk to him.

She knocked on his door as she always did prior to entering and opened it to find Susannah Hawkins already there bathing her son. The older woman smiled at her, and Hallie knew James had shared her news, and somehow, she didn't mind.

"Good morning, Hallie! I hope you don't mind, but since it's my son's birthday, I decided to spend the day with him. It would have been better to tell you last night and let you rest longer, but I just decided as I lay in bed last night. Please forgive my selfishness," the older woman said as she finished and covered him with a sheet.

Hallie retrieved his clean clothes and joined his mother. "Of course you should spend the day with him," she said even though disappointed, and a stab of guilt pierced her for feeling it. She slid James's sleeve on his arm near her, and then they rolled him to pull the shirt under him and slid the other arm into the garment. As they worked together to button it, she looked at James, who had a smile playing about his mouth as he watched her. She returned the smile. "Happy birthday, James! How old are you today?"

He grinned at his mother and said, "Mother, I don't mean to make you feel old by stating my age, but she did ask." He turned to Hallie and said with his eyebrows drawn in a dramatic feigned frown, "I am a very old twenty-seven-years today."

They all laughed, but a tinge of surprise caught Hallie. She thought him about twenty-four or twenty-five, the way everyone spoke of him. They emphasized her older age as one of the reasons for selecting her. Wait, no one here *knew* her exact age. Though older, yes, but not by as much as everyone seemed to think. She never thought about age. Mr. Richards must have guessed at hers. Her less than easy life must show. No man ever complained, and those she met found her pleasing enough. She shrugged it off. Why did it matter?

"Well, I hate to tell you, I must show no sympathy or awe as I am ahead of you, depending on how you look at it. I hit that mark four years ago," she said and the slight dropping of his mouth confirmed her suspicions.

The older woman stammered. "Well . . . Well . . . Mr. Richards *seemed* to think you were at least thirty-five years or more, Miss Price. Oh, I'm sorry. How rude of me." A flush crept up her face, but she recovered. "I am glad to know this. It means you are younger and stronger and working with us may show more longevity."

James did not blink. His grin just grew wider. "Everyone has me beat except for the new recruits. Even Eddie has me by six months. Now, are you ladies going to make me stay in this bed all day? It is my birthday after all."

They laughed, and the tension left as they finished getting him ready for the day. They then called in a private to help lift him into his chair. Hallie walked outside with them.

Susannah said, "Enjoy your day off, Hallie. You are welcome to join us for lunch."

The wind whipped their dress skirts around them, and Hallie reached down to smooth the cloth. She looked back to answer. "Thank you, but no. After I take the linens from James's bed to the laundry, I need to go find the chaplain and talk about a few things. So enjoy your day, both of you."

Mrs. Hawkins smiled back. "Thank you and please know how happy we are for you."

"Thank you."

Hallie touched James on the shoulder as she left.

She finished her visit with the army chaplain close to lunch. He listened with intense kindness and prayed with her. She saw Corporal Rigby heading toward her as she made her way across the yard.

Once he reached her, she asked, "Did Mr. Richards and the boys get on the trail as planned?"

"Yes, we rode with them until about seven o'clock. We had to diverge paths in order to finish our patrol," he said, hesitating. His green eyes sparkled as he continued. "I saw James and his mother a few moments ago, and they tell me you're scheduling a dunking in the nearest horse trough if the chaplain will do it. Is that so?"

Eddie disconcerted her. There never seemed to be level footing for her with him. One minute she thought he couldn't stand her, and the next he extended friendship.

She laughed. "That's true."

"Good. Congratulations!" He beamed at her, but then he sobered. "Just be prepared for a period where old memories sometimes wash back over you, and you have to remind yourself that you're truly forgiven and new."

He appeared to have firsthand knowledge. So she decided to ask about his conversation with James yesterday. "What happened with you and James in the past?"

His eyes filled with emotion. "I should be the one in that wheelchair. You see, I was going to be second on the field that day. James waited behind me. Our friend Joe went first. My cartridge box fell off my belt, and I stopped to retrieve it. Everyone surged forward. James took the next step—mine to take—on that field behind Joe, and the explosives the Rebs had buried went off. I stepped too late. It's a scene that has played over and over again in my mind, and I have to pray about it daily. Joe died, and it paralyzed James. Sometimes it's harder to forgive ourselves."

A calm certainty descended as she gazed up at this man who stood a head taller than she did. "It wasn't your fault or your place. That cartridge box didn't fall off by accident, and James could have stopped and waited for you to retrieve it, but he didn't. It happened and has been used for good." She stopped and gave him a rueful smile. "Listen to me giving out words of wisdom."

He chuckled. "We start surprising ourselves—I know." He paused and met her direct gaze. "Thank you. I needed those words. I came to counsel you, and you ended up counseling me. Well, I need to report back to the major. Have a good day, Miss Price."

"Please . . . call me Hallie, Corporal."

"If you will call me Eddie."

"I'll only do that when we are with James."

"Fair enough. Good afternoon," he said, tipping his hat.

Hallie watched his muscled, stocky frame walking away. She thought a moment and decided to say it.

"Corporal Rigby," she called, and he turned with a questioning look on his face. "You're shorter than James."

He grimaced and shook his finger at her. "So you *did* study that photograph last night? Well, now the illusion is shattered. Everyone here has thought I had the comparative stature due to

James being forced to remain seated. I told him the advantage was finally mine after the accident. You see everyone notices the tall men first when you walk into a room, and they always did when we went out together. He laughed and told me he still had the advantage as most people notice the wheelchair first. It's not fair, but . . . " He flashed a wicked smile as he pulled his hat from his curly blond head in a flourish and bowed. "I still hold everyone's attention longer once they notice my rakish good looks." He replaced his hat and held out his hands in a shrug as he walked away backwards. Hallie burst out laughing. He gave her a farewell salute before turning and continuing on his way.

This must be the Eddie who James knew. Their friendship made more sense. The man had seemed critical and sarcastic during most of their interactions; she liked seeing another side to him. Hallie needed to ask Mrs. Hawkins a question and also see about lunch, so she turned and walked with purpose. She arrived at the Hawkinses' door and knocked. She heard voices engaged in an intent conversation and started to leave. Then Susannah's voice beckoned, "Come in."

"I completely disagree, Mother. Miss Havisham is not a character in need of sympathy, pity perhaps, and in need of redemption for certain. She ruins Estella's ability to love, and her dishonesty significantly impacts Pip's life."

Who? Her puzzlement must have registered on her face. James smiled.

"We are discussing Charles Dickens's 'All the Year Around' series *Great Expectations*. I first read it when it came out as a two-chapter-a-week series, and now Mother has purchased the three-volume set. Have you had the opportunity to read it?"

She shook her head. "No, I'm afraid the only reading I've done since my schoolhouse days is what I've done here: the medical volumes the doctor has loaned me and your Bible."

He stared at her and a feverish look came into his eyes. "We shall have to remedy that. Our daily Bible readings will continue, but we will add a reading time after lunch for a chapter of some of the most significant volumes of literature I have. Reading is an adventure and a portal into the vast world that is too immense for most men to travel."

Mrs. Hawkins smiled at her son and then at Hallie. "I am

afraid you have done it now, Hallie. My son has always been an avid reader. He would often relight his extinguished bedside lantern in the middle of the night to read until we caught him."

Another knock sounded at the door, and Hallie, who remained standing, turned to answer it. Corporal Case stood there. He glanced behind her to look at James.

"Pardon me, Miss Price, Mrs. Hawkins. The major has requested Mr. Hawkins's presence at his office."

"Yes, of course, Corporal. Please tell my husband I will expect him for dinner on time this evening."

"Yes, ma'am," the young soldier said and moved inside to get behind James's chair.

"I'm sorry to leave the company of you ladies, but duty calls. I'll see you this evening at dinner," James said.

As the door shut behind them, Susannah rose and started stacking the books on the table in front of her. "I should have known Ronald would expect James to still work even on his birthday," she muttered.

Hallie's head rose from her brief study of the books retrieved from Mrs. Hawkins chair. "Work?" she asked.

An incredulous look emerged on Susannah's face. "Miss Price, you must know that the two-and three-hour meetings James attends at his father's office are not mere observation and idle conversation." She shook her head at Hallie's blank stare. "I see James has not changed about his strict confidentiality regarding his job, even with you. You see, my dear, even though he's no longer a soldier, he has an official job for our government that is on an unofficial basis. Confusing, isn't it? Let me see the simplest way to put it, because that's how they first explained it to me. He's a diplomat in a way. You see, James was to return and finish at Harvard and enter law school very much like his friend, the young Mr. Lincoln. This crushed our plans for the tradition of West Point when he chose to go to Harvard and pursue law. He's a very intelligent young man, and I am not the only one who has recognized it. He ranked in the top of his class, and his military commanders during his service recommended him for many promotions in rank, which he declined. Which I—forgive me; I am getting ahead of myself.

"Once the war started and he realized how heavy his father's involvement would be, he wanted to share it with him and enlisted. He wanted to support the nation and his father, not to make a military name for himself." She paused and sighed. "Yes, that fact made it even harder for his father after James was injured. However, the major is a soldier first and knows these things happen. Anyway, back to my original explanation of James's job. He is a consultant on matters of diplomacy regarding Indian matters. They asked him to be on the Peace Commission that is about to meet with the Indians, but he declined as he felt his physical limitations and fatigue levels would be a detriment to the Commission; however, if there is a stalemate in an important decision, they enlist James's advice before proceeding. He also helps with the wording of certain treaties and speeches needed. One of the soldiers acts as his secretary during these meetings with the officers and makes sure his correspondence is sent in a timely manner. Originally, they asked him to serve in this capacity in Washington, but there was no family who wished to have him live with them, as the major and I were sent to Indian Territory."

The woman paused and turned to look out the window before looking back at Hallie with a defeated expression. "You see, Hallie, the other piece of information you do not have, and which I share with you now because it will be learned once you move to Washington with us, is that we have a married daughter, Amelia. She was devastated but also very embarrassed by her brother's condition. Her husband is a judge, and they have a high standing in the community. Her solution to our dilemma at the time of the move was to place James in the soldiers' home there. He told us to do it, but I knew he would die if we left him there. We have not heard from our daughter since we moved." She sat down in her chair and gave Hallie a wan smile. "Are you still sure you want to go with us?"

Hallie went to her and knelt down in front of her, grasping her hands in her own. "Mrs. Hawkins I would be honored." She held the woman's gaze, and then they hugged. As she stood, she remembered the original reason for her intrusion on James and his mother's day. "Mrs. Hawkins, the reason I came to see you today was not due to your invitation to lunch or to intrude on you and James. I wanted to ask if you thought Mrs. McDonald would let me spell her for a bit. I mean, since you don't need me today, I would like to offer to sit with Mrs. Scott and play with young Charlie."

"That is so thoughtful of you. By all means, go and offer your services. Regarding lunch, I'm afraid, James and I were so consumed by the literature that we forgot to stop. I'll go get us something together before you go. Please tell Elizabeth to come and rest in my room if she wants," Susannah said with a broad smile.

At that moment, they heard a shrill scream filled with agony and the sound of horses struggling to be controlled by their riders. The ladies rushed outside in time to see Molly Scott running to retrieve her son from the Indian scout who had just ridden in with the patrol. The Choctaw man—a well-known Indian at the fort—held Charlie. He handed the boy to Molly, who snatched him away, clutching him to her breast as she backed away from the man in terror. The Irish infantrymen who worked on finishing repairs to one of the barracks had ceased work and stood staring at the scene. No danger existed. The gates remained shut, and they knew the other Indians present, as well as this man.

Elizabeth McDonald rushed out to get her daughter, but Molly pulled away and clutched Charlie closer.

The young woman looked around with wild eyes as if seeing her surroundings for the first time. She scanned the faces and called, "Hank! Hank!"

A soldier moved toward her with a slow steady approach. Her glazed eyes locked on him but did not see *him* in truth. "Hank, is that you?"

"It's going to be fine, Molly," Corporal Rigby said in a soft voice.

Molly looked confused, tears streaming down her face. "Hank, I saw them hurt you. You let them take me."

Elizabeth moved in again behind her and hugged her. "Molly, let me take Charlie."

The young mother looked down at her child, who began to cry.

"Charlie? Oh, my baby, don't be scared. Mama's here," Molly said and turned him in her arms so he could bury his face in her neck. She started rubbing his back and looked at her own mother for the first time. "No, Ma, I'll take care of him. Where are we?"

She looked lucid for a moment, and then her eyes landed on the Indian scout again, and she started to whimper. "No, no, no! Please, don't touch me!"

All watching her, could see that her trauma had gone beyond witnessing her husband's death and being taken from her family for a short time.

Corporal Rigby had reached her, and her eyes strayed back to him. "You're not my Hank." The reality registered on her face. "He's dead! Hank! Hank! Ma! Ma!"

As the older woman moved forward, Hallie ran across the road and took Charlie so Mrs. McDonald could enfold her own child in her embrace. Molly dissolved in her mother's arms, and the spectators could do nothing until Corporal Rigby moved forward to place a guiding arm around the pair to lead them inside. Hallie followed with Charlie, who calmed in her arms. She glanced back. James watched from under the porch outside the office along with the senior officers. She met his gaze for a moment before rushing inside.

The doctor came and gave Molly a little laudanum to calm her. He didn't want her given any on a regular basis. Once she rested, he returned to visit with Mrs. McDonald, Hallie, and Corporal Rigby. Hallie had fed Charlie a bit and put him to bed. They all had missed lunch, as well as dinner and were exhausted. Dr. Jones scanned their faces as he began.

"From what information I gathered from the scout and cavalrymen, who came in with the patrol, young Charlie ran out into their path as they were arriving. The scout had scrambled down to rescue him from being trampled. The intensity of the situation, paired with the memory of another event that included an Indian, must have triggered the breakthrough. Yes, I do count it a breakthrough in her condition. She still has a long way to go, and the care she needs is in Washington." He paused and took a deep breath. "I visited with the captain and major before coming here. It would be best to get her moved as quickly as possible. They are wiring Washington to request release to return in two weeks instead of waiting until December. I know this will impact all of you in preparing for the move, that is, except for the corporal here."

Hallie's gaze shifted to Eddie, "What's he talking about? You were with Major Hawkins's detail when he came here. Aren't you returning with him?"

He met her desperate look. "No, they're sending the small group of men who are considered to be the major's to Kansas to help with Indian, as well as railroad expansion issues. The major plans to ask for me to be assigned to him again by the spring or earlier if possible."

"Does James know?" she asked.

"Yes. He's concerned because the Indians might not agree to the proposed treaty that is to be signed at Medicine Lodge, Kansas, on the twenty-first of this month. He personally thinks all the promises won't be kept. He wanted to amend it, but the majority of the commission disagreed. James is concerned I might get caught in some more battles. Who knows, I may make a name for myself in my own right yet."

Hallie saw through his false bravado and started to respond, but Mrs. McDonald stopped her.

"I hate to agree with the doctor, but if that's what is best for Molly, and it won't cause trouble for the major and his family, we should plan to do it." Elizabeth McDonald turned back to the doctor. "Does this mean she may come back to us?"

The physician sighed. "This is a complicated condition of the mind, not unlike some of the severe stress-related conditions our soldiers suffer after battle. Today's events are a step forward, but it is no guarantee of recovery."

"We will pray for her recovery," Hallie said with conviction.

All nodded, and then the doctor left. Elizabeth went to check on Molly. She returned a few moments later with gratitude on her face.

"Thank you both. Now I'm going to send you home," she said.

"There's a tray of food on the table, which Mrs. Hawkins had sent over. Please eat and get some rest if you can. Good night, Mrs. McDonald," Hallie said.

Eddie took her by the elbow, and they left.

~

As they walked toward her quarters, Hallie took a sideways look at Eddie. He appeared lost in thought but turned to find her watching him.

"What's wrong?"

"I just can't stop thinking about the fact that James hasn't been without his best friend since his injury."

Eddie lifted his eyebrows. "Yes, he has. I had to continue to fight after James fell injured. They took him away after the field hospital realized there was nothing they could do for him. It really tore me up, but I still had a job to do. Once the war ended, I asked to be assigned to Major Hawkins. It was given more favorable consideration because of our friendship. The major made more military training opportunities available to me." Eddie stopped and turned to face her. "James is like a brother to me. I will miss all of the family, but I know he's in your excellent care," he said and then smiled. "Of course, your back will miss these strong muscles helping you lift him."

She smiled back. "Yes, I'm sure I will. It's too bad we have to part ways when we're just now able to abide each other. No, now don't deny it; you haven't been very fond of me to this point."

He kicked a small rock out of the way before he looked up at her. "Well, let's just say I've been too critical. You've taken exceptional care of him. It was just—"

"I know and your instincts were right. You did overhear Ted and me, didn't you?" she said as she watched him and could discern a little embarrassment on his face in the dark.

"Yes, I did, and we had no right to listen. Please accept my apology, but I think we may be even on the overhearing things score, right?"

She gave him an apologetic smile. "Yes, so *I'm* sorry. Why don't we start out fresh? Everything else in my life feels fresh since last night."

"I would like to start fresh," he said. He took her elbow and turned her toward her door. "Now, I will go and update the Hawkinses, and *I* will take James to his room. You are to go and eat the food I know Mrs. Hawkins will have had sent to your room and go to bed. It's been a very busy day. Now, Hallie, no arguments." He held up his hand as she started to protest and smiled as he shook his head. "You have friends here, and we help each other."

"I guess I still have some habits to break. Good night and thank you."

~

The two weeks passed like a blink. Amidst all the preparation that had to be done, James managed to get Hallie through the first volume of *Great Expectations* and started lessons in math and science. He wanted her to be prepared to start work with the doctor at the hospital once they reached Washington. Dr. Jones had already sent letters to the appropriate people and penned letters of introduction, which he placed in Hallie's hands. The treaty meeting had happened in part on October 21, but the Cheyenne and Arapaho still had not signed. They were expected to on October 28, which was just three days away. The Kiowas, Commanches, and Apaches had signed but not without issues remaining. James had been right.

~

The night before they were to leave, Hallie finished helping Mrs. McDonald complete their final packing. They didn't have much left but had added a few items while at the fort. Molly spoke only a few more times after the outburst. It impacted little Charlie. The morning after the breakthrough, Elizabeth had risen to find him cuddled up against his mother in her bed. Molly had wrapped her arms around him in her sleep but didn't speak again for two days after that.

Hallie sighed and shielded her eyes to watch the bustle of activity as wagons were loaded.

They'd be traveling by wagon until they reached the train station. After that, they'd travel by rail the rest of the way. James's wagon required special preparation with extra padding and stability for his spine and neck in the covered wagon bed. Hallie would ride in back with him. She crossed the street and went to his room, expecting him to be back from his meeting with his father and the captain, but found it empty. She heard a voice call her name and turned.

Eddie heralded her as he strode down the street. He reached her as soon as his long, lumbering strides would allow.

"Miss Price, James has asked for you to accompany me," he called. As he drew closer, he said, "Hallie, James asked me to come and get you."

"Where is he? Is he sick?" she asked.

"No, no, nothing like that. Our boy has decided he wants to

see the sunset one last time from the back gates of the fort. Come on; I don't want to leave him unattended for long."

"Corporal Rigby, please tell me you didn't leave James open to the elements and Indians," she asked as she hurried alongside of him.

"In a way, yes—now don't go getting mad at me. He wanted it that way, and besides I posted two guards just inside the gate until we returned and alerted the lookouts without him knowing it."

"Thank goodness one of you has some sense."

When they arrived, the corporal signaled dismissal to the guards, and the lookouts moved away from their upper vantage point. James lay propped up in the back of a wagon bed in much the same way as the night when she first saw him. Blankets surrounded him. He gazed outward but turned his head a bit and smiled as they approached.

"Care to join me? The view is quite magnificent."

"Not me, I don't want to be scalped." Eddie joked, but at the alarmed look on Hallie's face, said, "Things are peaceful right now. There's still one patrol out who will be coming in this way. I'll return in just a few minutes."

He raised an eyebrow at James. "I'm more considerate than some people here," he said. "Mrs. Hawkins needs to know we will be late for dinner, and I have to word it in a way as not to alarm her."

"You deserve a brawl over that one, my friend. Too bad I'm unable to accommodate you," James said. "We'll be waiting here."

Hallie watched Eddie stride away and threw up her hands in exasperation. She turned and found James watching her with his lopsided grin. It had always made her laugh, but for some reason, at that moment, it touched her heart, and she smiled back. "How can I be mad at you?" she asked, moving toward him. "I would ask for you to move over, but since that's out of the question, I just hope I can squeeze myself into the space left."

He laughed as she climbed in beside him. "There is plenty of room for both you and Eddie."

"Not with all these bags. What is all this?" she asked as she settled on the incline of bedrolls, blankets, and feedbags.

She squirmed for a few minutes more before finding a tolerable position. She turned to find him watching her with an amused glint in his eyes.

He then turned back to face outward. "Look! It won't be long until it sets. I wanted this memory, and I wanted you to share it with me. Washington has many sites to see, but they're nothing like this. Now, if we ever get to Virginia and to the coast, the ocean is something to see. Have you ever seen the ocean?"

"No, I haven't. Some of the boys used to tell me about Galveston and the waves there. Oh, that was thoughtless of me."

"Why was it thoughtless, Hallie? You have to accept your past. Remember the pleasant parts and forgive yourself for the mistakes which are no longer held against you. If you hadn't experienced those things, you would not be the open, nonjudgmental person you are. Now, back to the ocean. I'm sure it is beautiful there, but I'll tell you, it can make you catch your breath. You've got to embrace moments of beauty. Eddie has trouble with that. He always looks at survival first, and only then will he allow himself to consider it."

"How did you meet Eddie?"

"Let's just say I was at Harvard, and one evening as a group of us were out for a night of games, we happened on a young man about to be hauled to jail by the authorities. It seems he owed this man some money who had planned to do physical damage when Eddie couldn't pay but instead decided to press charges. I decided to accompany him and used my way with words, as well as the fact that my brother-in-law is a judge, to our advantage. We have been friends since then. He joined up with me, and you know the rest."

"Had he borrowed the money to take care of his sister?"

"Yes and no. She'd lost her job as a seamstress and left Eddie alone when she turned to a new line of work. If he could have found her, he would have helped. By the time I met him, Eddie fought for his own survival."

"I see. You do realize his sister was trying to protect him in her own way. It would be easier for him to fend for himself alone."

He frowned. "Do you know I had not thought of that until you said it. You should tell Eddie. Sometimes we think more of our intelligence and forget to have common sense."

She smiled, and his expression softened. The atmosphere between them changed, and James looked ahead. The sun sank lower, burnishing the sky around it. Hallie joined his gaze and caught her breath. She hadn't noticed the sunsets during her entire stay at the fort.

She felt his fingers move against her hand, which lay beside his arm. It felt natural to intertwine her fingers with his as they watched this majestic sight, neither one speaking. She turned and found him looking at her with the most open expression.

"Hallie, may I ask something for myself?"

"Of course, James. What is it?" She held her breath, sensing something different for them both.

"I resigned myself to the fact I would never marry, never have a sweetheart, after the accident. Believe it or not, I went through a very dark period. I didn't understand how God could let this happen to me. Then after many long nights in prayer, I found peace. Instead of focusing on why life as I knew it had been taken away, I started focusing on the fact I had been left to live at all. I found out that many of the boys with injuries like my own had died. Their organs had trouble functioning. So I found how blessed I was. My mind had not been damaged, and I could find ways to share with others who were walking down dark roads." He paused and swallowed hard. "What I'm—"

Hallie turned on her side. Her eyes searched his. "You never had a sweetheart . . . Even before the war?"

"Not to speak of, just boyhood fancies. I focused on my education, Harvard, and plans for law school. I thought there would be plenty of time for love later." He continued in a lowered voice. "Hallie, I wish I could reach up and touch your face right now. Please, do not misunderstand me. I wish to be proper and a gentleman; it's just . . . When I first met you, I appreciated your honesty and the way you didn't flinch at anything. Then I admired your detail and perfection in the way you cared for me. You studied and learned from the doctor. You were so careful to never embarrass me as you cared for all my needs. The way you stood up to Ted, who, by the way, made me wish I wasn't in this condition and could have thrown him out for you." He stopped when she smiled. "Then these last couple of weeks, since you've come to know our Lord, there has been a gentleness and compassion emerge that have been astounding. You have reached out to others beyond me. What I am trying to say is that I care for you beyond friendship. I know I don't have the right. It can't be, but what I wanted to ask . . . " His eyes caressed her face, and she held her breath. "Would you kiss me, just this one time? Tomorrow our lives will change. I just would like this one moment in time with you. Things can never be different for us, I know, but—"

She placed a silencing finger to his lips and noticed their softness for the first time. This moment differed from any other moment in her experience with men. Pure, simple, and more special than any of her flitting dreams from her girlhood.

"James, you're the most special man I've ever known. These past two weeks have also deepened my feelings for you, but I wouldn't even entertain thoughts of shared affection. I have decided to never marry again and to never have another relationship with a man. It's caused too much pain, but this is beyond words."

She watched his eyes and reached her left hand to his cheek before adjusting to place her lips on his. His lips moved in return, and emotion coursed through them in an aching and beautiful exchange; there were tears on both their faces as they parted, sable brown and azure blue eyes seeing deeper within the other than they had with any other. Neither spoke, instead turning to watch the last glimmer of orange sink below the horizon.

~

A short time later, Eddie appeared with a lantern, James's chair, and Corporal Case to help them. Hallie released James's hand and jumped up to assist them.

"Corporal Rigby, you missed it. The sunset didn't wait for you." She feigned irritation, but her heart rejoiced in his delay.

James had given her the most special gift—the honor of his first kiss and allowing her to share the sunset as they both for that moment forgot the rest. It also felt like her first true kiss. Sure, her experience offered many kisses, but none like the one they shared. She wished for a moment that they could have met each other earlier in life, but at the same time, life made it improbable. How strange to feel so grateful for all the circumstances that had brought them into each other's lives. This evening belonged to them alone; an oasis of memory. Neither would ever think to move beyond propriety as they returned to everyday life. She pushed further pondering from her mind as they lifted James into his chair and greeted the patrol who arrived just as they passed through the gates. Those gates closed, signaling the end of what James and Hallie had shared.

Chapter Six

In spite of it not being the rainy season, torrential rain continued to fall. The knock on the door a short time after the family had retired for the evening didn't surprise Lucy. Travelers who got caught in bad weather often sought a form of shelter on nights like this. Her father let them sleep in the barn, or if some of the hands were gone, as now, he often directed them to a spare bunk.

Mr. Kennedy's deep voice conversed with another; then Lucy heard her father invite them inside. This unusual breech *did* surprise her, and she wondered if a friend of theirs might be in trouble. Without wasting time on further speculations, she dressed and opened her door, just off the entrance.

Three men in slickers and cowboy hats stood outside her room. For a moment, she wondered if Ted and the hands were back earlier than expected from the drive, but the man speaking to her father far surpassed Ted in height, and his arm encircled the waist of the shortest of the cowboys with him—how peculiar.

Her father held a beckoning arm out toward her.

"Lucy, I am so glad you're still awake. Come meet our new guests."

The trio turned, removing their hats. Things became somewhat clearer at that point. As the shortest of the group removed their hat, long strands of copper hair dangled away from where the woman had coiled it on the top of her head. The handsome man beside her had dark brown, almost black-looking hair; a mustache; and green eyes. The third man didn't stand as tall as the other man and had dark blond hair with a trim beard and blue eyes. He appeared older than his companions by at least six or seven years.

Her father gestured with his free hand. "Lucy, this is Marcus Johnson; his wife, Florence; and Mr. Andrew Richards, the cousin of our Boyd Richards."

She nodded to Florence and stuck out her hand to greet the men. "It's nice to meet you. I'm Lucy Kennedy."

She waited for her father to further explain their presence.

"Lucy, the Johnsons have traveled from East Texas, and Mr. Richards has come from Georgia, as they have some legal papers, which require Boyd's signature once he returns. I told them we don't expect the men back for another week or so, but it's imperative they get his signature and, therefore, must wait."

Agnes Kennedy appeared at that moment, fully dressed and always ready for unexpected visitors.

"Welcome! Please take off your coats and warm yourselves by the fire. I have a few items left from dinner I'm warming for you."

Florence Johnson shed her slicker, revealing men's trousers and a shirt. She shrugged. "It's much easier traveling this way, less attention and more comfortable. Mrs. Kennedy, please let me help you. I've been in the company of men for too long a journey." She smiled at Marcus even as she said it.

Lucy liked her right then, and she could tell her mother did as well.

Andrew shook off his gear, apologizing for the mess they'd tracked inside. Mr. Kennedy gave a hearty laugh and assured him the foyer had seen much worse.

Marcus remained in his slicker and asked if he could move their horses to the barn. Mr. Kennedy told him to get his hand, Jim, who happened to be in the barn taking care of a sick horse, to help him. Marcus left and the women excused themselves.

Twenty minutes later, the women set the food on the table. Marcus returned just as Lucy beckoned her father and Andrew to the table. The two men rose from their seats in front of the fireplace as Marcus strode in from the foyer.

Andrew Richards soon dominated the conversation over the late-night meal. His accent heralded *far* from Deep South Georgian.

"Mr. Kennedy, are you sure they made it to their destination and are on their way for certain?"

"Yes, Mr. Richards. Ted, my trail boss, wired me from Abilene, Kansas, when they arrived. He wanted me to know there had been a bit of Indian trouble, and planned for further delays when going by a fort on the way home. They needed to see a Major Hawkins."

Marcus's eyes became alert and interested. "Did he mention Major Hawkins's first name?" he asked.

"Yes, Major Ronald Hawkins. Do you know him?"

Marcus smiled at Florence before he replied. "If it's the same soldier who was once Lt. Ronald Hawkins, yes, we do. In fact, he served as the catalyst that got us engaged."

"Well, well, this may be a tale I have to hear during our time together," he said. He cleared his throat and scratched his head. "I wonder how an ex-Confederate soldier ended up a major in the United States regular Army and how he got to a post at a fort in Indian Territory."

Marcus chuckled, and Florence giggled. "He's not an ex-Confederate. He was a Union soldier—when we met him after the war—that helped with reconstruction in Arkansas."

Mr. Kennedy made a disbelieving sound. "Yes, we *will* have much to discuss, but it's too late tonight."

The group finished eating and thanked their hostess for everything. Lucy's mother smiled.

"You're welcome. Now you need a good night's rest. Mr. Johnson and Mr. Richards, you can sleep in our son's room," she said. "Jason attends a new college established by the Massachusetts Technical Institute in Boston. He's in the first class scheduled for graduation."

"Where do you want Mrs. Johnson to sleep, Ma?" Lucy asked.

"I'm afraid you'll need to share your bed with Mrs. Johnson due to the circumstances." She gave their guests an apologetic smile. "We have a large ranch, but our house hasn't changed since my husband first built it for me."

Lucy intercepted the helpless look Florence sent Marc.

"Your home is very spacious and lovely. I hate to seem ungrateful, but we haven't spent a night apart since our wedding," Florence said.

Agnes smiled. "Well, we do have another small room off of the kitchen, which our trail cook occupies when he's here. He's an old friend. I'm sure he won't mind Boyd's cousin borrowing it. Is that proposition acceptable to you, Mr. Richards?"

The man gave a gracious nod. "I'm sure that would be fine."

"Thank you so much," Florence said.

Marcus placed a protective arm around her. "Please don't misunderstand my wife. She's the least particular person in the world except when it comes to me."

"That's as it should be, Mr. Johnson," Lucy agreed. She turned to Florence. "Mrs. Johnson would you like to borrow a gown? I know you've traveled in your present garb for a long time. Let me pour some water in the basin in Jason's room for you both to freshen up a bit, and I can loan you what you need for the night. We will get proper baths for you tomorrow."

"Please call me Florence, and yes, I would love to borrow a gown. I have a dress in my saddle bag, but it's sure to be the worse for wear with this weather."

"We'll freshen it tomorrow, and please call me Lucy."

Mr. and Mrs. Kennedy said good night to the couple and left to show Andrew Richards his accommodations.

Lucy showed Marcus and Florence to her brother's clean and spacious room. It had a double bed, a dresser with a mirror, basin, and chair. Lucy excused herself to fetch the nightgown for Florence.

Lucy hurried to her room and grabbed a gown and a ribbon. She stopped and picked up the pitcher of water her mother had left on the table for her.

Florence answered her knock on their door.

Lucy held up the gown and ribbon draped over her arm. "I'm afraid this will swallow you, but maybe you can tie it up with this ribbon."

Florence laughed and took them from her. "Thank you. These are just fine."

Lucy poured water into the basin from the pitcher she carried.

"Thank you, Miss Kennedy," Marcus said.

"Please rest well. Good night," she said, closing the door after her. Meeting them, stirred up all her foolish speculations about Boyd; for some reason, she couldn't get him off her mind.

~

The next morning Lucy gave a tentative knock on their door.

"Florence, are you awake?" Lucy inquired from the other side of the door.

Florence opened it with a sleepy yawn and stretch.

Lucy smiled at her. "I am sorry to awaken you, but I have had a bath prepared for you and did not want it to get cold."

Florence looked down. "I don't have a wrap to cover this gown. Wait." She grabbed her slicker. "This will have to do I'm afraid. What time is it?"

"It's fine. I've borrowed one of my mother's dresses for you as mine are way too long. The time is seven thirty. The men have been up and out since six. Your husband asked for us to allow you to sleep a bit."

Lucy ushered Florence into a room with an actual tub, which had steam coming from it.

"Here are some under garments and the dress. There's a bar of soap over there and a towel. I'll give you privacy now. Please come to the kitchen when you're ready and have some breakfast."

Florence turned as Lucy opened the door. "Thank you, Lucy. I'm not normally this disheveled, but I promise to return your hospitality if you're ever in East Texas."

"I think you're a pretty strong woman coming all this way like you did. It would've been easier to take the stage for me. Enjoy your bath." Lucy smiled as she shut the door.

Florence emerged within twenty minutes. The dress fit a little wide on her but perfect in length.

"Your hair is beautiful coiled up that way, Florence," Lucy said.

Her new friend smiled. "Thank you. I feel like a new person this morning. We slept so well." Florence closed her eyes and sniffed the air in the kitchen. "Everything smells delicious."

"Please have a seat," Lucy said.

Lucy and her mother dished up eggs and bacon. Agnes Kennedy carried the plate to the table and smiled at their guest.

"Good morning, Mrs. Johnson. How beautiful you look! That color of green is much better on you than it is on me. I might just have to take it in a few inches and give it to you. Please, eat. Coffee?"

"Oh, there's no need to do that, but thank you and yes, I would love a cup of coffee."

The three women visited as Florence ate. Lucy found it easy to talk to the young woman. She shared about her love of horses and working in town at the newspaper. Their guest reciprocated and Lucy learned Florence and Marcus were about to celebrate their one-year anniversary. They lived on a farm with Boyd's brother, Ben, and a couple named Daniel and Martha. The newspaperwoman in her tended to be curious, and so she asked the question that had been burning in her mind.

"Florence, please tell me to mind my own business, but I'm wondering why Mr. Richards, I mean Boyd Richards, our hand, doesn't live in East Texas with you?"

The small woman's gray eyes looked down and then met hers. "I'm afraid you'll have to ask Boyd that question."

The friendship and loyalty must run deep, and so Lucy did not push the issue. Anyway, many more things interested her about the man. Once Boyd returned, she could ask him. She nodded at Florence. "Yes, of course. I'm sorry I tried to pry. Now, let me show you some of the ranch if you would be interested."

"I would love it. My favorite thing to do as a girl was to explore," Florence said and finished her breakfast.

~

Marcus and Andrew leaned on the rails of a corral not far from the house with Mr. Kennedy and a few hands. A wild stallion bucked and ran back and forth inside. Lucy rushed toward her father in a determined stride, leaving Florence behind.

"Pa, I thought we were leaving that one for when our Mr. Richards returns? I mean we have let many of our brood out to pasture for the upcoming winter. We can just get this one again then," Lucy burst out without bothering to greet the others.

Her father gave her an indulgent smile. "Lucy, all that you say is true, but what you don't realize is Mr. Johnson is an accomplished horseman like his friend. We're also discussing a future business deal. They might buy some horses for their farm and soon to be ranch. It seems, without allowing me all the details, Ben and Boyd Richards have an inheritance—bequeathed to them by their late uncle—that will make this possible. That's why Mr. Andrew Richards is here. He's the executor of their late uncle's estate in Georgia. If Mr. Johnson wishes to try this stallion while he's here, I would appreciate it."

Florence joined them and descended on Marcus, who had straightened at their approach with a small flash of being caught in his eyes. "Marcus Johnson, you haven't broken a horse in over a year. I didn't travel all this way for you to break your neck."

Marcus picked his wife up and sat her on a nearby hitching post, ignoring the chuckles of the men. "Florey, you need to remember there are things I did quite well before I returned to Arkansas. I know what I'm doing. If I decide to do this, you will trust me to do it as I have everything else that I've promised you."

Lucy watched the emotions playing on her new friend's face and her admiration grew as she watched them. Instead of persisting and nagging, Florence spoke loud enough for all to hear. "Yes, Marc." One of his eyebrows went up at this demure response, but he said nothing and lifted her back to the ground.

The look on the other men's faces reflected respect of his control over his wife. Lucy suspected these two shared control.

"Now, what are you ladies planning for the day?" Marcus asked.

"Lucy is taking me to see some of the ranch," Florence said.

Mr. Kennedy motioned for one of the ranch hands. A man of about forty with a slight limp came forward. "Hitch, go get the wagon ready and follow these two. It's Saturday, and it wouldn't be a bad idea for you make sure there's nothing amiss."

"Yes, sir, boss," the man said. He then headed to the barn.

Once he returned, he assisted Florence and Lucy onto the wagon seat. Lucy took the reins. Hitch fell in beside them on his horse, a dappled gray mare. Florence took in a deep breath and smiled at Lucy.

"This is so different than our part of the state. You have such a far way to see with not as many trees. It's a different sort of beauty," she said.

"Really? Tell me about your home," Lucy said with genuine interest.

"There are so many trees, and in the spring everything is so green and lush. It's humid and hot in the summer but with such fertile soil for farming. It was hard on Ben with the drought he went through last year but better this year." Florence gave a wistful smile. "It's surprising how the land gets into your heart and soul. I felt that way about missing Arkansas during their first few months in Texas, but now I love it. Marcus is going to build our house starting this spring."

"It sounds beautiful. Is Ben older or younger than Boyd?" Lucy asked.

"Younger, he's eighteen but will be nineteen in a month. I told him he'd catch up with me for a short time as my birthday was this summer." Florence smiled. "Yes, we're a young lot except for Marcus, Boyd, Martha, and Daniel, who are still all under thirty. Boyd will turn thirty next fall. Anyway, back to Ben. He served in the war and lost a leg. That's why he chooses to stay close to home. He says he's seen enough beyond the farm, and it's too difficult to be slowed down when you travel. How old are you, Lucy?"

Lucy curled a strand of loose hair around her finger for a long moment trying to reconcile all this new information.

"Lucy?"

"Why, I'm twenty-five," she said and smiled. "I've never been married. There have been suitors, but I seem to have a penchant for scaring them off after a time. You see, I've been described as a very emotional but in control female that can't be tamed. Before the war, Pa had sent me to the East for school, but I had to come home once the war broke out. Afterward, given the challenges present, Pa chose to send Jason to college. He'd reached the right age and needed the responsibility. I'm not jealous of him. He's attending this college in Boston, which has a new educational method that allows field studies, as well as classroom instruction. He's studying science and ways to apply it to agriculture for better farming methods as part of his program. The degree requirements will be finished this coming year, and he'll return home." She paused to find her new friend listening with interest. "Florence, I hope you've found, as I have, that the Lord has perfect timing. If I'm ever to marry, it'll be in His time and to the man He has chosen."

Florence nodded. "I couldn't agree more. Would you like to hear about how Marcus and I were reacquainted after the war?"

"Yes, yes, I would. This is so much fun to have you to talk with." Both ladies laughed, and Florence told her their story as they continued to ride. Lucy glanced back. Hitch followed, but stayed far enough back so as not to intrude. He pulled away and checked on a few of the close-by horses and cattle at one point. They arrived back at the ranch house by lunch after a very enjoyable morning.

The men sat around the table as the women hurried in to help Mrs. Kennedy, who had been left to see to all the preparations alone. Her mother laughed and said she enjoyed having the kitchen to herself. Once Old Amos, the trail cook returned, he wouldn't allow her in the room to even make a biscuit.

Lucy and Florence helped her gather up the serving dishes, and they entered the dining room to a very hungry group. Mr. Kennedy didn't look up from his discussion about the British State of affairs with Andrew. It turned out the man hailed from England. He'd gone to Georgia to help his aunt settle his uncle's estate. However, the conversation ceased as the ladies joined them to say grace.

They then pursued less terse, polite, and common ground conversations as the meal progressed. After the meal, the hands returned to their duties, and the other men retired to Mr. Kennedy's study as the women cleared the table.

Mrs. Kennedy and Lucy brought out some needlework, asking if Florence would like to join them. She laughed and said she didn't enjoy the gift of the needle, except for when making clothes, but she sat to visit with them. They made plans to attend church services together the next day, and then Florence would accompany Lucy into town on Monday to observe her work with the newspaper. They hoped Ted and the boys reached home before the week's end.

~

Boyd tried to see if his companions shared any hint of excitement as they neared home but found himself hard pressed to find any sign of emotion on the tired, grimy, and unshaven faces. Ted had put them on the trail before dawn for the last leg of the journey. He wanted them at the Kennedy ranch before nightfall. Their present location made it evident that they'd make it with hours to spare. They didn't even take a chow break, just hard tack and jerky from their saddlebags. Boyd looked ahead and thought about his decisions. He needed to talk to Mr. Kennedy and write Ben another letter—time to go home and pull his weight. He'd left it to others for too long. In many ways, a tougher road may await him, however, he needed to do the right thing. One other consideration made his pulse quicken. It involved another person.

He'd prayed about it every day since they left the fort. Some things would have to wait until he got back before he could be sure of their direction. These thoughts recirculated until he noticed Ted pull alongside to address them.

"Boys, we should be home in about an hour. I need you to get cleaned up when we arrive as you know Mrs. Kennedy always wants us at dinner our first night home. You can go into town tomorrow night. I'll meet with Mr. Kennedy first, so you boys leave me some water. I'd say this was the most interesting cattle drive I've been on so far. Thank you for a job well done. Now let's go home."

The men murmured in agreement, and the mood became lighter as the pace quickened. Time passed in a blur of anticipation. A cold breeze chilled the air as the Kennedy ranch came into view. They could see a group gathered around the horse corral at a distance and a man on a fighting stallion within the rails. Ted signaled them to pull up for a moment before their presence could be discerned.

"Richards, it looks like the boss might have gotten somebody to replace you while we've been gone. Let's give him a moment to get control of that beast before we ride in," Ted said with a bemused smile at Boyd, who just shook his head.

Boyd turned his attention back to the man in the corral. Something about his style seemed familiar. He exhaled and turned his head to spit on the ground once the man took control. Ted motioned them forward. Whoops and clapping came from the yard as the wrangler trotted around the fenced area, but heads turned at the sound of their approaching horses. The man slowed the stallion and scanned the group of riders. Boyd had not taken his eyes off him and started to grin as the man pushed back his hat, cocking his eyebrow and flashing white teeth in return as he met his gaze. Boyd's smile widened as he noticed the two women who leaned against the fence, watching the show. A small woman with copper hair turned from her place beside Lucy Kennedy. He couldn't believe it. Boyd pulled up, dismounted, and strode across the yard and lifted the young woman, who had run to him, off the ground.

"Florence! I can't believe it," he said as he set her back on her feet.

She smiled. "You don't think I'd let him come to see you

without me, do you?"

Marcus dismounted and ducked between the rails to join them. Boyd grasped his hand and shoulder as they grinned like schoolboys.

"I knew there was something familiar about the man breaking that bronco. It's so good to see you. Did Ben get the letter I sent him from Kansas?"

Marcus frowned and shook his head. "Not before we left to come out here. What's happened?" He searched Boyd's face and then their eyes met. His friend's penetrating stare never missed much.

"We will talk after supper," Boyd said.

Marcus exchanged a look with Florence. He crossed his arms and looked back at Boyd. "No, I want to talk now. Let's go get cleaned up, and you can introduce me to your new pards. I've got some things to tell you about why we're here."

"Is everything all right at home? Is it Ben?" Boyd asked, steeling himself for what might follow.

An unfamiliar man stepped away from the group, and Marcus motioned for him to join them. "Boyd, I need to introduce you to your cousin, Andrew."

"My cousin?" Boyd asked, confused.

The man offered his hand, and Boyd shook it, not caring for the lack of firmness.

"I am Andrew Richards, your cousin and executor of our Uncle Robert's estate. As you know, he and Aunt Elizabeth had no children of their own. Therefore, he arranged for the liquidation of his assets and dispersing them among his three nephews, you, Ben, and me, as well as adequate provision for his widow."

Boyd frowned, removed his hat, and wiped the grit off his mouth with his hand as he fixed a disbelieving look on the man claiming to be his cousin.

"I thought Uncle Robert would have lost everything during the war or at least afterward as he depended on his slaves for so much."

The man laughed. "He wanted many to believe that, but the truth is much to the contrary. We need to talk in private, Cousin. I'm sure Mr. Kennedy would not begrudge us the use of his study after dinner." He turned to their host. "Would you, sir?"

The ranch owner studied Boyd and his cousin. "Of course, Mr. Richards, but I need it at the present to talk business with my trail boss."

"Thank you, sir," Andrew stated with evident satisfaction and nodded at his cousin. "I'll let you go get tidied up a bit before dinner. It is nice to at last make your acquaintance." He crossed the yard and disappeared into the house.

Boyd could almost hear all the questions being formulated in the minds of the men, who watched them with interest. He shook his head at them, letting them know he might discuss it later. All except Ted knew not to pry. Ted moved by the fence and stared at Florence. Marc frowned, about to step forward. Boyd placed a hand on his shoulder and motioned Ted over.

"Ted, come and meet my good friends, Marcus and Florence Johnson."

Ted shook Marcus's hand and tipped his hat to Florence. "Ma'am, it's too bad you're married. A pretty little thing like you is a rarity out here. Yep, too bad. I'd offer my hand."

"I'd break it," Marcus bit out. The two men sized up each other, and Florence flushed, looking at Boyd for assistance, but Lucy broke in on them.

"Don't mind him. Ted's just been on the trail too long. Too bad Miss Hallie's no longer in town." She smiled as she linked her arm in Florence's and looked at Ted. "But you knew that, didn't you? We heard many reasons for her leaving town. I'd like to know the real one."

"Then you'd better ask Richards here. He arranged it. Thanks for the welcome home, Lucy," Ted said. He followed Mr. Kennedy into the house.

Lucy turned to Boyd. "Well, do you care to elaborate?"

"Not particularly. I don't want Miss Price in your newspaper tomorrow," he said.

"Ouch. I know when to stop." She flashed her beautiful smile and tugged on Florence's arm. "I'll take Florence with me and let you men take care of your business. Welcome, home."

The two men watched the ladies as they made their way to the house and smiled as Florence turned her head and wrinkled her nose at them before going through the door with Lucy. Boyd inclined his head and studied Marc.

"Florence is good for you," he said.

A look of complete satisfaction covered Marc's face as he nodded. "She has renewed me in so many ways."

"I'm glad and have an apology to make," Boyd said.

Marc frowned. "What do you have to apologize for?"

"The two of you moved to Texas because of me. I should have gone home and helped Ben. You should have remained in Arkansas."

His friend laughed. "No, you're so wrong. This has been the best year. We have depended on each other, and we've had Ben, Martha, and Daniel. God used everything to put us where we needed to be. Now, I'm not saying we wouldn't consider returning to Arkansas one day but not for a while. We're grateful. Florence and I consider you family."

Boyd felt peace rush through him. "We are, Marc, in many ways. Are you ready to talk?"

Marc nodded, and they turned toward the bunkhouse. In the next two hours, they shared bathing provisions with the other hands, dressed, shaved, and talked. Marc laughed as he saw Boyd's clean-shaven face void of the familiar beard once again. The other hands respected their need to talk in private, and left once ready for dinner.

Boyd related the events of the last few months as he dressed and took care with his appearance for the first time in years. As he finished, he sat in the chair across from Marc at the small table used for card games, watching his friend. Marc's green eyes held a tinge of moisture, and he looked away for a moment before he spoke.

"Answered prayers for so many people and for so many lives—you, James Hawkins, Hallie Price, and our families all have a new direction. It'll be interesting to see all the Lord has planned. It's been a ride with more twists and turns than riding that wild stallion today. I wouldn't miss the rest of it." Marcus whooped, throwing his hat in the air.

Boyd laughed, and Marcus shook his head.

"I don't think I've heard that sound from you more than a couple of times since we came home from war. Let's find it more often."

"It's a deal, my friend. Now, I've got a favor to ask," Boyd said.

Boyd got up and crossed to his saddlebags on his bunk. He took out his Bible and removed a well-worn piece of paper from the back. As he returned to the table, he unfolded it and handed it to his friend. Marc stared at the sketched picture of the woman and baby—now smudged and starting to fade a bit. Although creased and stained, it still reflected the tender love and joy between mother and son.

"When did Ben give you this?" Marc asked.

Boyd shook his head. "He placed it in her Bible along with her last letter and put it in my saddle bags the night before I left this last time. Could you take it to him and ask him to draw it again? I'm afraid I've almost worn it through looking at it most days."

"Boyd, he has more sketches of them. In fact, he has sketches, almost like a book of ones he did after you left for war. He also has some disturbing ones he brought home," Marc said.

Stunned, he took a moment. "My brother has handled more than I have considered. How selfish . . . him pulled away from home as a boy to go to war . . . lost his leg, came home and buried his sister-in-law beside a nephew he'd wanted to protect. After all of that, his ungrateful brother came home only to desert him again and again." Marc started to interrupt, but Boyd held up his hand. "I know that is all behind me now, but it still hurts to recognize how blind I've been to the pain of those I love. My love was sure not complete before now."

Marc nodded. "I know what you mean. Why don't you come home with us and give this to him yourself?"

"I'm coming in the spring." He paused to watch his friend as he said the next words. "For good. The letter I wrote Ben from Kansas explained what I've told you and stated I would be joining all of you after I fulfilled my obligation to Mr. Kennedy for the spring."

"You're right to feel that way, but I'm betting Mr. Kennedy may be more interested in you doing a different kind of business with him," Marcus said.

Boyd narrowed his eyes and leaned forward on the table. "What are you up to, my old friend?"

"Well, it's a Richards family decision. Ben wants to transition from just farming to horse breeding and ranching. Once all things are settled with your uncle's estate, he wants to take his portion and go forward with Daniel and me as partners. He plans to give us five percent each of his final amount as we start, but we don't want him to do that."

Boyd's mind raced as his brother's dream caught fire inside the deep place of inspiration and possibilities still present within his soul. "How about we give you and Daniel ten percent each of whatever my uncle has bequeathed to us together? I'll come home with you if you let me have a few more days to take care of some things here. There are a few loose ends and areas I need to explore here before I can leave."

Marcus grinned as he stuck out his hand.

"That sounds like the best news I could have right now. Let's—"

A knock sounded at the door. Lucy stuck her head in the door.

"I'm sorry to interrupt you gentlemen, but Florence asked for me to retrieve Mr. Johnson so he could get ready for dinner. Ma said dinner is in twenty minutes and the rest of the men are visiting on the porch at the moment," she said.

Marcus passed the paper in front of him back to Boyd as he stood.

"Thank you, Miss Kennedy. See you at dinner, Boyd. We'll meet with Andrew afterward." He tipped his hat and said, "Ma'am," as he passed Lucy on his way out the door.

Lucy turned to follow him.

"Miss Kennedy, would you like to see a sketch of my family?" Boyd asked.

Lucy turned, blinking in evident surprise.

"Why, yes, I would," she said as she crossed and sat in the chair to which he gestured.

Boyd hesitated for a second before passing the aging paper to her. He swallowed as she looked at the sketch of the smiling, medium-framed, angular woman with sleek, dark upswept hair, laughing as she held a child of about a year on her lap—his late wife and son. His son laughed. Ben must have joked with them as he sketched them.

Lucy raised her blue-green gaze and met his. "I didn't know you had a wife and child. What are their names?"

"Nancy and Sam—I did have them at one time but came home to find they'd died during the war," he said, never taking his eyes from hers.

Tears sprang up in her eyes, and she reached up to wipe them as they started to fall. "I'm so sorry, Mr. Richards. How awful for you . . . I . . ."

Her tears fell in earnest as she glanced back down at the picture and then passed it to him. He took it from her fingers with one hand but reached across the table with his other hand to smooth away the wetness from her eyes with his thumb. His breath caught. He pulled back, stood, and crossed to his bunk to put away the drawing, sliding it between the pages of the Bible that lay on his bunk.

He turned, looking back at the woman who watched him with sad eyes. Her look held no pity, just sorrow. This confirmed his decision to tell her.

"I'll always love her and look forward to meeting my son one day when the Lord calls me home, but I now know life is not over for me."

She tilted her head and toyed with the ribbon around her collar. "You're different than before you left here. I can guess why, and I'm glad. I know she is too. Your love for her is so apparent I know she must have loved you as well," she said.

Boyd looked down and kicked at the floor with the toe of his boot. *Stop stalling, Richards.* He returned to the table. She lifted her eyes in seeming appraisal. He ran a hand across his shaven face and grinned at her.

An embarrassed flush appeared on Lucy's face. She rose, eyeing the door.

"Thank you for sharing this with me, Mr. Richards. I better go help my mother," she said and strode to the door, but he reached it before she did.

Contrition and concern filled him.

"I've made you uncomfortable, Miss Kennedy—the opposite of my intention. It's obvious I have made a mess of conveying things," he said with one hand on the now ajar door.

"Whatever are you talking about, Mr. Richards?"

He swallowed hard. "I'll always love Nancy, but I know she wouldn't want me to be alone for the rest of my life. That's what I wanted, but through much prayer, I now know isolation is not the answer. Life is never guaranteed, and meeting special people is rare. We can miss the pathway we're supposed to travel if we keep our eyes inward."

He could still see that she didn't understand. With the same slow movements he used when approaching a skittish horse, he reached up to cup her cheek in his large, calloused hand. His breath caught in his throat at the feel of the petal softness. Her eyes widened, but then softened in understanding, and she reached her own hand up to caress his face. Boyd held his breath as he treasured the soft touch before bending his head to brush her lips in a brief, tender kiss. He gave the door an accidental push with his foot. They both stepped back. Boyd didn't want her reputation compromised in any way; he forced himself to break the precious moment. However, she remained just outside the bunkhouse watching his face.

"I'd planned on asking your father for permission to call on you and to spend the spring courting you, but it looks like I'll only be here for a few more days. You see, I'm needed back home."

Her eyes flashed at him. "Then what was *that kiss* about?"

Boyd remembered Ted's warning about her volatile moods and held up his hands. This is not how he'd imagined it.

"Lucy, don't get riled at me. I'm sorry the skill of smooth courtship has evaded me this day. I want you to marry me and come back with us this week. If you are so inclined," he said and then lifted his hands in self-exasperation as he heard his own ineloquent words. He turned and started for the house.

"Boyd Richards, don't you walk away from me. You can't propose marriage and not give a lady the chance to answer."

He turned around and found the men on the porch watched them with interest. They stood too far away for any of the men to make out their exchange but loud enough for their audience to know they appeared to argue.

Boyd crossed back to her, taking her by the elbow and moving her back beside the door of the bunkhouse and out of sight. He closed his eyes and then opened them with expectancy and hope. Her gaze softened, and she smiled, flashing a dimple.

"You'll have to wait until after you've talked to my father. Let's see what he thinks about this crazy plan of yours," she said, eyes twinkling.

"I want to know what you think?" he said, propping his arm on the wall behind her.

She gave him a teasing smile. "I think you need to talk to me later, but I will tell you, I tend to like crazy plans."

His heart raced, and he grinned back as she ducked under his arm. Amusement filled him as she sauntered back to the house, throwing him a challenging smile over her shoulder.

~

Lucy passed through the group of men on the porch, ignoring the questioning looks. She found herself grateful that her father remained in his study talking to Ted. Florence met her inside the door.

"Lucy, where have you been? Marcus has bathed and is almost ready in the time you've been gone. Your mother is asking for you in the kitchen." Florence stopped short, and she clapped her hand to her mouth to squelch a squeal. She then grabbed Lucy's hand, dragging her into her bedroom. Lucy tumbled into the room and landed on the bed as the shorter woman leaned against the door and beamed at her.

"Is it Boyd?"

Lucy buried her face behind her hands before looking back at Florence's expectant face. A smile danced on her lips. "Yes—Oh, Florence, I will admit—I'd had thoughts about him but never dreamed of his interest."

Florence threw back her head and laughed. "Hallelujah! We thought Boyd was lost to his sorrow forever. Marc told me about the events of the cattle drive while he bathed, but I don't think Boyd told him about his feelings for you."

"Well, he didn't tell me about the cattle drive, but I know he has had a spiritual change. He told me about Nancy and Sam." She paused as sadness and guilt rushed in for a moment. "I'm awful, aren't I?"

The younger woman rushed to sit beside her, taking her hands in her own. "No, you aren't. You have no idea how long that precious man has punished himself and grieved. The surprise is how quick he has decided to approach you. Boyd's cautious, but I surmise he recognizes what a special woman you are and didn't want to wait another day before finding out if you'd have him.

Now, tell me what happened. Sorry to be so nosey, but as this could affect all our lives, it is necessary, plus just fun to know."

Lucy laughed, blushed, and then told her a brief summary of Boyd's words and the kiss.

Florence shook her head. "No, that's not like the Boyd Richards I know at all. He's the most in control, smooth Southern gentleman you could ever meet. You must have him rattled and to think he wants to propose marriage. He wants you to come back home with us. The question is, how do you feel about it and how will your parents feel?"

Lucy stood and walked to her window. She spotted Boyd crossing the yard toward the porch. Her heart raced and filled with joy. A smile lit her face as she turned back. "Florence, I'm no longer a young girl. Remember what we talked about in the wagon that day? I want to be loved when and if I marry. If Boyd can't do that now, it may be enough for me to love him. He could grow to love me."

"I understand what you're saying, but I learned love is not a clear path that's the same for everyone. As I told you, Marc and I had to discover the gift of love we share. Yes, Boyd will always love Nancy, but that doesn't mean he can't love you. You must remember Boyd had a very good marriage and was well loved by his wife. It's why he can and should remarry. The regrets he's had have nothing to do with failing at marriage but at failing to be present to protect her during an impossible time. I can't speak for Boyd, but I do know that he doesn't make decisions lightly and this one is taking a risk that involves faith. He has feelings for you now or he wouldn't have proposed, and he must have the expectancy of them growing. Lucy Kennedy, if you don't fan those feelings, you are a silly woman."

Determination welled up inside of her, and she set her chin as she nodded at her friend. "Done. Now, I just have to talk to my parents. I am past the age of needing their permission, but I want their blessing." She stopped and threw both hands to her cheeks. "I can't believe this is happening. My whole life could be about to change."

A knock sounded at the door, and her mother entered with exasperation written on her face. "Where have you two been? We have a group of very hungry men out here at the table. Come on and help me." She glanced from Lucy to Florence. A look Lucy knew well replaced the exasperation.

"Ma, I'll tell you everything later. I'm sorry we left you without help. Let's serve dinner." They rushed out to the kitchen, where Old Amos waited, tapping his foot.

"It's a good thing I'm home. The bread almost burned. Let me help you ladies. The men will want to be back on the trail with me if you can't feed them faster than this." His grin softened his growled remark.

A long period of quiet ensued as the group of ravenous men loaded their plates after the prayer. Easy joking and talking ensued thereafter, the men ever mindful of the presence of the ladies. Lucy looked up to find Boyd glancing at her a few times, causing her to look down to hide her smiles from the others. After dinner, he disappeared into her father's study with Marcus and Andrew.

~

Boyd finished reading over the papers Andrew handed him and their uncle's last will and testament. A mixture of shock and disgust filled him as he finished and glanced up at his cousin.

"You see, my dear cousin, our uncle was a very smart, self-serving scoundrel. He shipped cotton to England and owned a lucrative steel factory in the north, as well as retaining his Southern-made wealth. Of course, the last did not serve as well after the war. He'd written you out of his will, due to the way you took your rightful inheritance from your late parents and left Georgia, but your wife had continued to write him to let him know you were fine. When he found you had a son, he realized this preserved the family name. It's unfortunate what happened to young Sam and Nancy, but the will stands as it is."

Boyd could not believe Nancy had continued writing to his uncle. There again, it might have served as the reason his uncle helped him and his friends. Helped . . . if you could call it that. He shook his head. No, she must have corresponded with Aunt Elizabeth. Even given her less than affectionate nature, his aunt always made sure they felt wanted and had seen to all their needs and education. She remained his one regret when they left Georgia.

"Where is Aunt Elizabeth?" he asked.

"She is returning to England with me once we conclude this business. You may not know this, but our fathers both came from

England to America with our dear uncle. My father met my mother first then introduced her sister, Elizabeth, to Uncle Robert. They all married Richardses. My father returned to England to work for our grandfather a few months after the wedding, and the sisters have not seen each other in years. Aunt Elizabeth felt an extra responsibility besides being family when your parents died. She is weary and wants to come to England to live," Andrew related.

Boyd's conflicted feelings due to his uncle's character remained, but he knew they could use this for good. He reached for the pen and added his signature beside where Ben had signed before handing it back to Andrew. They shook hands.

"I must say I prefer England to this raw land of yours, but it's been quite exciting and interesting visiting here. I hope we may meet again one day and look forward to the few remaining weeks we will share as we sojourn back to your home. Then I must take my leave to collect Aunt Elizabeth," he said.

Boyd shared a smile with his cousin, frowned at the cocked eyebrow of Marcus, which dared him not to laugh before they all stood and went to the door. Mr. Kennedy waited at a polite distance from the door. Boyd had asked if he could speak with him after his meeting. Andrew and Marcus joined the men in front of the fireplace as Boyd followed his boss back into the study. The man motioned for Boyd to sit as he positioned himself behind his desk.

"I expect there may be some changes in our business association given your new circumstances. Is this what you wanted to discuss?" Joe Kennedy asked in his no-nonsense way.

Boyd leaned forward in his chair, meeting the rancher's gaze. "Yes, sir, in a way, but there is much more I need to discuss with you."

The man frowned but nodded. "I'm listening."

"First, I want you to know I'll stay and honor my commitment to you for the spring round-up and drive if you want, but I would prefer to purchase horses from you this spring for my ranch instead." He waited for a response as he wanted to conclude one area of business before becoming personal.

"Ted tells me you are a very good trail hand, and I know what a way you have with horses. Though I hate to lose you, this new association may be more beneficial to us both. Now, what else is on your mind, young man?"

Boyd swallowed hard. "I want to ask for Lucy's hand in marriage, and I want her to come back to East Texas with us when we leave on Monday."

Joe Kennedy grabbed a cigar and lit it. After a few draws, he stood, circled the desk, and stood in front of where Boyd sat.

"You what?" he bellowed.

Boyd stood and faced him. He didn't blink and repeated, "I want to marry your daughter."

"You don't even know her. Do you realize what you're asking? No man has held her interest. What makes you think she'd even have you? Until now, you were just another cowhand."

The double doors opened, and Lucy entered, pulling her flustered mother with her. Joe Kennedy waited for his daughter to close the doors before continuing.

"Lucy Anne Kennedy, what do you know about this?" he demanded.

"Just a little more than you do, Pa, but I have decided it's what I want."

"Hrphm! I thought you were now a mature, intelligent woman. Why does this make sense, daughter?"

"Joe, why don't we all sit down and discuss this," Mrs. Kennedy urged, taking her husband's arm.

"Agnes, don't tell me you knew about this too?" he asked in disbelief.

"No, I just learned of it before we came to stop your bellowing." They moved to the leather chairs and sat, each waiting to see who would continue the discussion.

Lucy licked her lips and started. "As you know, I am no longer a young girl to be wooed. It's past time for me to marry; therefore, I feel it's a decision I must make. Pa, you, and Ma have been so supportive, but it's time for me to be out of your house. Mr. Richards is a good man from all the information we learned before you employed him to everything we have learned since that time. He is now in the position to take care of me and is starting a new endeavor involving horses with which I am very capable of assisting him. If those logical reasons remained the basis of my consideration in this, they'd stand well on their own merit, but there's more." She paused and looked at Boyd. "I . . . I . . . you see

. . . I have feelings for him. Yes, they are new but very real."

Her parents turned their eyes on the man asking for their daughter's hand.

Boyd faced them. "Mr. and Mrs. Kennedy, you should know I'm a widower. My wife and son died during the war. We had a good marriage. The years since that loss have proven hard and long. I thought I'd never marry again. When I arrived here and met your daughter, I fought the attraction that I felt. There hasn't been anyone since my wife. Then, while on the cattle drive, I came to know the Lord, and it has changed me. There is now love in me like I have never known. If I could love my Nancy the way I did before, then I know there's now the capacity to love even more. Please know Lucy is not a replacement, and she is very different from my first wife. The things I've seen in her during our short acquaintance are new for me, and I want to spend the rest of our lives learning more. The timing is short, but I also know I don't want to leave here without her."

Complete silence fell when Boyd finished. Tears spilled from Mrs. Kennedy's eyes.

Mr. Kennedy stood and gestured with his cigar. "Well, I can see you two have your minds made up. Boyd, you take good care of her, or you'll answer to me." Boyd shook the man's hand. His future father-in-law continued, "I expect you'd better be talking to the minister tomorrow to prepare for a wedding this weekend." Mr. Kennedy looked at his wife and daughter. "Now, if you women will excuse us, we need to talk about the details of the next few days and plans for the spring. Please ask Mr. Johnson to join us and express my regrets for my absence to our other guests and bid them good night for me, Agnes."

Lucy smiled at Boyd, and he bade them good night, bending to kiss both her and her mother's hand. Her mother took her arm, pulling her through the door.

Chapter Seven

Boyd had been ambushed with questions as he entered the bunkhouse late that night after the evening at the big house. He conceded the fact that Mr. Kennedy granted him Lucy's hand. Some of the men had placed a few wagers as speculations started to emerge after dinner. This did not please Ted and he said as much.

"Richards, you have no right to her just like you had no right to send off Hallie. I'll hate losing you as a hand and wish you well, but also good riddance. If you stay around here much longer, we won't have any interesting, eligible women to pursue."

"Ted, don't blame him for your rejections," Frank said.

Ted rewarded him with a punch in the nose.

Boyd grabbed Ted before he could take out his anger any further as Frank struggled to his feet.

"Whoa, let's cool off a bit. How's about trying to be happy for me?" he suggested.

Ted threw him a glare and pulled away before storming out. They heard his horse hit the road to town a few minutes later. Billy let out a long whistle, shook his head, and threw his leg across a chair, sitting in it backwards so he could prop his arms on the back as he played his harmonica. Everything settled again and the card game proceeded for another round before the group settled in for the night.

Boyd lay on his bunk replaying the events of the afternoon and evening. He had never expected so much to happen in this quick of a fashion upon his return, but he felt at peace about every part of it. Nancy remained in his heart, but he felt this new love within him for Lucy. His heart had enough room for both now. Nancy had been very strong but easy going. She managed to find humor in most everything and remained practical; whereas, Lucy proved full of surprises and showed a rainbow of emotion. She challenged him with her quick mind, and he knew to watch for her quick flashes of temper that came on like a storm but could be calmed into gentle waves if handled well. So many things yet undiscovered, and he looked forward to the discovery of each one. He sighed, said a prayer, and drifted to sleep.

~

The dawn seeped light into the sky before long, but the group enjoyed a slight reprieve to sleep until Old Amos sounded the chow bell. However, Boyd stirred and decided to splash his face and dress. He stretched as he left the bunkhouse, scanned the sky, and placed his hat on his head. A movement by the barn caught his regard, and he saw Lucy emerging with his horse and her own saddled. She caught sight of him and called, "Good morning."

He walked to meet her. "Good morning."

"How about helping me exercise these two?" She wore a long, split riding skirt with boots, a ruffled blouse, and a coat. Her honey-blonde hair cascaded down her back with a ribbon. He marveled at the curling tendrils.

"Sure, let's go," he said with a grin and took the reins from her to steady her horse as she swung into the saddle before he followed suit. Once he settled on the saddle, she turned her head and flashed a challenging smile.

"Try to keep up, Mr. Richards," she said as she kicked her mount forward into a racing gallop.

He felt adrenaline flow through his veins as he leaned low over his mount, racing to follow her. She knew the land well, and she didn't slow until they reached the pond on the other side of the crest of the northern rise. They stopped in tandem. She laughed, flashing her dimple. He feigned fatigue, dismounted, and flung himself on the ground.

"Miss Kennedy, I do believe you intend to be rid of me," he said, frowning. He rolled to his back, placing his hat over his eyes.

He listened as she dismounted, crossed, and sat down beside him. She leaned over and raised his hat to find his eyes closed. He could feel her waiting and cracked open one eye to see her peering at him.

"You are going to have to do better than that, my good sir, or I'll tell my father I won't have you," she said before letting the hat drop back on his face.

He pushed it up, replacing it on his head as he raised himself into sitting position alongside her. She sat with her arms around her raised knees and stared straight ahead.

"Then we'd better get going." He sprang up and collected his mustang from where he drank at the he pond's edge.

She grabbed her mare and raced to catch him as he galloped across the open pasture. They slowed and eased into an easy trot. She must have ridden for most of her life.

"Lucy, you are quite a horse woman. I don't believe I've ever observed another female nor many males who could compete with you. When did you first started riding?"

"Thank you, Boyd. I was three years old when Pa first sat me in a saddle with him. I rode with him by the age of four, much to my ma's dismay. My brother, Jason, couldn't wait to catch up with me."

"I can understand that. My brother, Ben, always pushed himself so he could do things with me. He didn't like being left behind."

"No, not Jason, he wanted to be the one out with Pa and wanted me to stay home with Ma," she clarified.

"Aren't you close to your brother?"

"We were once, but he's competitive, and it's important for him to excel at everything he does. It's exhausting being around him because he always challenges everyone. You must be able to give a logical and accurate explanation for how you approach things, or he'll tell you why he thinks you're wrong. That's fine to a degree, but sometimes I just wanted him to be my little brother. Do you understand what I mean?"

"Yes, I do. Some think I should have done as my uncle wanted and gone to school at Harvard instead of leaving Georgia. Your brother might not approve of me."

"Did you have the high marks at school to qualify?" she asked.

"Yes, I did," he said.

"Then leave it there. You don't have to justify your choices to Jason, me, or anybody else. He's the reason I wasn't allowed to finish college," she stopped and turned her head away.

He sensed her unease. "What is it, Lucy?"

"Boyd, my brother has a bit of meanness in him," she said.

Her horse stomped, and she pulled on the reins to steady him. Her eyes met Boyd's. "You need to know about him. It's one of the reasons why my father sent him away to school. I hope he returns a mature and kinder person."

A fierce determination gripped him. "For your parent's sake, I hope so, but he won't be an issue for us."

She relaxed in the saddle and smiled at him. "Anyway, back to the two of us. We are educated enough and, what's more, have the intelligence we need to choose what to do in our lives. Also, none of it means anything if we can't show our love to others. I'm glad not to feel the need to make others second-guess themselves. Life does that on its own."

"Well said. Now let me change the subject. Look over there at the cattle resting, the wide-open sky—all magnificent, but none compare to the beauty of your eyes. Now that's something to appreciate," he said, softening his voice.

She turned toward him at the compliment. The wind stirred a wisp of curly hair at her temples, and their gazes held. He pulled his horse steady and reached over to stroke the tendrils away, caressing her cheek with the back of his hand. He wanted to protect her.

"Let me get you back to the house. We need to head to town after breakfast to talk to Brother Moore, and I don't want you tired out." She nodded and took the lead as they turned the horses toward home.

~

Marcus waited for him by the corral as they returned. He tipped his hat at Lucy.

"Good morning, Miss Kennedy. I hope you don't mind if I borrow Boyd for a few minutes. We will stable the horses so you can go on to breakfast."

"Of course not, Mr. Johnson, and thank you," she said, allowing him to take her reins as she dismounted. She gave Boyd a wave before she started for the house.

Boyd could tell Marcus had something on his mind by the way his jaw kept clenching. He followed him into the barn, leading the horses to their stalls. The other hands remained at breakfast, so they unsaddled the mounts and brushed them before they gave them some feed. Boyd shifted his weight to one side, looked down at the ground with his hands propped low on his hips as he waited for his friend to speak. After another moment of silence, he glanced up to find Marcus with one foot propped on a stall gate, leaning on his elbows with his mouth resting on his overlaid hands.

"Are you going to tell me what has created that storm cloud on your face?"

Marcus turned troubled green eyes toward him. "Boyd, this isn't the right time for Lucy. You need to come home, walk your land, spend time with Ben, and get reacquainted with Martha and Daniel for a while. There are memories to deal with that are still going to hit you once you arrive. John and I had to experience our own set of memories once we returned to Arkansas. You've never let yourself come home."

The truth of his friend's words punched his gut, but at the same time he remembered how he supported Marc and John when he accompanied them home to Arkansas.

"Marc, you and John faced your memories with me there. Why can't I have Lucy with me?"

Marcus crossed to him and placed a hand on his shoulder. "Because it's not fair to her. If you care about her, you'll go and prepare things for her. Don't make her walk into a house and share the same bedroom that was yours and Nancy's. We built Martha and Daniel a cabin last spring and plan to build Florence and me one this spring. It won't be a problem to build two. Ben can keep the main house. He has more than earned it."

Guilt and remorse washed over him as he pulled away, turning his back on his friend. A long silence ensued as he collected his thoughts.

"Marc, you're right. What was I thinking? I come back from the cattle drive and stampede over Lucy's life and think it's a boon to be ready to move on with my life. Lord, forgive me, but it felt good to stop grieving and start living," he said, turning to face his friend.

"It's so good to see you ready to do that, Boyd. Just slow down a bit. If Lucy is the woman God has intended for you, she'll want you to do this in order for both of you to be ready," Marc said.

"What does Florence think?" Boyd asked.

"She thinks Lucy and you are wonderful people who could

make each other very happy, but she doesn't want anyone to get hurt. The fact that I know you much better than she does makes her trust what I'm saying is true."

Boyd nodded. "Marc, I'm different in so many ways now than the man you've known. The man you knew would have never considered marriage again, didn't care if death waited at the door, and stayed self-absorbed and bitter. I guess my new outlook has me as excited as a child who wants to share everything good with those he loves right now. If you had confronted me in this way five months ago, I would have run out on everyone again but not now. Marcus, you must understand this one thing, I'm sure about Lucy. It's hard to explain. Being around her is so . . . it's just . . . contentment, pure contentment. She challenges me, shines her smile on me, and I'm satisfied just being around her. I almost lost my balance on a bronco when I caught her watching a few days before the cattle drive. It made me angry at the time, but I understand why now. I started to fall in love with her from the moment her brush almost took my hat off the first day I got here, which is another story. Please tell me how to tell her we need to wait until the spring. What if I leave her here and something happens to her before I can come back for her?"

Understanding appeared on Marc's face, and he straightened, exhaled, and then said, "Boyd, Nancy's and Sam's deaths are tragic, but now the testing begins. Do you trust God and his love? We are promised tribulation in this world, not a life without troubles. The difference for you now is learning His promises to you can all be trusted. He's not waiting to pull a cruel scheme on you by bringing a new love into your life to just take her away. That's where faith must be exercised."

~

They didn't hear Lucy's footsteps or know she stood just outside the open barn door. She returned to bring them each a plate of food as her mother cleared the table. Most of their conversation reached her ears. She started to leave but felt frozen until Marc's last words on faith. She knew what to do. With as much stealth quietness as possible, she backed away and turned to make her way to the house. She found her father and mother in his study.

"Ma, Pa, I need to talk to you," she said, shutting the door behind her. She wanted to make this easy for Boyd and didn't want to lose him. "I need your help and advice. You see, I think the spring would be a better time for a wedding. Also, it'd give everyone more time. Jason may even be home by then. We'll be taking horses to East Texas for Boyd's ranch then, and I thought maybe the both of you could accompany me at that time, stay for the wedding, and see where I'll live. My marriage will take me away from here, and I want time to say good-bye to my friends. I'll need to train someone to take my place at the newspaper, and I want one more Christmas with you. Pa, could you make this your idea and talk to Boyd? He'll respect that and won't think I'm uncertain, because I'm not. He needs time to go home and prepare his family for my arrival."

Her mother sighed in contentment, and her father took on a look of satisfaction. "Well thought out, daughter. This is clear thinking, and I'll go find Boyd right now." He crossed to her and dropped a kiss on her forehead. Her mother hugged her close.

~

Boyd thought he heard someone outside the door, and the footprints made by female boots where someone had lingered for a bit remained as he increased the opening of the barn door. As an excellent tracker, he noticed details. Marc stood behind him and noticed his regard of the dusty ground.

"Those are too big to be Florence's, but I wish it had been her," Boyd said. He took off his hat and ran his fingers through his hair. "I don't know how much Lucy heard, but I hope it wasn't the wrong pieces. What should I do?"

Marc nudged his arm with his elbow. "You may be about to find out that answer."

Boyd looked up to find Joe Kennedy striding across the yard. He wouldn't say anything until he heard what Lucy's father had to say.

"Mr. Johnson, will you excuse us? Boyd, I need to talk to you for a bit," he said.

"Of course, Mr. Kennedy. We can talk more later, Boyd," Marcus said before he headed for the house.

"What can I do for you, sir?" Boyd asked.

"Well, I don't want you to think your future father-in-law is not a man of his word, but Agnes and I have talked about how fast all this has happened, and we feel the need to amend part of the plans," Mr. Kennedy said. When Boyd remained silent, he continued, "Lucy is our only daughter, and we know when Jason marries it will be different because he's a son. There are more delicate emotions involved with leaving home for a female. We need her here until the spring. This will give you a chance to prepare your brother and your other friends for her arrival, but more importantly, you need to prepare to take care of my girl. Your cousin still has to finalize all of the business from your uncle's estate, and this will give adequate time. As you know, taking a wife is a serious responsibility, and seeing as your wife-to-be is my daughter, I intend to see you do it right."

Boyd could have chosen to be offended, but first and foremost—even if Marcus hadn't just told him something similar—the reasonable request made sense. Second, the fact that he suspected Lucy had overheard his and Marc's conversation and had gone to her father made him amiable to Mr. Kennedy's declaration. He didn't hesitate or waver in his response.

"Yes, sir, I do believe you're right. It's very important to start out our lives together under the best possible circumstances. I must assure you my cousin has promised to have everything finalized upon our return. The paperwork is all in order and awaiting my signature. Please know if anything compromised my ability to provide for Lucy, I would return here and, if you would have me, would work for you from sunup to sundown in order to care for her."

This seemed to please and satisfy his former boss. "Good, we're in agreement. I spoke to Lucy before coming to you, so she knows. It would be prudent of you to seek her out and give assurance of your coming marriage. Ted can oversee the spring roundup and preparations for the next trail drive. My son has written us of his return home at the end of April or the beginning of May after graduation. Therefore, Agnes and I will be able to stay for a few days when we bring Lucy. We'll bring your two breeding horses in the spring. This will complete two areas of business without tying up more of my men who'll need to be on the spring drive." He fixed a contemplative stare on Boyd for an uneasy moment before concluding the matter. "Son, you'd better get going, or my daughter may reconsider many things."

"Yes, sir, and thank you," Boyd said and hurried toward the

house.

~

Boyd found Florence in a chair on the porch with a book. "Have you seen Lucy?" he asked.

Her fond smile warmed his heart.

"Yes, she's doing needlework with her mother by the fire. Boyd, she will join us in the spring. Have faith," she said.

"Thanks, Florence," he said and dropped a quick kiss on the top of her head. This woman had become like a sister to him. He pulled open the door and strode inside.

Agnes Kennedy took Lucy's hand as he came into the room. Lucy looked pale and not like her normal self. He knew the reason and wanted to restore the joy and certainty from their morning ride.

"Mrs. Kennedy, I've just spoken with Mr. Kennedy and would like to talk to Lucy. Is it agreeable with you for us to talk in the study?" he asked.

"Mr. Richards, I encourage you to do that. The two of you need to spend as much time together as you can before you leave."

He sought Lucy's gaze, and she stood, laying down her embroidery. She kept her eyes down and proceeded him to the study.

Boyd followed her inside and closed the doors. In that moment, he felt like a stranger to her, and he didn't like it. He crossed to where she stood in front of the desk and took her hands. She stiffened, and he felt the degree of her upset. Of course, he should've expected this. She knew, as he did, this new course sounded more sensible, but it brought disappointment. He wanted her to be honest with him.

"Lucy, I know you overheard Marcus and me. It's the reason you had your father talk to me, isn't it?"

She nodded but wouldn't look at him.

"How much of the conversation did you hear?"

"I was bringing you some breakfast and didn't mean to stay to listen. It's just . . . I heard most of it." Her eyes reflected her despair. "Boyd, you don't have to marry me. I'll understand if you've changed your mind now or if you get home and decide different. You have had enough unhappiness since losing Nancy and Sam. The last thing I want to do is to jump into the middle of your life when it may not be right for you. I have a good life right where I am."

He could see all the conflicting emotions in her eyes. "I know you have a good life here. That's how I know you care for me. You were willing to leave all of it within a matter of days to go and make a life with me. Lucy, please don't pull away from me. Marcus and Florence want us to be happy; therefore, they've done what true friends do by making us face some realities. You don't have any areas of resolution in the way I do. My brother and I have never talked about the war, what happened to him, what happened to me, what happened to Nancy and Sam—because I wouldn't discuss it. Now, because of God, I can. Everyone at home, but especially Ben has been handling responsibilities that were mine ever since the war ended. I owe it to them to be there for a bit before I bring you there. It wouldn't be fair to you if I don't do this first. There is such sorrow in my heart at my selfishness. I had no right to ask for your hand because of those unresolved things, but even as my mind knows this to be true, my heart is glad I did."

Lucy twisted away from him, wrapping her arms around herself. Had she changed her mind? The risk of heartbreak hung between them. His mouth tightened as he waited in grim resignation. She dropped her arms to her sides and faced him with an unexpected smile.

"Boyd, take all the time you need. I'll be here, and if you still want me as your wife when spring comes, I'll be there." She shut her eyes and tilted her head upward as she took a deep breath. "You must know something . . . " Her eyelashes fluttered open, revealing blue-green depths of emotion. "I love you."

Boyd's heart thundered in his ears as her words touched his soul. His eyes never left hers. He opened his mouth to speak, but she shook her head.

"No, no, no, please don't say anything you don't mean. I just wanted you to know how it is for me. At this point in my life, it's a gift to know I have found the man who creates this wonderful emotion I've never felt before. You've given me the gift of this love in my heart. It's new for me, and even if your heart doesn't have room for more than a corner of emotion for me, it will be enough. Boyd, every time I discover something new about you, it makes me want to know more, and I will never tire of learning you." She smiled at the look on his face. "Please, I know you're not perfect; neither am I. You and I are strong-willed people with deep convictions. It will keep things spirited."

Words left Boyd and he knew anything said at this point might not be accepted. He must show her his commitment by his actions, but now he must show his emotions. No time to court her and with nothing to lose, he gathered her close. The shock on her face softened to reflect the love she felt in her heart as he bent to kiss her, cherishing her. Lucy's breathing quickened along with his heart. Boyd's lips slowed as they moved over hers and caressed the petal softness as he ended the kiss. She opened her ocean-colored eyes, which reflected waves of emotion as they searched his gaze. She filled him with wonder and deep contemplation. It overwhelmed them both, and Lucy buried her face in his chest for a moment before laying her head near his shoulder, wrapping her arms around him, and hugging him close. His arms dropped for a moment—*she will be my wife*—as his mind raced; then he gathered her close and laid his head on the top of hers.

Boyd didn't know how to feel. Lucy had opened herself to him in such a gentle and affectionate way. Nancy had loved to dwell in his embrace at night, but during the day, they might brush hands as they worked together, but she never sought hugs. Neither had he. His aunt and uncle had cared for them, as had Nancy's parents for her, but they'd not taken much time to display affection. The way they worked hard for their family demonstrated their love. They found the world a challenging place with much work to be done to survive, and children must learn to deal with things as they happened. This upbringing made them take most things in stride without expecting too much. They shared a deep love, laughed a lot, and worked hard together. They interacted in a different way. Lucy relished hugs, and he enjoyed her.

Lucy lifted her head and released him as she said, "I'd love to stay here with you, but I'm sure my parents would frown upon it, and I have to go to the newspaper office. I'd planned on going by there on our way to talk to Brother Moore to let them know I'd be in later today, but now I can be there by nine o'clock."

Boyd took both her hands in his as she started to step away. "I'll go with you. Andrew mentioned he needed to mail the second copy of the papers he had me sign. If they reach my aunt before he returns, she'll have the judge finalize everything, and the money will reach us sooner. He'll hand-deliver the original papers to the judge in the event of anything preventing the mail from reaching her. Ben told him about more holdups of stages to get the Express boxes this year; as the mail delivery is involved, he doesn't want to take any chances. Oh, that brings up a very important matter that I must discuss with your father. He has proposed you take a stage this spring; it may not be the safest way to travel."

She smiled and shook her head. "Boyd, you'd better pray with Brother Moore about this worrying of yours. There are no guarantees on anything. Let God take care of the details. He has brought us together; and if His plan is for us to share days, weeks, months, or years, it's not for us to know."

He grinned. "You're right. Do you still have areas where you struggle since you came to know the Lord?"

She cringed and laughed. "I sure do. My temper is too quick fire. Brother Moore says I have the temperament of Simon Peter in the Bible. My zeal and passion are well placed, but my reactions when things aren't quite as I had envisioned them are disproportionate."

"Thanks for the warning," he said, rolling his eyes. "Now, let's get you to town. I'll go get the wagon and let Andrew know to be ready."

"I'll go change into more appropriate attire. Mr. Jenkins would frown upon my riding skirt to the office," she said and swept past him to the door. He followed, opening the door for her. He nodded to Mrs. Kennedy as he passed through on his way outside.

The trio left within twenty minutes. Lucy had changed into a brown-checkered dress with a bustled skirt and billowed sleeves with tight cuffs. She parted her hair in the middle and swept it up in a coil on the back of her head. She glowed as Boyd assisted her into the wagon beside Andrew.

~

Marcus Johnson came down the steps of the ranch house and headed toward the barn as the group departed.

"It's Johnson, right?" Ted called from where he worked on a horse's bridle by the corral.

Marc had taken an instant dislike to Mr. Kennedy's top hand after his open appraisal of his wife. Still, he didn't abide rudeness, so he made his way over to the well to join him.

"Yes, I'm Marcus Johnson," he said, waiting to see Ted's purpose in all of this.

"I saw you use a Hackamore instead of a bridle bit on that horse yesterday?"

"Yep," Marc said.

"Your choice. Not mine," Ted said. "I heard Billy telling Ol' Amos that the plans have changed. Mr. Kennedy has asked him to go with them to take Lucy and some breeding horses to your farm this spring."

"Yep," Marc replied.

Ted smirked. "Well, now, maybe I'll be able to get what I want after all."

Marc's green eyes narrowed under his hat. "What would that be, Mr. Dalton?"

"You see, there were two possible paths for my life that I've been pondering for the past few years. The first considered the reform of a soiled dove from town, but your friend sent her to the fort in Indian Territory to be a nurse to some invalid there. The second pushed to work my way further into a permanent place here on Mr. Kennedy's ranch by a marriage to his daughter. It's not an obvious match and Lucy can be pretty prickly, but she's no spring chicken. Better to see her married to me than an old maid. Richards has snaked me on that too." He paused with a wicked look in his hazel eyes. "For now."

Marc acknowledged the rugged cowhand had the chiseled looks many ladies found attractive; however, his contrary disposition didn't endear him. "It seems to me she prefers a different type man than you, sir."

"Yes, but I can be charming when the need is present. I've bided my time. She might take a shine to me, and her parents could keep her close. Now, don't get hasty and jump to judgment on me. Also, her brother, Jason, will be home in a few months. He might not want his sister moving away."

Marc sat on the well wall and stretched his long legs out in front of him as he crossed his arms and twisted his mouth in contemplation.

"I think I'll wait until we are well clear of this ranch before I tell Boyd of your plans," he said.

Ted frowned. "Why's that? Don't you want Lucy to marry Richards?"

"It's not that, no; on the contrary, I think she'll be good for him given a little more time. The simple fact is you might be separated from a few of your teeth or lose your job once he informs Mr. Kennedy of your plans," Marc said without looking at Ted.

A humorless chuckle echoed off the walls of the well as Ted bent over the structure in disbelief. He straightened and nudged Marcus's boot with his toe. "You must be thinking of the man I met before the cattle drive. Now he has found religion and is much tamer. He'll be acting like a tenderfoot before long."

Marcus pushed back his hat, giving Ted a good-natured smile. "You don't understand, do you? What motivates him now is even stronger than the anger that spurred him on before. He will protect what he feels has been put in his care. Those of us who have placed our lives in God's hands would prefer peace to conflict, but it's not always possible."

Ted looked at him in grim disbelief. Marc straightened, removed his hat, and examined the brim for a moment before he looked up to speak again. "One more thing, Mr. Dalton, you need to learn more respect for women, or you'll never have a wife. Lucy strikes me as a very intelligent and perceptive woman who has chosen to remain unmarried until this point. She has now met the right man, and it's not you."

Ted glared at him for a moment before he returned to his work. Marcus remained calm, replaced his hat, and headed to the barn to check on the new horse. He wanted Billy to saddle him, so he could try the stallion again in the corral after he and Florence returned from their planned ride.

He found Billy cleaning the stalls and explained his plan. The young man stopped and sent a wary look toward the restless stallion in the stall and shook his head as he looked at Marcus.

"Mr. Johnson, I'd be happy to oblige you, but it may be best if I wait until you get back and help me. That animal still seems like he wants to fuss a might."

Marc chuckled and slapped Billy on the shoulder. "Sure, you may be right, Billy. We should be back within an hour—"

He stopped as he heard a scuffle outside and Florence

screamed, "Marcus!" Billy caught his gaze, and they rushed out to the yard.

Ted had Florence by the wrists and pressed against the corral railing. Marc perceived a flash of movement on the porch as he dashed forward, grabbed Ted by the back of the neck, and applied enough pressure to inflict sufficient pain to cause Ted to release Florence. Marcus stepped in front of his very irate wife to thwart her plans of retaliation and knocked Ted to the ground in one movement. Mr. Kennedy finished his descent from the porch steps and reached them as Ted hit the ground. Marcus clenched his jaw in anger as he watched the instigator struggle to his feet.

"No disrespect intended, Mr. Kennedy, but I suggest you pull the reins on your top hand here. I better not ever find him with his hands on my wife again," Marc said with his green eyes flashing at Ted before he whirled to check on Florence, who stood behind him. He could feel her indignation and knew fear gripped her a bit, so he didn't say anything. He just gathered her close until the tension left her, and she laid her head against his chest, holding him.

"Ted, in the house, now. I'll meet you in my study," Mr. Kennedy barked, and Ted complied without one backward glance.

The rancher turned to Marcus and Florence. "Mrs. Johnson, I want to apologize for Ted's behavior and be assured he will make amends to you both once I'm finished with him. I know you're upset, but would you mind telling me what happened?"

Florence lifted her head to look at Marc, who nodded before complying with their host's request. "I was on my way to meet Marc for our ride when Mr. Dalton stopped me as I passed him. He said a woman like me is wasted on my husband and tried to kiss me. Well, I kicked him. He grabbed me by the wrists and pushed me against the rails to try again when I called for Marc."

Marc cut Mr. Kennedy short as he opened his mouth to reply. "You should be aware of Mr. Dalton's intentions to try and court Lucy once we're gone. I didn't want to cause a problem as I thought Lucy quite capable of warding off any of his advances. Now I'm not so sure."

The older man's lips thinned into a grim line. "I appreciate that, Marcus, but be assured nothing of that nature will ever occur. You need to understand something about Ted before you determine it's time for me to let him go. He's been with me since the year before the war, except for last spring when he rode with Mr. Goodnight to get the trail experience to get us started. Instead of fighting the Yankees, he fought the Indians who threatened my home with me. I'm very aware of his coarse nature but have found him to be a reliable and trustworthy hand. He's someone I've trusted with all I own, but my daughter is not an option. Even if I found her interested in him, I'd warn her off of Ted. He's been closed mouth about his upbringing, but his regard for women is very limited. So, once again, please accept my apologies. I'll leave it to your discretion in whether or not Boyd needs to hear about this before you leave. If you should choose to wait until you are a few days from here, you should give him my assurances that Lucy is safe."

Marc nodded, but he knew Florey would be sure to tell Lucy even if he chose not to tell Boyd. Ted's roughness reminded him of the actions of one young man in his wife's past. She shuddered and moved back into the shelter of his embrace. Mr. Kennedy returned to the house, and Marcus moved her away from him to look at her wrists. She pulled back to smile at him.

"I'm fine. Let's go for our ride," she said and strode past Billy, who had watched it all in disbelief.

"Mr. Johnson, I don't think I would tell Boyd about this. He's ready for his new life, but it would be easy to slip back. Ted's not worth it."

"You're right, Billy. Hey, be ready to help me with that bronco when we get back," Marc said and moved on to the barn.

"Yes, sir, I'll go see if Ol' Amos has something I can eat. This excitement has made me hungry," Billy said.

Marcus laughed, thinking of how Ben, Boyd's younger brother, stayed hungry all the time. He strode to the barn, feeling a little levity until he found Florence in tears against the neck of her horse. Words formed in his head but died on his tongue. He'd learned many things this past year of marriage. His wife needed tenderness more than words when upset. He moved to hold her. After a few moments, she glanced up at him. "I'm tough, huh? I hope your male pride is satisfied that I need you to protect me," she said and then leaned up on tiptoe to kiss him. "Thank you."

Marcus stroked the escaping strands of hair at her temples

behind her ears before bending to kiss her. He straightened, and then leaned back with a wry grin.

"Does this mean you'll let me win the race today?"

Her eyes twinkled as she turned to finish saddling her horse. "Not a chance." She swung up into the saddle and smiled as she waited for him to do the same. They guided their mounts outside and headed for the open range of pasturelands.

~

Boyd, Lucy, and Andrew arrived in town and stopped at the newspaper office first. Lucy needed to work for about an hour before they met with Brother Moore. They wanted to request his guidance and prayer. The men dropped her off and proceeded to the telegraph and mail office for Andrew to mail the second copy of the signed inheritance papers. He kept the original. In the event the mailed copy didn't arrive, he planned to deliver it to the judge in Georgia in person upon his return. Andrew also planned to send a message to their aunt by telegraph to let her know of his actions.

Boyd left him to tend to business with a promise to meet for lunch at the small family restaurant instead of the saloon at noon. Andrew wanted to explore the town after he finished his more official duties.

He received a warm greeting from Mr. and Mrs. Thornton when he stopped by the mercantile to place an order for Mr. Kennedy. They welcomed him home and inquired about the cattle drive. He gave them as brief of a summary as he could. They promised to have the items ready to pick up after lunch.

A cold wind blew as he drove the wagon back to the newspaper to pick up Lucy. As he jumped down, he caught a glimpse of her with her head bent over her desk, reviewing a paper with Mr. Jenkins. Boyd paused and leaned against the hitching post, enjoying the scene. She frowned, deep in thought, and turned to look at her boss. The man nodded. Her obvious intelligence struck Boyd and emphasized the multifaceted layers of this intricate woman. It winded him. He hoped she didn't get bored with what he could offer her.

She turned toward the window, caught sight of him, and smiled, flashing her dimple. His heart skipped a beat. Mr. Jenkins also waved, and Lucy gathered her things together. She came out the door a few minutes later.

"Your timing is perfect. We just finished the changes for tomorrow's edition, barring any unforeseen events this afternoon," she said.

He grinned as he stepped up onto the boarded walkway. "I'm at your disposal. Andrew is well occupied for now and has offered to buy us lunch once we're done at the church. Are you ready to find the good minister?"

She smiled as she took his arm. "Yes, let's."

~

Brother Adam Moore looked up at the sound of the doors opening. They laughed at his look of surprise and his deep chuckle soon joined them. "Well now, Mr. Richards, I know that I have been praying for you, and it's obvious the Lord has been at work. Would you mind filling in the details?"

"It might take some time to tell you about the events of the past few months. Do you have some time for us this morning, Brother Moore?" Boyd asked.

The minister gestured to the front seats. "Please have a seat, Mr. Richards and Lucy. I do indeed have time for you."

They settled themselves, and Boyd began. Brother Moore listened with quiet reserve except for an occasional clarification question until Boyd finished. Then he turned to address Lucy first.

"Lucy, I've known you most of your life and have seen you grow into an intelligent and thoughtful woman. However, I've known you to be impulsive and temperamental at times." He held up his hand to silence her as she opened her mouth to speak. "No, now let me finish. You have come to me many times since I baptized you, frustrated at yourself for your quick temper or disproportionate reactions. This is a very serious decision. First, you'll soon move away from your family and friends. They can't reach you without a journey if you need them. Second, you have agreed to marry a man who is still in love with his late wife. This means you'll never have his whole heart. These realities may sound harsh, but they are offered in love. What are your thoughts, Lucy?"

Lucy glanced at Boyd. Grimness gripped him, but she reached for his hand and turned back to the minister. "Brother Moore, you do know me very well, however, not on the subject of this man. I sensed something different about him from the moment I met him, but a barrier surrounded him before he left on the cattle drive. I now know why. He didn't know the Lord before and bitterness and grief over his wife's death consumed him. Nancy will always be in his heart. If she weren't, I don't think I would have agreed to marry him." She paused at their puzzled looks. "Let me explain. Their love was real, and that means it will never die. However, I don't think that means he will not be able to love me. That's insulting to both of us. It means he will love me well—with all that is left in his heart—and I trust in that. God opened Boyd's heart to me once He filled it with more than enough love."

Her eyes sought Boyd's as she finished. He blinked away tears.

Brother Moore nodded and turned to Boyd. "Well, what do you have to say, Mr. Richards?"

Boyd's voice had a gruff edge as he responded. "I know God has blessed me in my life by sending two women of such rare qualities. Nancy and I shared a love unlike many people ever find, but I now know it could've deepened if she'd lived. Because, while I fought in the war, she came to know the Lord. But she's gone. Now, I wonder. Would I have been open to the Lord if I hadn't experienced those things that brought me to my knees? Brother Moore, God transformed me. My heart has just started to stir, and my feelings for Lucy are so pure and strong that I can only anticipate how deep they'll become. My brother, Ben, and my friends at home will become family for Lucy. She'll be loved and appreciated. No one can know what the future will hold. We can only trust God for it."

The minister took them each by the hand. "I am satisfied with you both and will hold you up in prayer daily. While you prepare for her arrival and set things in order at your farm, I'll help watch over Lucy until it's time to go in the spring. Bless you both. Let's pray."

He prayed with them, and they left to meet with Andrew for lunch.

~

Boyd and Lucy found Andrew Richards already at the restaurant when they arrived. He sipped on a cup of tea and appeared pleased with the world.

Boyd grinned at his cousin as he held a chair out for Lucy.

"What has you so self-satisfied, Cousin?" he asked.

Andrew rose and waited until Lucy settled in her chair. He resumed his seat.

"Well, chap, I have had a very pleasing morning," he said. "I got all the documents sent regarding your inheritance and finalized some other business with Mr. Kennedy's attorney."

Lucy leaned forward at the mention of her father. "Excuse me, Mr. Richards, but did you say you had business with my father's attorney?"

Andrew winked at Boyd. "She's quick, mate," he said before his eyes shifted to Lucy. "My dear Miss Kennedy, I would not be worthy of my vocation if I yielded to further discussion of this matter. Now, as circumstances necessitate, I will change the subject; you must call me Andrew. There are far too many 'Mr. Richards' in your association and another in your soon-to-be brother-in-law, Ben."

Lucy blushed under his cousin's sparkling blue gaze, which belied the serious look on his face.

"I see charm is strong in the Richards family, Andrew," Lucy said. "Boyd, it's a shame you haven't met your cousin before now. He intrigues me, but not as much as you do."

Boyd rewarded the smile she gave him with a brilliant one of his own. He fixed his eyes on his cousin.

"Tell us a bit more about yourself, Andrew."

Andrew took a nonchalant sip of tea and returned the cup to the saucer. He cocked his head to the side as he met Boyd's gaze without one sign of intimidation.

"Well, let's see, my dear cousin, besides the obvious relations we share as a family. I have a lovely wife named Liza and a delightful two-year-old daughter named Mary."

Deep emotions washed over Boyd. Sam had a cousin, but young Mary would never know him. How could Andrew leave his family alone for so long? Andrew held up a hand as Boyd started to speak.

"I have been gone for eight months and am very ready to get home, old chap. You do not have to put me right. I miss them dreadfully, but my father's health prevented him from coming and as the eldest, it is my responsibility. My younger brother's wife is expecting, and it went beyond consideration for my sister to come."

Boyd looked down and stated, "Cousin, Texas and Georgia are not the safest places to be at this time. Texas still hasn't been readmitted to the Union, and travel is slow as the railroad system isn't yet refined enough for passengers in our state at this time. I have to say that Marc, Florence, and you took a chance traveling the way you did. If I had my vote, you'd be in England now, not to seem ungrateful."

Andrew fixed a level and respectful gaze on him.

"All sentiments are appreciated, dear cousin, but as we must deal with what is reality for us, let's make a deal: you get me back to your home unharmed, and the same military escort that brought me to your home will see me back to Georgia." He laughed. "You look puzzled, shall I explain? You are not the only one concerned about my journey. My government for whom I serve as an envoy has secured safe passage in many ways. Let's just say I have papers that made any checks by Union officials not a bother. I knew Texas is still considered as the fifth military district before I embarked on this journey. Plans accommodated all obstacles."

Boyd whistled in appreciation.

"Very impressive, cousin, but the Indians and bandits don't care about your papers," Boyd said.

Andrew smiled. "As I feel I must remind you of the strength of your friend, Marcus. We did have one unfortunate situation with bandits, as you call them, but Marcus diffused it. So, Cousin, do we have a deal?"

Boyd shook his head and reached for his cousin's hand. "Remind me to have a talk with Marcus. Yes, we have a deal."

Lucy cleared her throat. "If you gentlemen don't mind, I would rather eat than ponder the journey to come."

The anxiety on her face belied the smile that she shone on them. He grabbed her hand and squeezed it.

"Everything will work out as it's supposed to. Now, please tell us what is best to order here."

Mrs. Vaughn, the wife of the owner, soon came for their orders, and the conversation turned to lighthearted topics. Once their meals arrived, their conversation turned into companionable exchanges.

~

Several unknown horses stood tethered to the corral as the trio arrived back at the ranch in the early afternoon. Lucy soon satisfied Boyd's curiosity when she let out a delighted exclamation.

"Uncle Michael is here! Oh, you two must come to meet him this very instant," she said as she looked around, searching for a hand to take the wagon. "Billy! Come get the wagon. I want to introduce Boyd and Andrew to Uncle Michael."

The young hand came out of the barn. "Yes, ma'am. Hey, Boyd, you're in for a treat. Michael Kennedy is a bit of a legend around here."

Boyd waved at Billy as he and Andrew hurried to catch up with Lucy, who had already reached the door. They arrived a few paces behind her as she interrupted the group of men in her father's study and threw herself into the arms of a stocky, muscled man of about fifty years of age.

"Uncle Michael!" she exclaimed and kissed him on his dusty cheek.

The man frowned, but his eyes gleamed with affection as he set his niece away from him.

"Lucy, how many times have your father and I told you not to interrupt our meetings?"

She pulled the first pout Boyd had seen, and he could see her uncle adored her. The burly man smiled and pulled her into another quick embrace before turning to face Boyd and Andrew.

Before he could speak, one of his men, a tall lanky fellow with hair the color of corn silk stepped away from the fireplace. "Hey, Captain Richards, how've you been?"

Boyd squinted as he tried to place the man's face. He looked about his age. Then his eyes widened at a memory of a dirty, blood-streaked face of a soldier. He carried him to the field hospital during the battle of Fredericksburg.

"Caleb?" He moved forward with his hand outstretched.

The man flashed a lopsided grin as he shook Boyd's hand. "Yeah, I wasn't sure you'd remember. I kept my arm. It came close, but the doctor saved it. I'm one of the lucky ones."

Michael Kennedy cleared his throat. "Caleb, would you mind introducing me to this man?"

Caleb released Boyd's hand and stepped back. "Major Michael Kennedy, meet Captain Boyd Richards. Richards helped save my life at Fredericksburg."

The two men sized each other up as they shook hands.

"I understand you have asked for my niece's hand in marriage. Do you intend to stick by that intention after you return home?"

"Yes, sir, I do. There are just a few things I have to set in order before that can happen."

"As it happens, I'm going to help to see that you do just that," the former major said. "My brother made me aware of your situation upon my arrival here, and as my men and I are on our way to Nacogdoches to attend to some business, we can accompany you back to your home. That way I'll be able to navigate the way when we bring Lucy this spring."

Boyd frowned and scanned the room to find Marcus leaning against the mantle by the fire. They'd learned to read each other well during the war, and his friend's expression told him not to underestimate the major.

Boyd nodded and glanced to his soon to be father-in-law with a look of silent inquiry. His former boss sat behind his desk and leaned back in his chair.

"Michael, I think Boyd is wondering about your line of work. How much should we tell him?"

The man's brown eyes skimmed his brother before fixing an indulgent stare on Boyd. "The short of it is this, Richards: I was a ranger before the war; and as our government isn't yet . . . um, how shall I say it, back to itself. My boys and I travel the state lending assistance to Texans in need of our skills. Our benefactors are men who still hold wealth and power without advertising it."

Boyd glanced at the seven other men, including Caleb, who sat or stood about the room. All hardened ex-Confederate soldiers. They could be considered both good and bad depending on your perspective. Boyd decided to welcome them as the extra protection they might need

He inclined his head and encompassed the group with a slow respectful perusal. "Gentlemen, I'm glad to be in your company," he said as his gaze returned to Lucy's uncle.

The man's smile broadened. "Lucy, my dear, I think you've chosen well. Now, I think you should go find your mother and Mrs. Johnson and let us finish our discussion."

Lucy brushed a quick kiss on her uncle's cheek and smiled at Boyd and Andrew as she left, closing the door behind her.

~

Her uncle's men emerged two hours later and trickled outside. Lucy and Florence sat with their heads together over an embroidery pattern as Boyd and Marcus approached.

"Florey, I hate to interrupt, but we need to get packed. We leave at first light tomorrow. The major won't wait until Monday," Marcus said.

Florence handed Lucy the needlework as she stood. "I guess you'll have time to teach me once you come to us in the spring, or should I say, try to teach me? I'm afraid you are much more adept with a needle than I'll ever be. Well, I'll see you at dinner."

Boyd waited until Florence and Marcus left the room before sitting down beside Lucy. He looked down at her hands and traced the long, delicate but strong fingers. She shuddered and he looked up to find her gentle eyes on him, tinged with sadness.

"I know. Lucy, I wish you could come with me now, but my heart tells me this is the best way. The time will pass faster than we think."

A tear fell from her eye and splashed on his hand. His heart trembled, and he gathered her against him. Thoughts raced through his mind and then stopped as a prayer stumbled from his lips: "Father, Please keep us all in your care until you bring us together again. In Jesus's name, Amen." She lifted her head and gave him a watery smile.

"Thank you."

He placed his hand to her cheek, and she leaned her face against it.

"Lucy, do you have a sketch of this house?" he asked.

She straightened as her eyes searched his. "Well, yes, I do. Why?"

"I want to take it with me. I'll show Ben, Martha, and Daniel where we've been."

"I'll go get it," she said.

She returned a few moments later. The detail of the sketch pleased him. Perfect for his purpose. Love coursed through him and he smiled at her.

"Thank you, Lucy. I'd better go and get packed as we'll hit

the sack right after dinner tonight. Would you have a few moments for me before retiring?"

Her dimple flashed, and her eyes twinkled. "I do indeed, Mr. Richards."

He grinned and turned on his heel to head for the door.

~

The rest of the day and dinner sped by. Boyd hugged Mrs. Kennedy—such a short woman compared to Lucy—and she returned his hug with an affectionate light in her blue eyes. It seemed odd, Lucy's dad had brown eyes and her mother had blue eyes, but she had blue-green eyes. Lucy said she inherited her grandfather's eyes. He wanted to meet everyone in her family but knew neither the time nor the opportunity existed. Her father planned to see them off in the morning, but they asked the women to say their good-byes now. Boyd turned as he watched Lucy hug Florence, Marcus, and Andrew. He waited and waved to the trio as they each said good night. Lucy walked toward him.

"Shall we sit on the porch, Mr. Richards?" she asked.

"Of course, Miss Kennedy. After you."

They sat in the two chairs her parents often used after dinner as the evening drew to a close and the stars appeared in the sky. Tonight it encapsulated their time. The moon shone between feathery clouds, the wind stirring a gentle breeze across the porch.

"I wanted to share the sunset with you today. It was so brilliant and made me think of all the things I want to complete with you," Lucy said in a voice soft as the breeze in the darkness.

Regret tinged his voice as he reached for her hand. "I know you were trying to let me pack, but I'd have come to share the sunset with you. Lucy, I look forward to sharing so many sunsets, sunrises, and wonders with you."

"I promise to come and get you for the first sunset I see on our ranch when I get home in the spring," she said with a smile.

He swallowed hard. "Say that last part again, Lucy."

She squeezed his hand and repeated, "When I get *home* in the spring."

"Our home will be ready and waiting for you. I love you, Lucy Kennedy," Boyd said, his voice rough with emotion as he bent his head and kissed her.

~

Lucy honored Boyd's request and remained in bed as she heard the group gather to leave the next morning. She heard Florence and Marc as they passed her door to join the others out in the yard. The horses' hooves and soft whinnies reverberated through the morning air. Leather saddles groaned as the riders mounted in preparation for the journey. Her father's voice reverberated as he bid farewell to the group and mounted the stairs of the porch. At that point every emotion in Lucy caused her to spring from her bed and fling open the curtain to watch the travelers depart. Her eyes searched the group until she located Boyd's back, and just at that moment, he turned for one last look; their gazes collided, and the world seemed to stand still for a precious moment. Boyd held his horse steady for another breath before he raised his hand. He caught her return wave and smiled one last time. He turned to embark on the trail ahead. Lucy watched as they grew smaller on the horizon before she shifted her gaze toward her father, who'd turned on the top step to find her at the window when Boyd waved. Her father motioned for her to join him. She threw on her riding clothes and ran out the door into his comforting embrace. He held her for a few minutes as tears poured down her cheeks. Then he set her at arm's length.

"Lucy, let's go for a ride and talk about which stallion we should start yours and Boyd's ranch with. We'll need to also find a suitable mare. Even though winter is almost upon us, the spring will be here soon. I would like us to arrive there by no later than the end of May if your brother can arrange to be home by then."

Joy and anticipation soon replaced her sadness as she focused on all the preparations needed during the next few months. She accompanied her father to the barn as ideas circulated like a small cyclone in her head. They rode over the expanse of the Kennedy ranch engrossed in a companionable discussion about plans for the future.

Chapter Eight

The breathtaking verdant beauty of East Texas captured Lucy as the topography changed. Towering oak, pine, pecan, and many other trees she couldn't begin to name shimmered with new green leaves that danced in the breeze. The scenery and towns captured her admiration. After they went through Tyler, her adoration of the eastern part of the state deepened. Contentment should have filled her as their journey reached its last miles, but it didn't. Lucy knew the moment she resumed her seat in the wagon on this fine morning that one of her fits danced below the surface. She disliked this part of herself and fought the onsets as much as possible; however, this time, her weariness made it impossible. The many weeks of unkind travel culminated. She checked her mother's travel-worn face and dirty travel clothes and let all her irritation flow.

"Uncle Michael, my mother and I are in need of a real bath today. You, as well as the other men, have availed yourselves to the rivers and streams at your discretion. Propriety has not allowed us the same. I thought you might suggest it as we passed through Henderson last evening, but you didn't. Now, are there any towns left before we reach Boyd's ranch?"

Her uncle bristled at being called out in front of his men, but he turned toward his brother as Joe cleared his throat to get his attention.

"Michael, we must admit Lucy and Agnes are remarkable travelers. I share their desire to arrive in a more presentable state than any of us seem to possess at the moment."

Major Michael Kennedy rolled his eyes, and a few of the men snickered but swallowed hard as Lucy glared at them all. He held up his hand to stop the torrent of words that threatened to erupt from his niece's mouth.

"We will reach Mt. Enterprise in a bit, and I'm sure baths are available at the local hotel. I only ask you ladies to be quick about it. We are already behind schedule. Mr. Richards expected us yesterday from my initial calculations, based on the time it took us in the late autumn. My men will need to continue on to Nacogdoches without me as they're expected today. I'll join them after the wedding. Will those plans suit you, Lucy?"

Lucy felt butterfly flutters in her stomach. "Yes, thank you, Uncle. Oh, and, Uncle Michael, how far is Mt. Enterprise from the ranch?"

"About seventeen miles."

"Oh," she said and turned to intertwine her fingers with her mother's. They shared a smile.

"We're almost there, sweet one," her mother said.

The major motioned everyone forward, and they headed out on the last day of their journey.

~

Boyd's head jerked up as he heard his front door burst open and then slammed shut. He heard the uneven gait of his brother as he stormed into Boyd's bedroom.

"Boyd, I need—What are you doing in the tub?" Ben stopped as he stared at him.

Boyd relaxed back into the still somewhat warm water.

"Well, I figured I shouldn't let the water I had hauled in for Lucy go to waste. They've been delayed. Besides I want to be clean when I see her."

Ben shrugged and looked back toward the door.

"You need to finish and get out now. We've got another visitor here, and, knowing her, she's liable to burst in here at any moment."

Boyd frowned as he stood up and reached for one of the cotton sackcloth towels Florence had made for him as a gift when he finished building this house. He shook his wet hair as he stepped out of the tub.

His brother ran his fingers through his similar golden blond hair.

"Marie Sanders."

Boyd chuckled as he pulled on his pants and shirt. "What does the local schoolmarm want with you?"

"As you know, Mr. Penney has stepped down due to his age, and they hired this girl. She is seventeen and just passed her test. Well, you know Mr. Penney helped me finish my studies since the war interrupted them. He'd come over one or two nights a week and drop work off for me, and I'd get it back to him. I'm almost finished and asked him to keep helping me, but he thinks Miss Sanders would be better. Boyd, I won't finish if she has to teach me."

Boyd studied his brother as he pulled on his boots. "Ben, she has the knowledge, or she couldn't have passed her teaching exam. She's not that much younger than you. What's really bothering you?"

Ben threw another look of trepidation at the door before he sat beside him on the bed.

"I met her when we first moved here from Georgia; we were just kids. Then after you left for war, Nancy and I started going to church. Marie went there with her family. Her mother died when she was seven, and her father has raised her and her three sisters. Well, she'd come over, and Nancy let her help a bit and even more after the baby came. She stayed with Nancy the day the soldiers came and took me away. After I came home, she turned up right after I buried Nancy. She and her sisters had been sick with the fever that took Nancy, so she hadn't visited in a few weeks. We didn't say much. Then, I saw her on the day the preacher baptized me in the river. It was a wonderful day until I tried to crawl out of the river with this wooden leg. Well, it got stuck as the preacher tried to help me up the bank. Everyone else kind of averted their eyes as not to embarrass me, but not her. She stood there watching me struggle, smiling and beaming as I made it up the bank. Boyd, I had to repent as soon as I crawled out of the water. I sinned in my frustration at her."

Boyd laughed, and Ben punched him until Boyd knew to stop him before it became a true brother scuffle.

"Ben, Ben, stop a moment. Let's think about this. My recollection of the girl before this autumn is vague. She seems to be a young lady who has something nice to say each time I see her at church. What's the problem?"

Ben glared at him. "That's just it. She never seems to get riled."

Boyd lifted his eyebrow. "Ben, you, my brother, are smitten."

Ben gaped at him. "I am not." He strode to the window and looked out at the yard. Boyd came to join him. He saw the young lady in question; Marie talked to Florence and Martha as they made soap in large pots. As they watched, the diminutive young lady with brown hair coiled at the nape of her neck looked up and waved, her hazel eyes twinkling with good will. She said something to Florence and Martha, who looked up at the house and waved to Ben and Boyd. Marie then headed toward the stairs and onto the porch within seconds. Boyd smirked at Ben and strode to the door to greet their guest.

She held her hand posed to knock as Boyd opened the door.

"Good morning, Miss Sanders, how may we help you?" Boyd greeted.

The young woman smiled and beamed at them. "Why, good morning! Yes, I'd like to help your brother, Ben, finish his studies. I think it's so wonderful that he wishes to finish his schooling. You see, so many of our young men didn't care to do that when they returned."

"Yes, I do agree, Miss Sanders. I think Ben will benefit from your knowledge. He's very intelligent as I'm sure you know."

Ben elbowed him as he pushed in front of him.

"Miss Sanders, I appreciate your enthusiasm. It's just I'm more comfortable receiving my lessons from Mr. Penney. You understand, don't you?"

The young woman stood there with an unflinching smile on her face. "No, I'm afraid I don't. Mr. Penney is no longer available, and as I'm the only teacher around, we must work together. I do understand you not wanting to attend classes with the rest of the children and young people in the community at your age, but I do not mind coming by a couple of nights a week. Why don't you give me the opportunity, Mr. Richards?"

Ben frowned. "I'll have to think on it. Excuse me, ma'am," he said as he brushed past her and proceeded down the stairs. He picked up speed as he navigated the familiar yard on his way to the field where Marc and Daniel were working. Martha's voice caused him to pause but not stop.

"Mr. Benjamin Leon Richards!" Martha called.

Boyd didn't envy Ben. Martha viewed Ben as a younger

brother and friend. Daniel and Martha had to adjust after growing up as slaves on his uncle's plantation to living here as equals. They'd grown up with Boyd and Ben in a much different setting. Now, they had their own cabin and a baby daughter who had been born close to Christmas. They shared everything as friends and family. Some of the local people didn't accept the arrangement they had as part owners of this ranch, but Ben, Marcus Johnson, and now Boyd all stood firm about their status. However, at times like these, Martha's mother's voice echoed through her lips. Her mother raised the Richards boys with input as needed from their aunt. Whenever Ben had stormed off in anger, she stopped him by calling his full name. But she didn't have the sway her mother had because Ben didn't turn. Sadness showed on her face. Martha shook her head as Florence met her gaze before letting go of the stir stick and going to pick up her daughter from the small basket by the pecan tree. The breeze stirred, and Martha leaned to kiss the perfect, soft, brown cheek of her little Emily.

Boyd and Marie came down the stairs at that moment.

"Once again, Miss Sanders, thank you for stopping by, and please forgive my brother's rudeness. I promise he'll let you know by the end of the week. We're expecting company, so he won't have time before then," Boyd said as he walked her to her wagon.

"Yes, I understand you are to be married again. I'm so happy for you. The ladies of the church are anticipating her arrival. We'll bring dinner and come to meet her once she's had a chance to catch her breath. The preacher has told us her name is Lucy."

Boyd wished the preacher hadn't shared this information with the church. However, Boyd realized being part of a community meant others shared in your life.

"Thank you, Miss Sanders; I'll let her know to expect you. Good day to you," he said as he helped her up into the wagon.

"Good day, Mr. Richards." She turned to the ladies in the yard and said, "Martha, Florence," before taking her seat and flicking the reins to leave.

Boyd watched her depart and scanned the perimeter, taking in the original cabin where Ben lived; Martha and Daniel's cabin; Florence and Marc's new house—designed like their homes in Arkansas— made of flat boards. Each house sat on two acres with a half of an acre between each of them. A wooden corral type fence stood around the acreage on which the houses sat to separate it from the rest of the farm and ranch land. Marcus took up Boyd's idea about a house to resemble the home his bride had known as a child. Boyd had taken the drawing Lucy sketched of the Kennedy ranch house and built her a home as close to a replica as possible.

At first, he wanted Marc, Ben, and Daniel's assistance alone. However, as the magnitude of the construction become apparent, he enlisted the help of others in the community. His widespread neighbors seemed pleased to help. It broke the former state of isolation, which surrounded the Richard's farm. The last month required late night work by lamp light to finish the inside. He hoped she liked it.

"They'll get here today. I just feel it," Florence said.

Boyd turned and smiled at her. One of his favorite people, Florence had become almost as close a friend as Marcus.

"I'm ready, Florey."

"So, am I, Boyd Richards," Martha declared, shaking her head and smiling. "You need to be getting back to your work instead of staying under our feet."

Boyd grinned. "I'm just going to clean up my bath and make sure the house is in order one more time. If they aren't here after lunch, I'll get back to the field."

Boyd crossed toward his new house and thought about the last few prayer-filled months. Renewed grief descended after he came home and faced the absence of his wife and son; acceptance as he looked through his brother's sketches, which captured much of the time he'd missed right after he left for war; and renewed memories of laughter shared as he visited with his family and friends. A peace then settled upon him about Lucy. The time of building their home healed him in many ways and filled him with hope. Now he felt like a schoolboy as he awaited her arrival. He prayed for her not to change her mind, but knew in his heart she loved him. The anticipation almost made him jump out of his skin.

~

Lucy smoothed her damp hands down the skirt of her clean cotton dress in nervous anticipation.

"We are now riding beside the Richardses' property," her uncle announced.

She turned and gave her mother a small smile. After their

quick baths at the hotel in Mt. Enterprise, Lucy had twisted her still wet hair on top of her head. So strands now curled and tried to escape. She hoped she didn't look as much in disarray as she felt. Her mother's face registered disbelief and then delight as she stared ahead. She heard her father chuckle and turned to see what had caused their reactions. Four houses came into view. All set away from the road on the land to their left, and one of the houses looked like a replica of the Kennedy home in West Texas.

"Well, well, Lucy, I'd say Mr. Richards has been improving the place since I last stopped here," her uncle said.

Boyd's thoughtfulness touched her. She took in the lush green foliage and rolling pastures that surrounded the homes in front of her—home. Someone waved from the yard. Florence stood by a soap pot beside a black woman who had to be Martha. She heard her uncle quiet some grumbling coming from his men.

These men had decided to ride with them to the ranch. They'd leave for Nacogdoches after lunch. She wished they'd left them at Mt. Enterprise. Astonishment filled her and she started to whirl on them, but her father reached over her mother to touch her arm and shook his head to silence her. Well, he could stop her words for now, but not her actions.

As they came to a standstill in the middle of the main yard, Lucy jumped down from the wagon without assistance and ran to give Florence a hug.

"Florey!" she exclaimed, and her friend gathered her into a hug of welcome.

"Lucy, you made it. Boyd will be so happy."

"I can't wait to see him," she said and then turned to the tall dark woman who stood behind Florence. Lucy met the woman's gaze. She placed an arm around Florence's waist. "Please introduce us."

"Lucy Kennedy, meet Martha Richards."

Lucy released Florence and hugged Martha.

"I've heard so much about you, and you must let me know if being a Richards is a good thing," she said.

Martha smiled. "Well, Miss Kennedy, it's been good the last few years even if the years in Georgia with Boyd's uncle weren't the best. Welcome to the family."

A small cry from the basket behind Martha drew Lucy's gaze.

Without hesitation, she crossed and drew out the small bundle, turning to beam at Martha.

"She's so precious. What's her name?" Lucy said, turning to Martha, who hovered at her shoulder.

"Thank you, Miss Kennedy. Her name is Emily."

"Martha, please call me Lucy."

"Now, you must let me see this child," Agnes Kennedy said as she approached and took little Emily from Lucy with tender hands.

"Martha, I'd like for you to meet my mother, Agnes Kennedy."

The four women conversed in the shade of the pecan tree as the remaining members of the travelers engaged in a low-toned but heated conversation that ended in Michael Kennedy's men leaving with instruction to wait for him in Nacogdoches and to never set foot on the Richards property again. The prejudice and ill will from the war emanated from her uncle's men, but Major Kennedy's reputation and influence had far reaching implications; enough to benefit or harm those who required his focus.

The dust from the men's departures had just settled when three men emerged from a plowed field behind the largest log cabin. All eyes turned to watch them approach, and the sole remaining rider dismounted as the group waited.

~

Boyd had started toward his study when he heard more voices in the yard. He wanted to burst out the door. Instead, he walked back through the house one more time. He took a deep breath as he opened the door and froze. Lucy stood by the pecan tree with the other women with Emily in their midst. Could she have grown more beautiful than he remembered? The light of tenderness in her eyes as she talked to Martha and Daniel's little girl amazed him. His breath caught in his throat as she turned and her eyes found him. She smiled with a flash of her dimple, and he doubted his legs' ability to take him down the steps, but he soon found himself across the porch and in the yard. She met him, stopping just before reaching him. All the onlookers seemed to fade into the background. Something about Lucy drew him, exposed him, and overwhelmed him with more feelings than he knew how to deal with.

"Hello," they both burst out and then laughed.

Lucy looked down for a moment, but then lifted her eyes to meet his gaze. Her eyes filled with tears, and Boyd lost all restraint. He gathered her close, and she buried her face in his chest. The long journey had brought her to the haven of her new home, which he hoped had more to do with his arms than the house that stood behind them.

Joe Kennedy crossed to his wife and placed an arm around her. No one spoke until the three men coming from the field arrived sweaty and dusty. The youngest one hobbled forward and told the hound dog that loped beside him to hush. "Leave it to my brother to make my soon-to-be sister-in-law cry moments after she arrives. Lucy, you just come to me when he behaves badly, and I'll set him right. I'm Ben," he said, sticking out a dusty hand.

Lucy laughed and wiped away her tears as she turned to meet his younger brother. Ben stood almost as tall as Boyd but with the lean build of a youth. His maple brown eyes differed from Boyd's tawny, golden brown. Boyd had told her about his brother's artificial leg, but it didn't show. Their cousin Andrew had brought a doctor with him from Georgia to fit him with a better one. Still wooden, but it had a rubber foot attached that fit inside a shoe, making him more stable and his injury less obvious. He covered it with his pants, and although uneven, he had a pretty rapid gate.

She ignored his brother's hand and his dusty condition, hugging him instead. Lucy laughed as his dog jumped up on both of them, licking her.

"Thank you, Ben. I'll keep that in mind," she said, giggling and petting the dog.

He grinned back until Boyd bumped him and told him, Marc, and Daniel to clean up before they wiped any more of their field dust on his fiancée.

"Take that hound with you," he added.

Marcus laughed, brushed a brief kiss on her cheek, and introduced her to Daniel before the trio excused themselves to get cleaned up for lunch.

Florence and Martha ushered Mr. and Mrs. Kennedy, Lucy, and her uncle toward the Johnsons' house with Emily in arms. Lucy threw a helpless look over her shoulder at Boyd. He started to follow but stopped when he noticed the wagon and horses still in the yard.

He then noticed someone else still with Mr. Kennedy's rig. A young man stood in the yard beside his horse holding the reins of two other mounts—a mare and a second stallion that looked very familiar. Recognition coursed through him.

"Billy! I thought you were on the spring drive by now," he said, starting forward, but stopped and turned to call to the retreating trio. The three men, who had almost reached their houses, doubled back and soon joined them. "Ben and Daniel, this is my friend, Billy Cooper, who I told you about. Billy, this is my brother, Ben, and my friend Daniel. You already know Marcus."

Marcus circled around to the black stallion and mare, who kept nervous eyes on the dog sniffing at their hooves. In the midst of the exchange of handshakes, he procured the reins from Billy. The hound soon tired of his inspection of the new arrivals and trotted off as Marcus led the mounts out a bit. He talked in gentle tones to calm the black.

"Billy, this is the one I broke, isn't it?"

Billy grinned. "Yeah, that's him, and I think he still needs a few more lessons on his manners. Those two are the pair Mr. Kennedy brought for Boyd and Lucy to start their horse breeding."

Daniel frowned and approached the mare, running a gentle hand along her side. "If I'm not mistaken, this filly has already bred, and the first Richards colt will be with us in a spell. What surprises me is Mista Kennedy allowing that to occur before such a long journey."

Billy looked down. "Well, it wasn't really his fault. You see, these two didn't take to each other real well when first introduced. I didn't want the stallion to hurt her or for us to have problems on the trail. So, a month before we left, I started working with them at night . . . putting them in the same corral and feeding them together. Well, I supervised, but one night I fell asleep until they woke me and the rest of the ranch with their romancing. I'm grateful he didn't cripple her, and I didn't lose my job. Miss Lucy took pity on me and promised to take on the responsibility of tending the mare during our trip here. Believe me; we could've made better time without the need for frequent breaks and rests."

Ben laughed. "Sounds like something I'd do."

Billy flashed him a grateful smile, and Boyd knew the two would soon be fast friends.

"Ben, why don't you help Billy stall these two in the barn and then go get cleaned up before the women come looking for us."

Boyd smiled as he watched his brother's uneven gait alongside Billy's rolling, bow-legged lope as they made their way to the barn. He exchanged smiles with his other two friends.

"'Bout time that boy got to spend time with someone other than the likes of us. He's forgotten how young he still is," Daniel said.

"Maybe Billy can talk some sense into him about Marie," Marcus said.

Boyd grinned. "Or . . . he could give him some competition and make him take notice."

Marcus punched him on the shoulder. "You'd better leave that alone. Don't start stirring up mischief just because you're about to settle down."

Boyd feigned innocence. "Why, Marcus, I only want him to find the same happiness."

Marcus grimaced and chuckled. "Lucy and Marie are not the same."

Daniel crossed his arms, rocked back on his heels, and cocked up one eyebrow.

"Now, I know I done heard you two fine gentlemen wrong—talkin' 'bout about Miss Marie that way," he said and waited for the appropriate shame to show on their faces. He held up his hand as they started to sputter denials. "Now, I know you don't mean it and realize what a treasure she is even though . . . " He paused before he grinned. "She can make a man's head ache with her persistence. Still, you ain't foolin' me none."

They busted out in laughter and ambled toward Marc and Florey's house.

~

The atmosphere during lunch yielded a myriad of emotions: the awkward feel of strangers turned friends, bridging into a family with strong ties. Lucy relished the interplay of each person there. She treasured the gift of her parents and uncle at this table with her; her family blended with the faces of those soon to be her new family. Her brother's absence didn't bother her.

Jason remained contemptuous about her marriage plans. He came home focused on the implementation of all the new ideas on agriculture. Her parents justified his attitude as a desire for responsibility. They left him in charge of the ranch during their absence.

Her perusal faltered as she encountered the tender, golden gaze that made her heart skip a beat. Panic welled up but subsided at the love in Boyd's eyes. She blinked as he moved from his chair across from her to stand behind her.

"Florence and Martha, you've outdone yourselves with this delicious lunch, but now I find myself in need of a walk. Please excuse Lucy and me," Boyd said as he assisted her from her chair and turned to her parents. "Mr. and Mrs. Kennedy, please feel that you're at home and pass the afternoon as you please. Marcus and Daniel will be happy to show you and Major Kennedy the farm."

Boyd ushered her out of the door before she could say anything and before anyone, including her father, could object. She could do no more than hold tight to his hand as they ran down the steps from the porch of Marc and Florence's house. Boyd slowed as they reached the middle of the main yard. He watched her catch her breath. They burst into laughter as their eyes met.

"I've never seen my father with such a conflicted look on his face. Boyd, you must learn to be a better host to your guests," she said with a twinkle in her eye.

He grinned then tried to look repentant but failed. "I promise to learn from you after we are wed," he said. "Now, what would you like to do? Walk our land, see our house, go wade in the branch?"

A gentle light glowed in her eyes, and she looked down to retrieve his hands before seeking his gaze again. "I love the sound of things that are 'ours,' and I want to do all of them, but there are two things that we must do first or they'll be lurking in the shadows until they're done." She saw his puzzled frown and smiled as she said, "I need to see yours and Nancy's home . . . and Nancy's and Sam's graves. Boyd, in order to make this my home, I need you to bring me into the total family, and that will always include them."

Boyd looked down as he nodded. He dropped one of her hands as he guided her by the other. They walked to a large pecan tree that stood about twenty yards from the oldest—a moderate-sized cabin—of the homes. The wind stirred the leaves of the old tree in a greeting as they approached. Two thick and well-built carved crosses with the names Nancy Richards and Sam Richards and the dates of their births and deaths burned into the wood. Boyd dropped her hand and knelt to brush away a few leaves and sticks. Lucy watched him straighten and waited. Her throat constricted with emotion as the spring wind stirred her hair and rippled through the poplin cloth of her dress. She'd pictured this moment, but the reality overwhelmed her. A sudden impulse to run coursed through her. Could she handle the huge undertaking of the role he offered? Today made it real—to touch and feel the land and see the home where a very real woman and child had lived, laughed, loved, and now were . . . gone. She looked behind her toward the wagon. Boyd straightened to stand beside her, taking her hand. Emotion filled his voice as he spoke.

"God, Father, I'm not sure how to do this, but I want Nancy and Sam to meet Lucy. It's up to you on whether they hear me now or if we have to wait. I know I've talked to them on this very spot, all the while knowing they're not here but with you. Still, I need to say these words. In Jesus's name—Amen," he prayed. A long pause ensued before he continued. "Nancy, this is Lucy Kennedy. As I've told you over the past few months, she is a kind and passionate person with a blazing spirit for life. I think you would have wanted her as a friend. We're to be married this week. Please let Sam know." He paused, his eyes beseeched Lucy to understand. "I love both of you, and I love Lucy too." His voice trembled as he brushed away the tears that had started in his eyes.

Lucy squeezed his hand as he displayed vulnerability for the first time. The tough cowboy no one wanted to cross allowed her to see him at his most transparent. She turned, bolting toward the wagon. She ran as fast as she could until she reached it, dug through one of her trunks, and extracted a wrapped parcel. Clutching her treasure, she rushed back to Boyd. He looked stiff and stricken. A guarded expression covered his former open one. She reached him and extended the gift she held. He hesitated but took it as she gasped for air. A look of wonder transformed Boyd's face as he opened it.

"How did you do this?"

"I must ask your forgiveness because I sketched the plans from the sketch of Nancy and Sam your brother had done. The one you keep in your Bible. I went to the bunkhouse when you weren't there and borrowed it. Billy almost caught me, but I slid it back and scurried out as he entered. One of my friends converted it to an etched image and put it under glass to shield it from the weather. Then we fashioned this wreath from young sapling branches to surround it. I wasn't sure where you'd want to place it, but I thought we could insert different flowers and greenery into the wreath as the seasons change." She stopped herself from further babble. Boyd's face made it hard to gauge his feelings. She wanted him to say something.

Boyd stared at the miniature portrait within the wreath frame and knelt to position it against the base of the pecan tree, between the two crosses. He stood and turned back to gather her in a gentle, long hug. Raw emotion deepened his voice as he spoke next to her ear. "Thank you, Lucy. I'll secure it to the tree this evening." A gentle kiss followed before he took her hand to lead her to the cabin behind them without another word.

The door emitted a poignant creak as they entered Boyd's first cabin. "Please overlook the less-than-orderly state of things. Ben is not known for his house cleaning. Martha and Florence are appalled even now. They'd kept it tidy during their time here," he said. He swept his hand toward the room. "Please look around. There are two bedrooms over there."

"It's fine; I mean, it's a well-built cabin. I know Ben is just a boy. You forget I helped my mother clean the bunkhouse when the men were on the trail. Not that this is like the bunkhouse." She threw her hands to her mouth, horrified at her words.

Boyd smiled and gave her a slight nudge in the direction of the adjoining rooms as he laughed "Lucy, go look around. I'm ready to go to the branch."

She complied. The rooms each had sturdy, handcrafted beds, trunks, and chairs. Uncertain of what she might find, she took her time, but she soon realized not a trace of Boyd existed in the rooms nor Nancy. This cabin belonged to Ben.

Boyd stood with one foot propped behind him and his head tilted back against the door. He straightened as she joined him.

"It's not like I thought it would be. Where are her things?" she asked.

His gaze didn't flicker. "It's just a cabin, Lucy. Martha

153

wanted the trunk Nancy had brought from Georgia and the rocking chair. Marie, a friend of ours, took care of her clothes and the few things of Sam's. The cradle I made for him is the one Daniel and Martha's daughter is now using. This ceased to be my home while I was away at war; I just didn't know it. Now I have a home again."

"I want to go see it."

"No, Lucy—I mean *you*. You're my home. The house I've built for us will be a home because of you." He reached out and stroked her cheek.

Lucy couldn't speak. Instead she stepped forward and placed her arms around the man who would be her home and laid her head on his chest. Boyd's arms drew her close, and she felt him kiss her head. She breathed in a deep sigh, allowing herself to rest within his arms. The arms she dreamed about for months. Neither spoke for a few moments. Neither needed words.

~

Boyd opened his eyes and gazed at the walls of the room that held so many memories. Flashes of the shared pride and excitement on the day they'd completed the cabin, sitting on the floor for their first meal inside these walls. The firelight had captured their youth, as well as Ben's last few years of childhood. He smiled to himself. Those remained treasures of memory, and now he could move forward with the regrets forgiven. This cabin belonged to Ben. The one place his younger brother called his. Lucy stirred and he looked down to meet her glowing blue-green gaze. Happiness flickered there. He wanted to see her eyes blaze with laughter and joy.

"Lucy, it's time for you to see our land. I'll race you to the branch."

He grabbed her by the hand, pulled her out the door, and then let go to race passed her with a brief smile thrown over his shoulder.

~

Lucy laughed as she raced to catch him, holding the skirt of her dress to keep from tripping over the long folds of material. The beauty of the emerald terrain, thick with clover and xanthic jonquils intoxicated her as she dashed across it. The tall, sturdy trees stood in clusters in the pastureland. She noted a pond and then almost lost her balance as she topped a ridge that sloped into the bottomland Boyd now raced across. What appeared to be the edge of a forest loomed in the distance and Boyd stopped there to wait for her. Her legs and lungs burned from exertion even as her heart pounded with exhilaration as she reached him. Sweat trickled down his forehead, and he shook the droplets from the tips of his sun-streaked hair and grinned.

He took her hand and led her into the shade of the trees. She reveled in the cool shade for a moment before the sparkle and babbling song of fresh water caught her attention. Lucy took in the canopy of bright spring leaves on the arched branches. The sound and feel of the wind drifted through this place of peace, and solace enwrapped her. The musty, rich smell of moist earth, leaves, and moss wafted through the air. She remembered the rain they'd traveled through two days ago and knew it had reached this land. She smiled at a new thought, "their land," and turned to find Boyd still a bit winded from the race. He leaned against a tree and watched her enjoy the most perfect place in the world.

"I gather this is the branch?" she asked.

Boyd grinned and nodded in affirmation. "Welcome to East Texas, Lucy."

She clasped her hands in delight as she approached the edge of the meandering stream. "Do we have access to water like this on all our property?"

"I'll just say, we've had no trouble with the two wells we've dug close to the houses or the ponds," he said with satisfaction. His eyes made a panoramic appraisal of their surroundings. "Lucy, we have good land. It nourishes my soul to look at it, to feel the soil on my hands as I work, and to hear the wind through the trees. Just wait until you see it at night. I know how broad the sky is on your ranch without all of these trees. It's pretty there too, but the night here is so alive. The insects, frogs, and animals living in all this make music that pleases your ears even as the moon and stars shine above the rustling trees. I love seeing the wonder on your face. It echoes my own since I've returned."

Boyd walked a few feet away, placed his hand on the trunk of a leaning tree, and took in a deep breath as he gazed at the leaves floating on the surface of the rippling stream. He glanced back at her and gave her a rueful smile. He turned back and stared at the thick expanse of trees on the opposite bank.

He kept his voice soft and modulated as he said, "I blinded myself to so much for so long, Lucy."

She moved behind him, placing tentative hands on his shoulders. "Our land is the loveliest I've seen, and this place is a haven we will share. I promise to not let you get so distracted or consumed by things that you take it for granted or stop seeing it."

Boyd turned with tenderness in his eyes. Lucy fell more in love with him. Today she met a Boyd Richards with the weight of the world lifted away. Moments of regret still overtook him at times, yet she caught a glimpse of the pre-war man on this land. Their land. Although, she somehow knew she preferred him now. A heaven sent light glowed in his eyes; one she shared. She smiled, and a current of joy sprang between them.

He took her in his arms and kissed her; cradled in his strong, gentle embrace, time seemed to cease. The course of their emotions deepened until they both had to step away.

The sound of slow, plodding hoof beats and two voices calling their names caused her to turn. They could see Ben and Billy on a mule in the green bottomland. They moved into a patch of shadow but then re-emerged close to the edge of the trees. Sunlight danced on the top of the leaves that framed where Boyd and Lucy had entered. Boyd placed a finger to his lips—his smile full of conspiracy—to silence Lucy, who stifled a laugh.

"Boyd, I know you're in there. We saw you two dash off in this direction. Mr. Kennedy appeared a little alarmed, but Lucy's mother looked delighted. Anyway, show yourselves," Ben called.

Lucy affected a pretend pout but took Boyd's hand. He shrugged his shoulders in resignation.

"Ben, we're here. You and Billy might as well come cool your feet in the water a bit."

The two young men soon found them. Ben wore the look of a satisfied younger brother who'd disrupted his older brother's plans, but Billy looked flushed and apologetic. Boyd proved he knew how to handle both. As Ben stopped in front of him with a satisfied grin, Boyd gave him a push into the water.

Ben sputtered as he tried to right himself and reattach his artificial leg, which had been dislodged by the unexpected motion. Then he burst out laughing as he sat in the cold stream.

"I deserved that," he admitted, grinning at them.

"Yes, you did, little brother," Boyd said, winking sideways at Lucy. He reached down and pulled his half-soaked brother from the stream. Boyd turned toward the other tall, gangly youth who now stood beside Lucy. "How about you, Billy? Do you want a turn?"

Billy grinned, sat down on a tree root, and removed his shoes. "No, I'll just wade for a bit. I don't need no help."

They convinced Boyd to wade with Billy while Lucy and Ben observed from their seat on a fallen tree at the water's edge. Billy told stories about the last cattle drive with Boyd. Ben told stories about Boyd's and his childhood that made Lucy laugh until she cried. They swatted away the gnats and a few flies that droned by without much awareness.

Ben's laughter slowed after one last tale, and he cleared his throat. As all eyes turned on him, and he adapted an expression of mock seriousness.

"I hate to bring this delightful outing to a close," he drawled, "but I need to take my fine mule and journey to the church on an errand of most importance."

Lucy smiled and played along. "My dear Benjamin, please enlighten us as to the nature of your errand with the local preacher."

He gave her an exaggerated look of disbelief before he shook his head at his older brother who still stood in the stream.

"My dear brother, I don't believe Miss Kennedy realizes the preacher is unaware of her arrival. He must be notified if there is to be a wedding tomorrow."

Lucy gasped. "Tomorrow?"

All eyes turned on her, and she gave an apologetic smile. "I'm just surprised. I thought it would take a few days to prepare for the ceremony after we arrived."

Boyd shot Ben a warning look. "Lucy, what my younger brother lacks in tactfulness, he makes up for in being organized and well prepared. He has arranged to have the pastor available at a moment's notice for our ceremony. We knew it should be this week. The ladies of our community have made us items and are anticipating a luncheon in our honor after the ceremony at the church. If you want to wait a few more days, that's acceptable.

You should have some time to settle."

Billy chose that moment to emerge out of the water and slipped on the bank. He splashed Boyd in his fight to regain his balance. He succeeded and tromped over to sit beside Ben.

"Ben, I'm going with you," he said, somehow oblivious to the tension and expectancy in the air.

Lucy's attention returned to Boyd. He wiped his face on his sleeve and shook droplets of water from his hair as she turned. Time slowed for a moment as the impact of Boyd Richards washed over Lucy. The tiredness from the long journey disappeared along with her initial nervousness, The true reason she came remained— him—a flesh-and-blood man and the best person in every sense. No problem on that score. She recalled their gentle, sweet kiss just an hour earlier. How attractive . . . it now settled into every fiber of her being like the tingle in the air before a lightning storm.

"Oh my." She blushed as her eyes met his. He felt it too. She decided the time had come for many things: first, a response for Ben, and second, a hasty retreat to Florence's house.

"Ben, you may notify the preacher that tomorrow will be just fine. Now, if you gentlemen will excuse me, I do believe I need to see to my parents."

She nodded and hurried through the trees and into the open pasture, where she could breathe. The sound of splashing caused her to once again pull up her skirts so she could run. Her feet moved faster than ever before, and she crested the hill to the house right before Boyd reached her. He whirled her around and, before she could catch her breath, kissed her without preamble. The image of branded calves came to her mind, but it blurred as emotions thundered between them. The kiss seemed endless, and Lucy couldn't find a coherent thought. Just as she thought her legs might buckle, Boyd broke away. She opened her eyes to find him staring at her with a look that thrilled yet frightened her a bit.

"Lucy, I hope you know what you're getting into here," he rasped. "What I meant to say is that this is forever. I want to see you every day for the rest of our lives. I won't leave you here when I travel; you will come with me. You are my home now."

Tenderness filled her. "You're mine too, Boyd Richards." She reached up to stroke his face as she spoke. He covered her hand with his as their eyes locked.

"How would you like to have a look at the house I've built for you?" he asked with a smile.

Happiness danced between them as she nodded, and they crossed the ground to the yard. They heard Ben and Billy arrive behind them and turned.

Ben grinned at them. "I think we'd better hurry along to the preacher, Billy."

Both young men laughed as they tried to hurry the mule toward the road.

~

The small country church sat nestled under the branches of tall, broad oak trees to the left of the dirt road they'd traveled for the last fifteen minutes. During that time Ben had learned more about Billy. The young man had lost all his family except for his two youngest sisters in an Indian raid at the age of eleven. He, along with his sisters, had lived with his aunt and uncle until the year Billy turned fifteen, when the rest of the family had moved to Louisiana. Billy's uncle had declared him a man and told him to make his own way in the world. He avoided the big war but learned cattle and dealt with Indians when the Kennedy family decided to hire a young, inexperienced hand. They and the other cowhands become his family. Ben didn't sense any bitterness in his new friend. No, the nonchalant way in which Billy told his story demonstrated the attitude of one who had learned to accept things as they came yet still expected adventure at every turn.

Ben saw the ladies of the community at work on a quilt frame set up in front of the church and groaned as one dark-haired member of the group rose at their approach.

His companion leaned from behind him. "What's wrong, Ben?" Billy asked.

Ben whispered, "Marie Sanders."

He didn't have time for a further explanation as the young lady in question set upon them. Her eyes twinkled as normal, and her ever-present good will beamed.

Ben swung his right leg over the mule's head and jumped to the ground on the opposite side as if an animal barrier between them could shield him from her onslaught of bright salutations. His awkward dismount brought smiles from some of the ladies.

He glared at Billy's smirk, but averted his eyes from Marie's face. After a brief period of uncomfortable silence, Billy cleared his throat, forcing him to return his attention their way.

Marie stood there in all her patient radiance. He eyed the road.

"My dear Mr. Richards, how nice to see you. Does this mean the Kennedys have arrived?"

Ben could tell she wanted an introduction, as well as an answer as her eyes darted toward Billy. He heaved his breath and nudged Billy, who jumped off the back of the mule and faced the expectant schoolteacher. Ben fixed a pleasant smile on his face.

"Yes, ma'am, they arrived a bit before lunch. This is one of their cowhands, Billy Cooper," Ben said without giving her any details. He sensed her eagerness to speak and tried not to frown before he continued. "Billy, this is Marie Sanders, our community school teacher and neighbor."

Billy removed his hat and stammered, "Ma'am."

"It's nice to meet you, Mr. Cooper. Please come and let me introduce you to the other ladies."

Billy reddened, and Ben frowned but shrugged and followed Marie's small form. Ben knew they had little choice but hoped the preacher would emerge from his small house next to the church.

The ladies all fawned over Billy and expressed admiration for the rigors of his long journey. Billy shifted his feet as if he wanted to run. Ben understood the impulse as soon as the group turned their attention to him with questions about Lucy and the wedding. Ben answered, and they expressed excitement.

"Ben!"

He looked up to find the preacher approaching.

"Ladies, we'll leave you to your quilting and planning," Ben said with a nod, and then he saw Billy's face. The young man stood transfixed by the young, golden-haired woman seated beside Marie. Ben knew the young lady noted his attention as she blushed and tried to hide a shy smile as she focused on her needlework. Time to finish the business at hand and get Billy back to the farm. "Excuse us." Ben pulled Billy away from the group, and they met the minister before he reached them.

They made plans for a service late the next morning with the ladies to provide a luncheon for everyone on the church grounds after the ceremony. They shook hands with the preacher and headed for the mule.

"Should we help the ladies?" Billy asked as they walked past the group, who now prepared to leave.

"No," Ben said. "They can handle it. We need to get home. I still have work to do before dark, and I'm sure you need to tend those horses."

Billy seemed reluctant but followed him anyway. They rode in silence for the first few miles, and then the question Ben had anticipated came.

"Who was the girl sitting beside Miss Sanders?"

Ben grinned. "That's Miss Mattie Davis. She's one of the prettiest girls in this county."

Billy's tone turned serious as he responded. "You seem to have a lot of pretty ladies around here. Is Miss Sanders spoken for?"

Ben tried to keep his shock and irritation in check. "No," he started, "but I thought you expressed interest in Miss Davis."

Billy chuckled. "I sure was taken with the sight of her, but I liked the spirit of Miss Sanders. Which one do you favor?"

"Me—why do I have to favor either? I'm not looking for a wife, and neither should you. You aren't settled, and women need a man who is. I'm settled, and I don't want some woman who wants to come in and unsettle me."

"I might be—before too long—if Boyd agrees with Mr. Kennedy's plans," Billy said.

Ben frowned, and the wheels in his head started to turn. He'd better find out these plans while Billy wanted to talk.

"What plans?"

After a long silence, Billy answered.

"Well, since I'm sure Mr. Kennedy is talking to Boyd about this while we're gone, I'll tell you. Now, Ben, you can't bring it up with Boyd until he chooses just in case I'm wrong. See, Mr. Kennedy has bought the land across from your farm—"

Ben pulled the mule to a stop and turned to face Billy.

"He did what? Boyd had planned to buy that land and tried a month ago, but it had already sold. Now I know who bought it, but why would Mr. Kennedy do that?"

"He bought half of it as a wedding present for Boyd and Lucy to use for breeding their horses and half for me to clear to develop into a small ranch. Mr. and Mrs. Kennedy plan to turn their land

and ranch over to their son in a few more years. Mrs. Kennedy would like to be close to Lucy. Mr. Kennedy doesn't want to compete with your farm or ranch business, but feels he can help expand the family holdings."

Ben turned back toward the road and urged the mule into motion. He should've known Boyd's marriage to the daughter of a wealthy rancher would bring more changes than another woman on the place. Nancy's family had never visited given the times and events. Nothing stayed the same. He knew that well, and it might work well. The land could've gone to someone they didn't know. Then the other change hit him.

"So, you'll stay on here, Billy?"

"Yeah, and you're sure I can choose to call on Miss Sanders or Miss Davis? Since you're not interested," Billy said with a laugh.

Ben frowned. "Sure, but as you don't know them, let me offer my insight. Miss Davis is one of the most docile creatures you could meet. She is demure but quick witted with a nice laugh and smile. If you're considering, she's the better choice for you."

Riding in front of Billy, Ben missed the look of satisfaction followed by one of pure mischief cross his new friend's face.

"Well, I don't know. You see I'm used to spirited creatures that need a gentle hand. Maybe, Miss Sanders would be better," Billy said.

"No, you don't understand. Miss Sanders is settled and steady already. It's just she . . . well, she likes to will things into happening," Ben said in frustration.

"I think that could be a help to a man."

Ben had had enough of this. If Billy wanted to court Marie Sanders, why should it matter?

"Fine, Billy, you decide which one you want. It doesn't matter to me. Besides I think you need to get to know both ladies better before you decide."

"I'll keep that in mind. Thanks, Ben," Billy said.

~

Lucy loved her new house. With its design close to identical to her home in West Texas, but with added touches that made it theirs alone. Each window had a built-in bench in front of it. The mantle had been hand carved by Daniel, who had also handmade the furniture. There were built-in shelves in the study and kitchen, and petrified wood composed the fireplace. Her parents had expressed their approval and relaxed in such familiar surroundings for the rest of the day.

Boyd and her father shut the doors of the study after dinner and talked for hours. During that time she and her mother prepared for the next day.

Her father had chosen to afford her the luxury of ordering her wedding dress from New York. It remained in a truck where they'd packed it with care for the journey, along with special accessories. She hoped the other ladies wouldn't think her too extravagant. Her mother said, in his own way, her father allowed the extravagance to make up for not letting her finish college. Although appalled, Lucy decided to enjoy it. As she watched her mother remove yards of delicate lace and silk, she gave herself permission to enjoy its beauty. Such times in life merited the enjoyment of gifts someone chose to give. She relished the dress more because she didn't ask for it.

"Lucy, you'll be so beautiful in this," her mother gushed as she smoothed the garment.

Lucy joined her and allowed her hands to brush across the elegant garment. Her mother slid her arm around her, and for just a moment, she laid her head to the side to rest it on the top of her mother's. It still amazed her that her physical stature exceeded Agnes Kennedy's. The woman had rushed in to rescue her from bad dreams, cared for her during illness, and defended and protected her in the myriad of situations that had arisen on the ranch. She refused to think about the inevitable good-byes at the end of the week. Her one consolation remained the fact that her parents planned to return and build a new home on the land across from them in a few years. Her mother gave her a squeeze and kiss on the cheek.

"Ma, I love you," Lucy said, facing her mother before bending to give her a hug.

"I love you, my darling daughter. Now, we must go and see if our men are finished with their business. We have a big day tomorrow, and I know we're all trail-weary tonight. Florence said they'd come over before first light to help with breakfast and to get you a nice bath before preparing for the trip to the church."

When they reached the study, the door stood open.

"Now, where did those two go?" her mother said.

"Wait, listen, Ma," Lucy said.

The sound of voices out on the porch reached them. She shared a smile with her mother.

Her father smiled as they opened the front door. "There you are. I thought you might've retired without me, Agnes," Joe Kennedy said as they opened the front door.

"If the study door had still been closed, Lucy and I would've been forced to do just that. So, Boyd, if you don't mind, I will request my husband now join me and bid you good night," Agnes Kennedy said with a gracious but weary smile.

"Of course, Mrs. Kennedy. It does my heart good to know we can look forward to your presence as a neighbor in the future," Boyd said.

Agnes moved to stand in front of Boyd. "My dear man, you're soon to be my son-in-law, and I hope you'll look on me in the capacity of a mother. I'd be honored."

Lucy could tell this touched Boyd even in the darkness. His voice—low and gruff—filled with emotion as he responded.

"Yes, ma'am, thank you."

Her mother drew herself up as tall as her five feet four inches would allow before she stepped forward and hugged Boyd, who dropped his arms to encircle the small woman. Her father cleared his throat, and Lucy knew he intended to rescue Boyd.

"Boyd, I believe it's bedtime. Our plans for the horses and ranches are solid, as are your plans for caring for my daughter. Good night. Agnes, let the boy go, and we'll find the first real bed we've seen since we left home. My back doesn't handle the trail as it used to. Lucy, we will expect you to retire soon."

Lucy kissed her father's cheek as her parents turned toward the door. Boyd moved to lean against a porch post. When the door shut, he turned and motioned to the two chairs that seemed to be beckoning them to sit for a spell. She smiled and accommodated. Boyd then sat beside her and propped his feet on the porch railing. A nice breeze blew, and the night came alive with sounds Lucy hadn't heard interspersed before. She remembered Boyd's description of these sounds at the creek that afternoon and smiled.

"So, this is the night-time music score you told me about,"

Lucy said, shutting her eyes and breathing in the sweet air.

Boyd didn't respond, and she opened her eyes to find him watching her with a look of pure contentment. He nodded and stood to lean on the post again.

"Lucy, do you remember the young man I told you about? James Hawkins? The one Hallie Price is taking care of now?"

"Yes, he's the one who was injured in the war and can no longer walk. Why?"

He turned and sat on the rail. "I guess that's the way most people would describe him, unless you met him. Well, I wrote to his parents after we returned to your farm. I just received a letter back this past week. They're in Washington now, and James is a consultant for the current administration and Miss Price is training with Dr. Jones at one of the hospitals there, as well as continuing to help take care of James. They're so grateful to have her with them. His father wrote that the journey from the fort was very hard on James and he remained ill for a few weeks after they arrived, but he quoted Mrs. Hawkins as saying, 'God and James pulled out another recovery.' Lucy, the first night I met him, I found a man more whole than I was at that time. He's a man so free of bitterness because of his relationship with the Lord. The reason I'm thinking about him now is because we wouldn't be here without my meeting him. I had run from the Lord for so long and tried to ignore the words of my friends, my brother, and even Nancy. It's so amazing how circumstances occurred and I met him. His testimony and attitude brought everything together. James got me to open the Bible, and even as I continued to fight it, I knew. It just took the counsel of a preacher and the simple faith of a small child to cause me to surrender. If I had chosen to keep running, I'd have lost my life forever, and I'd never have been open to anything new again, but surrender gave me life in every way. God saved me, and he used a man in complete humility to draw me. I'd like you to meet James and his parents one day."

Lucy stood and went to him, her heart tender and full. "I'd like that. I'm sorry my words seemed insensitive before. Please know, I'd be honored to meet your friend. I need to give him a big hug."

Boyd reached up and smoothed away the tear that coursed down Lucy's face. He reached out and pulled her to him. He pulled back and smiled. "Just not too long a hug. He's a fine looking gentleman." Boyd laughed.

Lucy smiled at him. "No other man can make my heart race the way you do." Her heart skipped a beat as his grin broadened. She brushed her lips against his before pushing away. He stood, and she smiled and teased him with her eyes once she reached the door.

"Good night, Mr. Richards."

He gave her a warning look and a smile. "Good night, *Miss* Kennedy. You know when we end our day tomorrow it will be 'Good night, Mrs. Richards'?"

Lucy's cheeks burned, and she retreated inside the sanctuary of her new home. She could hear Boyd's soft chuckle and smiled as she entered the bedroom just off the entrance.

~

The next day started before the sun had even decided to overcome the night. Boyd had cleared the house before breakfast with Joe Kennedy close on his heels.

"Boyd, if I know my daughter, it would be best to be far away during this preparation. I hate to tell you this, but she gets very high-strung and emotional at times of great excitement."

Boyd's first recollection of Lucy flashed in his mind and he grinned. "Like throwing brushes?"

The realization that they shared a common memory crossed his future father-in-law's face. "That's right. I had forgotten she almost knocked your hat off the first day you arrived."

"My hat? More like my head. I've never ducked faster in my life."

"Well, my boy, I guess you do love her. Now, where can we find a peaceful breakfast?"

Boyd gestured toward his brother's house. "I can guarantee Marc, Daniel, and your brother are already there. Ben can cook a decent breakfast, and if I remember right, Billy can make coffee. Cook would let Billy help on the trail every now and then."

Mr. Kennedy rubbed his hands together in anticipation. "Lead on, son."

~

The familiar irritation crept in, trying to pop the bubble of joy present when she first opened her eyes to the songs of the birds.

Florence, Martha, and her mother fluttered around with breakfast preparations as she sat in the wonderful warm tub of water that Daniel and Marc had prepared earlier. They'd also prepared one for her mother, who'd taken advantage of it before dressing and rushing to help the other ladies. They told Lucy to relax and take her time, but, as the irritation spread, she found it difficult.

Her mother appeared as she stepped from the tub and helped her into the dressing gown made for her to wear until time to dress for the wedding.

"Lucy, breakfast is ready, and the house is man free So, we can relax with Martha and Florence," Agnes said.

Lucy smiled at her mother's verbal preparation. She'd done it since Lucy's childhood. Whenever she got out of sorts, Agnes pointed out the positives to help Lucy focus on them instead of whatever hysteria brewed beneath the surface. It did work on occasion, and Lucy breathed a sigh as it seemed to work now.

"The delicious smells are calling me. Are you sure Boyd has left the house?"

"Yes, dear, he knows not to see you before the wedding. Now, come and eat the wonderful feast our friends have made. There are biscuits, gravy, eggs, and steak."

"What? I can't eat all of that and expect to fit into my dress." Lucy laughed.

Her mother replied with an impish expression. "You can try."

As they joined arms and left the bedroom, they announced, "Here comes the bride ready to be wide."

Martha and Florence laughed and hurried to hug Lucy as she arrived in the kitchen. The table held so much food that Lucy felt sure the men would soon join them. The ladies ushered her into a chair. Little Emily slept in her cradle close to the table. They joined hands and shared smiles as they bowed their heads for the blessing. Once Agnes finished giving thanks, they passed their plates and filled them before conversation started to flow again.

"I can't believe you made all of this for me. It's wonderful. Now, Martha, I have a question for you," Lucy said.

Martha's face registered surprise. "For me, Miss Lucy?"

"Yes, you see, I know the stories about my parents' wedding, and Florence has shared Marc's and her story with me. The one story I don't know is yours and Daniel's. Do you mind sharing?"

Lucy asked.

Lucy noted the reserve on the dark, angular face and in the ebony eyes. Martha shared a look with Florence before she began.

"It's not the same kind of story. You see, I came to the Richards plantation when I was ten years old. The missus asked for me to be placed in the house to work. That's when I first met Mr. Boyd and Mr. Ben. They'd arrived there just a few months before themselves; after their parents had died. You know children have a sense of the feelings of other children, and they either use it to be mean or to develop friendship. Mr. Boyd—just a little older than me—started looking out for me. If he saw the older house slaves misusing me or if 'n Mr. Richards spoke ill to me, he'd let his aunt know at first, then as the staff started respectin' him, he'd take direct control. Erma, the head kitchen woman, used to say, 'That boy gonna get hisself in a mess. You can't change the way things is.' I guess she'd never met anyone like Mr. Boyd.

"Well, Mr. Robert decided the boys needed to start helpin' oversee the field help before school. That's when they met Daniel. He worked in the field with his father and older brother. None of the field boys dared look Mr. Robert Richards's nephews in the eye 'cept for one, my Daniel. So, after dinner at night those three boys started playing together in secret. Before long, I got invited, and then one day Mr. Boyd brought this sweet little girl from one of the poor farms down the road to join us. Miss Nancy was the first white girl to speak kindly to me. It just happened natural like. We all knew down deep we should feel guilty and scared, but it was the one fun part of our lives—those few minutes each night as the sun set—until Mr. Robert caught us after 'bout a year. He threatened to sell both Daniel and me if we continued, so things changed but none of us ever forgot.

"The day Mr. Boyd was of age enough to do it, he married Miss Nancy, packed his brother's and his things, got their inheritance from his parents' estate and left. After they left, Daniel and I started seeking each other's company. You were allowed some time before all lights had to be out at night, and Daniel would jest turn up to talk. After the war started, things got harder, Mr. Robert became even tougher and angry. Mrs. Elizabeth kept me close to the house, and I stayed there at night off the kitchen. All the slaves wanted freedom, but we didn't know where to go if'n we got it. The missus is a smart one, and it's cause of her doin' that got Daniel and me married.

"One night, with Mr. Robert away, the missus asked me to answer the door when a visitor arrived. Their minister didn't look too happy to be there. Then Mrs. Elizabeth asked me to get Daniel and bring him to the house. He'd never been to the house before. We were told we'd be married. Unheard of, but the minister performed the service, pocketed the money the missus gave him, then left in a rush. She gave us some Yankee money in two small pouches—one for us and one to take to her nephews—and a small travel bag with a change of clothes and some food. I wondered how she came by all that Yankee money, but I kept my mouth shut. She told us to go and find Mr. Ben and Mr. Boyd. She said she'd known 'bout our friendship and sending us could help her nephews.

"Let me tell you, that's the toughest journey we've ever known and we were 'bout starved when we got here. Then we had a terrible episode durin' the first month. The local people weren't so acceptin' when Daniel went to town without Ben. One day a group attacked him on the way home, and we had some major healing to do. Mr. Ben was beside hisself. That night those men tried to sneak in and finish my Daniel." She paused to exchange a glance and chuckle with Florence, who'd appeared to have heard the story before. "But they done messed with the wrong Richards man. Ben had us in his room since Daniel was hurt, and he slept close to the door in the big room. Well, those two men just cracked the door when Mr. Ben jumped on 'em with his wooden leg. That was before Mr. Andrew brought his new leg. That first one—hmm, hmm—I mean oak and hard. He cracked them over the head and called me to help him tie them up. He then put on his leg and pulled them out into the yard for the night. Then he sat on the porch with his gun 'til morning when he took 'em to the sheriff. No 'am, they ain't none too happy, but they haven't messed with us since. No easy road, but you know the rest."

Lucy's mother mirrored her amazement.

"That's some story, my dear," Agnes said.

"Yes, that's one of the most courageous things I've ever heard. I'm honored to know you and am glad you'll be part of my wedding today," Lucy said.

Martha shook her head. "No, ma'am, I'm 'fraid not."

Florence nodded. "Lucy, we're able to do things right here on our land, but you better understand this is still basic confederacy mentality here in East Texas. We don't go to each other's churches, and our children will not go to each other's schools. I'm sure you noticed your uncle's men's reactions. They left because they don't agree with a black couple living as equals with whites. Boyd, Ben, and Marcus have all gained respect in this community, so it's tolerated. Many have paid Daniel to build furniture for them. There are just certain things that can't be changed now, and I have a feeling it could be many years before more change is tolerated. There may not be slavery, but that does not mean there is equality," Florence said.

Lucy reached to cover Martha's hand with her own. "I want us to be good friends, Martha, and we'll manage that any way possible."

Martha smiled and squeezed Lucy's hand. Then, without warning, Florence jumped up and excused herself. She ran for the back door.

"It wasn't anything I said, I hope," Lucy said. She saw Agnes and Martha smile at each other.

"No, dear, I have a feeling Florence might give little Emily a playmate in the near future," Agnes said.

Lucy jumped up and ran to the window. Florence stood bent over, with her hands on her knees, and Marcus ran to her from the direction of Ben's cabin. The men must have seen her through the window. She smiled and returned to the table.

~

Marcus reached Florence just as she straightened and leaned against the maple tree.

"Florey, what's wrong?" he asked, placing his hands on her shoulders and squatting so he could see her face. His green gaze scanned his wife's pale face with concern.

Her gray eyes met his, glanced away, and then returned with a soft light dancing in their depths. A gentle smile tugged at the corners of her lips, confusing him even more.

"Marcus Elias Johnson, is there anything wrong in your being a father?"

Her words penetrated but not their truth. He thought her ill when Ben saw her by the tree and came to get him. She never got sick, except for a slight cold after they left Arkansas.

"What?" He stood before she could respond, walked away a few feet, and then returned to sweep her up into his arms. He started walking toward their house.

"Marc, I'm fine. Having a baby is natural. I need to go help Martha," she said, watching the muscle twitch in her husband's cheek.

Marc glanced down at her earnest face. "Florence Elizabeth Johnson, why didn't you tell me?"

"I wanted to wait until after Boyd and Lucy's wedding."

"That's just like you to think about them first," he said, leaning down to touch his forehead to hers. He then stopped and placed her on her feet. He grinned like a schoolboy. "Look at the boy and girl from Rockport, Arkansas, all grown up and having a child of their own. Florey, I love you. I can't wait to write our families."

"Dawn and John will be so excited to know our little ones will be close in age. Now we'll have to make a trip home next year for a visit."

He frowned. "Yes, but not until our baby and you are strong enough. Maybe, the railroad will expand down here, and we can go by train."

"Yes, I'd like that. Now, please walk me back, so I can help Lucy finish getting ready. This is her day," Florence said, reaching up to kiss him.

He gathered her close and marveled at the life growing within. He pulled back after a few magical moments. "Let's go."

~

Boyd watched Marc and Florey as they walked hand in hand back to his house. Ben walked up beside him.

"I'm right. That's the way Nancy and Martha acted when they were first pregnant," Ben said.

"Now, my Martha never got sick like that. She just felt puny for a bit each day," Daniel said as he joined them.

Boyd waited for the old feeling of anguish to hit him. It didn't. Instead, joy for his friends filled him. A sigh escaped, and he grinned at the two men.

"Look at you two. Quite the experts on expectant mothers."

He turned toward the other men still talking around the table. "Mr. Kennedy, how about Agnes?"

His future father-in-law coughed and then grinned at his brother's look of discomfort. "Michael would prefer another topic, but I'll say it differed with both children. Agnes had more of the episodes you just witnessed when she carried our son than with Lucy."

"My ma differed with each of my brothers and sisters too," Billy added.

Michael Kennedy snorted and stood. "I've had enough of this hen party, gentlemen. This is a farm and ranch. Isn't there some more work to be done?"

"Yes, plenty, and not much time left to do it. Let's grab Marc on our way out so we can double up as the morning will be cut short," Boyd agreed.

"Now, Billy and I did some of the chores already. We may need to leave a bit undone as we have a wedding to attend in a few hours, and besides Daniel will still be here," Ben said.

"Good try, Ben. We'll get it done," Boyd said, grabbing his brother by the back of his shirt and starting for the door.

~

They finished dressing Lucy. The elegant silk gown fit her well, accentuating her height and shape. Her mother pulled up Lucy's thick, honey gold hair with a few of her natural curls spiraled tighter to dangle down under the small headpiece. It took all three women to use the buttonhook to fasten the soft white kid leather shoes on her feet and the delicate lace gloves with pearl buttons on her hands. The gloves had belonged to her grandmother.

All the ladies stood back in silent admiration. Martha spoke first.

"Miss Lucy, I've seen many elegant plantation ladies come for parties in Georgia, but you done beat 'em all. Yes'm, I do wish I could be there to see the look on Mr. Boyd's face . . . no, the other ladies' faces. Them ladies gonna be jealous of you."

Lucy's heart leapt in delight and fear. "Do you think so? Oh, I don't want the ladies to hate me."

"Lucy, don't you worry about a thing. Once they get to know you, it'll be just fine. Besides, who are you wanting to impress today?" Florence asked.

"Boyd." She smiled.

"Let the other women envy all they want. It's your day," Florence said.

They all laughed until her mother glanced on the mantle clock.

"It's time to go. The men will be there and others should start arriving. We don't want to be too late," Agnes said.

The one person the women hadn't discussed entered the house as they moved toward the door. Her father stopped at the sight of her in her wedding gown. Her mother moved to his side to squeeze his arm.

Lucy watched her parents and felt a new flood of emotions. In a rare moment, she missed her brother being there and got angry at his absence.

"Where is Jason anyway?" she fumed, pushing to where her overcome parents stood.

Mr. Kennedy bowed his head and bent down to kiss his daughter.

"You're beautiful, my dear. Jason would have come if he could."

"No, he wouldn't have."

Mrs. Kennedy squeezed Lucy's hand—giving her husband a wan smile—and helped usher their daughter out to the door. Marcus, Ben, and Billy had left for the church with Boyd a few minutes earlier.

"Who's Jason?" Martha asked, shifting little Emily in her arms.

"Her brother," Florence said as she rushed out to save the small train on the silk gown during its descent down the stairs and into the wagon.

Lucy didn't relax again until almost halfway to the church. They exchanged stories from their childhoods. By the time the church came into view, Lucy felt more like a sweet, nervous bride.

About ten buggies, wagons, and a few more tethered saddle horses stood outside the church. She just hoped all these new people liked her. Two young ladies waited outside the church doors. Florence smiled and waved at a brown-haired woman, but groaned at the sight of the red-haired woman beside her.

"What is it, Florey?"

"Your welcoming committee, one is a good friend, Marie Sanders; the other is ready to hate you on sight. Her name is Jane Simmons. She was so pleased when Boyd came home with us and became a nuisance. I mean we all know Ben gets irritated at Marie because he has feelings for her down deep, but Jane became a disruption to Boyd's work and healing. Ben asked me to take her aside to explain the realities to her. Needless to say, I didn't make a friend," Florence said.

The wagon stopped in front of the church.

"Oh my, that would explain the look on her face, or do you think it's my dress?" Lucy whispered.

"Both." Florence giggled as Michael Kennedy assisted her to the ground. He then helped Agnes, and it took both he and Joe to assist Lucy. Marie had pulled Jane forward to meet Lucy.

"Marie Sanders, Jane Simmons, meet Lucy Kennedy, her parents, and uncle," Florence made hasty introductions.

"Ladies," the men said in tandem.

"Nice to meet you," Lucy said.

"Likewise," Jane said, "I just feel I must tell you that your dress won't be well received. You should've tried something plainer for our little area."

"Oh, do hush, Jane Simmons. I think the other ladies would be appalled to hear you say we're limited to simple dresses. I find it marvelous that Miss Kennedy has chosen to share the most up-to-date fashion in wedding dresses. We need the stir of something so breathtaking. I think it's wonderful," Marie said.

Lucy knew she wanted to become friends with the small brown-haired woman.

"You may call me Lucy," she said to Marie with a dimpled smile.

"What about me?" Jane asked.

"Wait and have Boyd introduce me again after the ceremony. I hope we can start over then, Miss Simmons," Lucy said.

"Let's get you inside. Jane and I will get the doors," Marie said with a bright smile, grabbing Jane's arm and ignoring her shocked expression.

Lucy's mother and Florence each gave her a quick kiss before they moved to the front of the church where Mrs. Kennedy sat and Florence stood waiting for her. Everything began to change from that point. Her eyes registered Marcus and Ben standing beside Boyd. Her uncle slid past and moved to a scat on a bench. The entire church of strangers turned as she and her father moved through the doors. A collective gasp and indistinguishable murmurs followed. Her father's firm arm beneath her hand strengthened her.

Only then did she allow her eyes to find Boyd; once their eyes met, his love held her. The look on his face left no doubt about the feelings in his heart. No one else mattered in that moment, and she knew Boyd would mask such raw emotion at any other time.

The slow walk down the aisle seemed endless. She smiled at her first memory of him. His quick reflexes had saved him from her wayward brush. He'd impressed her even then.

Now, his golden gaze led her like a beacon until she stood by his side. Her father responded to the preacher and kissed her cheek before he left her side.

Boyd moved forward and took her hands. Elation coursed through her, followed by peace. His eyes met hers and her heart overflowed. Boyd's sure and strong voice repeated his vows. Hers mirrored certainty and love.

Then the preacher uttered the most beautiful seven words Lucy had ever heard, "I now pronounce you man and wife."

Lucy brushed away a tear of happiness and flashed a smile as Boyd bent to kiss and hug her, and whispered, "I love you, Lucy Richards," in her ear before he straightened and turned her toward the church.

~

The rest of the day surpassed her expectations. She found most of her new neighbors to be very kind people, hardworking and family oriented. Some of the ladies appeared shy, but once they found her welcoming, things became easy. The food tasted wonderful, and after the meal, the ladies presented Boyd and Lucy with the quilt they'd made. Lucy shed tears of gratitude. The older ladies who had done some of the initial piecing had hearing issues, and Lucy adjusted her voice to thank them. The silver-haired matriarchs smiled. The men congratulated Boyd. The crowd thinned and dissipated, leaving those bound for the Richards/Johnson ranch. A treasured day full of love, endings, and new beginnings.

Lucy leaned against Boyd as they traveled seated behind Florence and Marcus in the wagon. Her parents, uncle, Billy, and Ben rode in the other wagon. Florence turned to smile at them as they neared the turn into their home.

~

Boyd reached up to slap Marcus on the back and received a nod of understanding, which needed no words.

The sun began to set as Boyd lifted his new bride from the wagon; the horizon painted in the hues of the peaches hanging from the now grown trees brought from Georgia all those years ago, as well as the reflection of the deep red dirt of the rich soil of East Texas. The trails leading them to this moment had taken many lifetimes within this lifetime; people and places shaped by the diversity of roads traveled. His brother and Billy took the wagons to the barn as his in-laws, Marcus and Florence made their way toward their house. His keen awareness of the woman beside him—his wife—held his regard. She turned and smiled at him with sparkling eyes and a flash of a dimple. His heart knelt in surrender. He pulled her to stand in front of him, placing his arms around her as she leaned her head back against his chest.

"I promised to watch the coming sunsets with you. This is the first of a lifetime, Mrs. Richards."

She turned her head to look up at him and smiled at the sound of her new name.

"I'll take each one as a blessing to be shared with you, Mr. Richards," she whispered.

They shared the sunset, as awed by the love they shared as the amazing sky ablaze before them. Both held a promise for many tomorrows. He bent to kiss her, the gentle light in his golden gaze affirming their vows. The Maker of the trails had led Boyd home.

About the Author

Lana Lynne Higginbotham (writes in the fiction genre under the pen name: *Lana* Lynne): Lana is a Speech-Language Pathologist and a writer/author. She is the author of these historical fiction novels under her pen name, Lana Lynne: *Home Always Beckons (subtitle: A New Sunrise) (*First Publication 2009; revised-Second Edition coming in 2018*); Trails of Change (subtitle: A New Sunset*)(First Publication 2010; revised-Second Edition 2018); and *Sunbeams at Twilight: A Life's Echo (First* Publication 2012-first printing 2012, second printing 2014, revised-Second Edition 2018). *A Compass of Stars in Your Eyes (*First Publication 2018*)* is her newest historical fiction romance.

Her first contemporary Christian novella is *Whimsy Michaels and Her Amazing Room (*First publication 2018).

Other writing credits: A creative nonfiction novel, written with a coauthor: *Life Between the Letters: The Chuck and Mary Felder Story (*First Publication 2014*)* by Lana Lynne Higginbotham and Mary K. Felder. Blog writer: a weekly blog post (2012-2014) contributor and served as part of the "Venture Galleries Author Collection" blog team (2013) under her pen name, Lana Lynne.

Lana lives with her husband in East Texas. They are empty nesters and proud grandparents. Learn more by visiting www.lanalynne.com.

Research Resources:

Author's Note: This is a work of historical fiction. Research consulted for background information and historical accuracy of people, places, and items utilized in a fictional sense for this story. No quotes. References only. Websites listed are per last date visited as listed. Some may no longer be available. The Endnote section follows this one per the four notations within my story. These are so noted in order for the reader to reference and find more information on the terms utilized or topics discussed by my fictional characters. They are listed twice per research listed and as linked to the notations within the story.

Background Information Research from Books and Web Sites

Adams, Ramon F.; Botkin, B.A.; Dodge, Natt, N.; Easton, Robert; Gard, Wayne; Lewis, Oscar; Morgan, Dale; Russel, Don; Winther, Oscar Osburn, *The Book of the American West*, editor-in-Chief, Jay Monaghan; Art Director, Clarence P. Hornung; published by Jullian Messner, Inc., 1963

Barnes, Joseph K., Surgeon General, US Surgeon General's Office, *The Medical and Surgical History of War of The Rebellion (1861–65), University of Texas at Tyler Library, Micro lm #s LAC 22396–405, Med V 2pt1; p. 425–465 Chapter IV "Wounds and Injuries of the Spine," Vol 2, Book 1 #LAC 22399, Vol 1, Book 2 "Appended Documents" p.10–13, p.84–85, p.206–208.*

Dickens, Charles, *Great Expectations*, afterward copyright 1963 by The New American Library of

World Literature, Inc., and Bibliography copyright 1980 by The New American Library, Inc.

Dobie, J. Frank, 1964, *Cow People,* Seventh University of Texas Press Printing, 2001, by arrangement with Little, Brown and Company

Douglas, C.L., *Cattle Kings of TX,* Branch-Smith, Inc., Ft. Worth, TX , 1939 Cecil Baugh and 1968 Mrs. C.L. Douglas, new material-1989 by State House Press

Foreman, Grant, *Advancing the Frontier,1830–1860,* copyright 1933 and 1968, University of Oklahoma Press; Norman, Oklahoma, p.253

Fort Worth Convention and Visitors Bureau: "Mini History" and "Chronology,"11/98; "Key Dates Regarding Cattle Raising in Texas" prepared by Douglas Harman, Fort Worth Convention and Visitors Bureau

Fugate, Francis L. and Roberta B., *Roadside History of Oklahoma,* Mountain Press Publishing Co., Missoula, Montana, 1991

Gard, Wayne; Krakel, Dean; Frantz, Joe B.; Winfrey, Dorman; Frost, H. Gordan; Bubar, Donald, Jenkins, John H., *Along the Early Trails of the Southwest,* Austin and New York: 1969, The Pemberton Press, Jenkins Publishing Co.

Rutkow, Ira M., *Bleeding Blue and Gray: Civil War Surgery and the Evolution of American Medicine,* Random House, 2005

Web Sites

"The Handbook of Texas online: Rusk County," *Handbook of Texas Online*, s.v." http://www.tshaonline.org/handbook/ online/articles/RR/hcr12.html (accessed 12/7/2008)

"The Handbook of Texas online: Mount Enterprise,TX," *Handbook of Texas Online*, s.v." http://www.tshaonline.org/handbook/online/articles/M M/hlm93.html (accessed 12/7/2008)

"Robert Todd Lincoln." http://en.wikipedia.org/Robert_ Todd_Lincoln (accessed 9/26/2009)

"Fort Scott National Historic Site—Soldier vs. Settler: Railroads in Southwest Kansas." http://www.nps. gov/archive/fosc/posofsek.htm (accessed 8/2/2008)

"Railroads in Kansas." http://kansasheritage.org/research/ rr/rrhistory.html (accessed 8/2/2008)

"Portraits of Texas Governors." http://www.tsl.state.tx.us/ governors/war/page2.html (accessed 8/4/2008)

"The Evolution of Artificial Limbs," Hancock, J. Duffy, MD, Professor of Surgery, University of Louisville School of Medicine, 1929. http://www.innominate-society.com/Articles/The%20Evolution%200f%20

Artificial%20Li ... (accessed 8/30/2009)

"African American Research, Part 1," *Ancestry Magazine*, 3/1/1996-archive, vol. 14, N0.2., http://www.ancestry. com/learn/library/article.aspx?article+2052 (accessed 8/24/2009)

"Boone County, Kentucky, Slaves and Owners Enumerated in the 1850 U.S. Census Slave Schedule." http:// wwww.boonecountyky.us/slave-schedules-1850.htm (accessed 8/24/2009)

"Great Expectations," p.1–7. http://en.wikipedia.org/ wiki/greatexpectations (accessed 4/12/2008)

Morrison, W.B., transcribed and submitted by Carter, Sandi and Clark, Marlene, *Fort Arbuckle, Indian Territory,* "Fort Arbuckle." http://www.chickasawhistory.com/FTA1.htm, (accessed 4/13/2008)

Lawton Fort Sill Chamber of Commerce, "Things to See and Do," "Fort Sill National Historic Landmark and Museums." http://www.lawtonfortsillchamber.com/ index.php?pr=Things_To_See_and_Do. (accessed 4/13/2008)

Along the Chisholm Trail (Beginnings), "Head 'Em North" (Fort Arbuckle). http://www.thechisolmtrail.com/begin6.htm (accessed

4/13/2008)

Rossel, John. "The Chisholm Trail." February, 1936 (Vol. 5, No.1), pp3–14, Transcribed by Elizabeth Lawrence, Kansas Historical Quarterlies. http://www.kancoll. org/khq/1936/36_1_rossel.htm (accessed 4/13/2008)

Robbins, Peggy. "The Confederacy's Bomb Brothers" Issue 6.1, *National Mine Action Centers, Journal of Mine Actions, April 2002.* http://maic.jmu.edu/ JOURNAL/6.1/notes/robbins/robbins.htm (last accessed 12/11/1009)

WheelchairNet: The history of wheelchairs. http://www.wheelchairnet.org/WCN_ProdServ?Docs/ WCHistory.html (last accessed 2/5/2010)

"Texas Governor Edumund J. Davis: An Inventory of Record at the Texas State Archives, 1869–1874," http:// www.lib.utexas.edu/taro/tslac/40016/tsl-40016.html (accessed 8/4/2008)

"Texas Adjutant General's Department: An Inventory of reconstruction Records at the Texas State Archives, 1865–1873, undated." http://www.lib.utexas.edu/taro/ tslac/30022/30022-P.html (last accessed 2/5/2010)

Andrews, Elizabeth; Murphy, Nora; and Rosko, Tom."William Barton Rogers: MIT's Visionary Founder," October 2004, pp.1–10, http://libraries.mit.

edu/archives/exhibits/wbr-visionary/ (last accessed 7/10/10)

Endnotes

Author's note: There are no quotes from these works. They are for background historical research information and are noted for further reading. This story is a work of fiction. (Associated notes are listed twice per numerical and document notation)

.   1 Chapter 1, Prices of cattle in 1867-
For more information on range of prices:
Gard, Wayne; Krakel, Dean; Frantz, Joe B.; Winfrey, Dorman; Frost, H. Gordan; Bubar, Donald; Jenkins, John H., *Along the Early Trails of the Southwest*, p. 139, Austin and New York: 1969, The Pemberton Press, Jenkins Publishing Co.

.   2 Chapter 1, For more information on Early Trails:
Douglas, C.L., *Cattle Kings of TX*, "Trails and Troubles," p.266–274, Branch-Smith, Inc., Ft. Worth, TX , 1939 Cecil Baugh and 1968 Mrs. C.L. Douglas

.   3 Chapter 2, This term for extra horses on the cattle drives is found in many resources. For more information on the use of the term *remuda*: Adams, Ramon F., p.p. 323–376, "Cowboys and Horses of the Ameri- can West," Part Six of *The Book of the American West*, editor-in-Chief, Jay Monaghan; Art Director, Clarence P. Hornung; published by Jullian Messner, Inc., 1963

.   4 Chapter 4, This term for extra horses on the cattle drives is found in many resources. For more information on the use of the term *remuda*: Adams, Ramon F., p.p. 323–376, "Cowboys and Horses of the American West," Part Six of *The Book of the American West*, editor-in-Chief, Jay Monaghan; Art Director, Clarence P. Hornung; published by Jullian Messner, Inc., 1963

[i] 1 Chapter 1, Prices of cattle in 1867- For more information on range of prices:
Gard, Wayne; Krakel, Dean; Frantz, Joe B.; Winfrey, Dorman; Frost, H. Gordan; Bubar, Donald; Jenkins, John H., *Along the Early Trails of the Southwest*, p. 139, Austin and New York: 1969, The Pemberton Press, Jenkins Publishing Co.

[ii] 2 Chapter 1, For more information on Early Trails:
Douglas, C.L., *Cattle Kings of TX*, "Trails and Troubles," p.266–274, Branch-Smith, Inc., Ft. Worth, TX , 1939 Cecil Baugh and 1968 Mrs. C.L. Douglas

[iii] 3 Chapter 2, This term for extra horses on the cattle drives is found in many resources. For more information on the use of the term *remuda*: Adams, Ramon F., p.p. 323–376, "Cowboys and Horses of the American West," Part Six of *The Book of the American West*, editor-in-Chief, Jay Monaghan; Art Director, Clarence P. Hornung; published by Jullian Messner, Inc., 1963

[iv] 4 Chapter 4, This term for extra horses on the cattle drives is found in many resources. For more information on the use of the term *remuda*: Adams, Ramon F., p.p. 323–376, "Cowboys and Horses of the American West," Part Six of *The Book of the American West*, editor-in-Chief, Jay Monaghan; Art Director, Clarence P. Hornung; published by Jullian Messner, Inc., 1963